JANET PYWELL

Someone Else's Dream

A heart-warming story of love, adversity and friendship

Cover photograph:

Harbour Street, Whitstable by Tim Hinchliffe Photographer

https://timhinchliffe.co.uk

First edition

ISBN: 978-1-9998537-8-5

This book was professionally typeset on Reedsy.
Find out more at reedsy.com

Foreword

For anyone who has had to start their life all over again.
May you be lucky enough to make lifelong friends.

"Life is not made up of great sacrifices and duties but of little things in which smiles and kindness given habitually are what win and preserve the heart and secure comfort."

Sir Humphrey Davy, 1778—1829
English chemist and inventor

Chapter 1

Our flat is above the café. When we saw it for the first time we fell in love with its bay window overlooking Harbour Street and the flat upstairs with its two double bedrooms; one with a patio door leading to a small deck at the back. The view from the rooftop to the sea on the horizon was a dream and I'd thought it all had potential. Cassie had said it was quaint.

Now I realise it is pokey, riddled with damp and there's far more work to do than either of us had anticipated.

'I can't find anyone to work in the kitchen.' Cassie is frying ribeye steaks. 'It's impossible to get staff.'

I am standing in the doorway watching her. The galley kitchen is the only area of our flat that isn't littered with packages. My gaze wanders over the lounge still filled with boxes, untouched from our move three months ago. We haven't had time to unpack or decorate and on days like today I wonder if we've even made the right move. Everything seems so chaotic, disorganised and there's so much work to do. It's overwhelming.

I wander into our bedroom and it's overflowing with Cassie's clothes, hanging out of boxes and a chest of drawers and a wardrobe that refuses to close. The second bedroom is stacked with books, DVDs and music in labelled cardboard boxes. You can't even open the door to the deck at the back.

Scruff-bucket is curled up asleep and purring inside a box on top of my sweater. I stroke her neck and she stretches appreciatively. 'You could win the longest cat competition,' I whisper, then I wander back through to the kitchen.

The flat is less than half the size of my last apartment in London which was new and modern and immaculately painted and decorated. I miss the space and I have a sudden pang for the familiarity of my old city life; for order and cleanliness.

The sizzling ribeyes make my stomach rumble. They cover the persistent smell of damp from the musky walls and I crack open the sash window.

'Cheers, Amber!' Cassie hands me a wine glass without taking her other hand from the frying pan handle.

We clink our glasses together and our lips meet in a brief kiss.

'I thought your friend Marion knew someone who wanted a job?' I say.

'She's taken a job in one of the big supermarkets on the far side of town – more money, she said.' Cassie's Scottish accent is soft and warm.

She forks the meat onto the plate and takes chips from the oven.

I stand beside the bistro table in the window and look down into Harbour Street. The shopfronts are prettily decorated and have colourful awnings in blues, greens and pinks. The window displays are filled with seaside themed gifts; striped cushions, lighthouses, oyster shells and wooden signs saying; Gone Fishing and At the Beach. A multitude of colourful lamps, wooden lanterns, carvings and seascape paintings adorn the art gallery, and in the boutique, trendy, expensive, casual beach wear, sandals and flip-flops are on display. Wedged between the shops directly opposite our café is a boarded-up travel agents that looks weathered and neglected.

A couple, walking hand in hand, huddle together against the cold wind and disappear into the Indian takeaway next door.

I refill our glasses and look appreciatively at our supper. It's been a long week.

'You look exhausted, Amber. You worry too much,' Cassie adds, sitting opposite me.

'This place is such a mess. I don't know where to begin sorting it out. There's never enough—'

'Oh, Amber, stop worrying! Look, I don't have time to keep house for you and open my business. There aren't enough hours in the day. Close your eyes and you won't notice it.' She grins. 'What does it matter if everything isn't organised and in the right place? Don't you think this is much more fun than everything being so perfectly tidy and organised?'

'You told me you liked tidy.' I cut the steak and relish its juices on my tongue. 'You said you didn't mind me being a neat-freak.'

'But this is more thrilling, isn't it?' She uses her fingers to eat a chip. 'It's like camping.'

'It's been over three months, Cassie. I would actually like to unpack and find a space for our clothes—'

'It's not the end of the world is it? You're not going to make a fuss, are you?'

'No, but—'

Cassie silences me by pushing a chip between my lips, and I smile.

3

'Lighten up, Amber. You've become very serious and it doesn't suit you. Don't you remember the fun we used to have when we met? You'd meet me after a show and we'd go for dinner to that little Italian in Covent Garden?'

'Of course I do.'

Cassie had been a singer and dancer in the West End. She had never taken the lead part but she had been in the chorus of most of the musicals in London in the past four years; *Grease, Les Mis, Billy Elliot.*

'That was in the days when you loved me...'

'I still do.' I smile.

'You don't show it.'

'I'm sorry. It's all the work and commuting every day to London. I seem to spend more time on the train than anywhere else.'

'Give it all up. Come and work with me in the café, Amber,' she says excitedly. 'We'd be a real team.'

'I can't.' I pause with wine glass halfway to my lips. 'You know it would be my worst nightmare. I would hate to work in a café. It's the last thing in the world that I would want to do.'

I see her smile fade. I don't want to spoil our evening completely, so I don't add that unless she opens the café very soon and it starts earning some money, I won't be able to finance this venture for much longer.

* * *

It's taking shape. We've spent the weekend painting the café walls white, hanging bulbous orange lights from the ceiling and a chalk board above the counter.

4

'The cash machine has arrived.' Cassie puts a cardboard box on the counter and pushes curls of red hair from her eyes with the back of her hand. There's a frown across her face when she says, 'The guy from the printer's shop wants a logo.'

'Have you designed one?' I smother a yawn.

It's Sunday evening and I am exhausted. After working all week and decorating the café over the weekend there hasn't been much time to rest and now I have a headache that is creeping gradually down my neck.

'I thought you'd design it,' Cassie says. 'You're more creative than me and you know how to do logos and stuff. Besides I thought you would want to be involved.'

'Okay. We can look at it later if we have time. Right, what else needs to be done?'

'You mean down here or upstairs in our flat?'

I stare at her. What we saw as an adventure is fast turning into a nightmare but I'm determined to stay positive.

'Let's tackle one thing at a time. Let's make a list. Perhaps you can get some of these things done this week.'

I grab a notepad and pencil and leaning on the counter I begin to write.

'Electrician – ring for coffee maker, Plumber – dishwasher and leaking downstairs tap, phone company Wi-Fi installation…'

'Carpenter – shelves,' adds Cassie. 'Downstairs or do you want him to do upstairs in the flat so we can unpack all those boxes with your books?'

'Let's concentrate on down here then you can open the café and we can get some money in. At the moment it's all money going out.'

'I'll need money for advertising,' Cassie says. 'A couple of thousand.'

'What?'

'There's a glossy local magazine that all the wealthy people read—'

'We can't afford it,' I say firmly. 'Let's do a small ad in the local paper and try and get a free editorial. You know, the sort of thing, 'well-known actress opens local café'.'

'I'm not well-known!'

'You're an actress, Cassie. Tell them you appeared in *Les Mis* and *Grease* and *Matilda*. They'll love it. They will be queuing for your autograph.'

'I don't want fans – I want people who will buy coffee.'

'Cassie, we are in the middle of Harbour Street. This is the place you wanted – the one you chose – the one you said you dreamed of. We have footfall passing by everyday: locals, tourists and day trippers from London all heading to look at the pretty harbour. We won't need to advertise in expensive magazines if we provide good food and great coffee, we can build up a reputation, which is what we need.'

'But—'

'The best form of advertising is word of mouth,' I insist.

'Marion says that all the shops advertise. She puts an advert in every month for her boutique.'

'She can afford it but this is a café and we are on a budget. Now, what about someone to help in the kitchen? Have you thought any more about the menu?'

'Marion says we should do all-day breakfasts.'

'But what do you think?' I am smothering a yawn and tapping the pencil.

'Marion says—'

'Well it isn't Marion who is running the café – it's you!' I reply tersely.

'You really aren't interested in helping me, are you?' Cassie's eyes blaze fiercely. 'You really don't care.'

'Of course I am, I do—'

'All you think about is your work. You spend all week in London in your bloody lawyer's office and when you come down here, you're too tired to help. You have no idea what I go through—' Cassie's eyes well with tears and she adds angrily, 'Thank goodness I have Marion.'

'Of course I care, sweetie. I really do. I've just been under a lot of pressure. Martin's been acting strangely at work and talking to me about his clients and… Look, I'm sorry, Cassie.' I reach out and pull her into my arms. I can't face the thought of an evening arguing. 'Come on. Let's go for a walk and talk about this outside. We've done a lot today and the café looks much better. Let's shut up shop and go look at the sea. It's silly to live so close to it and not go out and enjoy some sea air. It will do us good.'

'It's spring in a couple of weeks.' Cassie seems mollified. 'It might get warmer in the flat.'

'Exactly. Let's see if we can catch the last of the sun. It might even be a beautiful sunset.'

'Can we have dinner out?'

I suppress a sigh and dry her tears. 'Of course.' Then I lock the door behind us and take her hand, squeezing her fingers. Eventually I manage to coax a smile from her tearstained face but as we cross the road and head toward the beach, breathing in the salty sea air, I can't help but wonder what she has done all week and how I can keep affording meals out.

* * *

A week later, Cassie announces she's fed up with the café. 'It's so exhausting,' she complains.

'But you haven't even opened yet.'

'That's the point, Amber. If it's like this now, imagine the stress when it's open and I'm working all those hours every day.'

'Come for a walk and let's talk about it,' I say.

But she groans, clutches the pillow under her neck and rolls over. 'I want to sleep until mid-day,' she mumbles, so I decide to leave her and go out for some fresh air.

I walk with determined strides with my hands tucked deep into my trench coat pockets and my chin wedged inside the collar. The wind whips at my hair and I relish the wild recklessness that it inspires in me. It matches my mood as do the churning waves crashing onto the pebbles beside me. My mind is a pattern of swirling complex thoughts, and my eyes stream with wind-made tears. I wipe them away angrily with the back of my hand.

A flock of geese fly in dart-like formation skimming the water before landing beyond the breakwater. They honk and flutter settling noisily, and a barking golden Labrador is held back by its owner.

My time is too precious to sleep. It's the beginning of April and there's still so much to do. I gaze at the sea and watch the families around me and I'm suddenly lonely – feeling very alone.

Back in Harbour Street the pretty shops are coming to life, opening shutters, lowering colourful awnings, and yawning into life.

The tall blond man from the souvenir shop is hanging up crab lines and children's buckets and spades and when he smiles, I wave back.

Our café is still closed and inside the air is cool and a faint tang of curry still lingers in the air. It had been warmer to eat down here last night.

The room is long and the orange lights hanging down from the ceiling are already festooned with cobwebs and the floor is littered with boxes; new tables and chairs.

I throw my coat onto a peg and begin cleaning, taking a broom to the cobwebs, wiping counters and sweeping the mess. Then I unpack boxes of china, cutlery, serving dishes and pans. I wipe down the coffee machine and organise cups, mugs, glasses and saucers. I throw empty boxes to one side and unpack the cash register that has lain for two weeks in its box.

Behind the wall of the café is a narrow toilet, the exit to a patio garden, and a small kitchen where the microwave is splashed with remnants of tinned tomato and crumbs spill from the toaster onto the tiled floor.

It is after one o'clock when Cassie appears, her eyes red with sleep and her hair tousled.

'I told you I would unpack everything this week.'

'We could open this week,' I say with cheerful optimism.

'I can't manage the café on my own, Amber. Toast?' Cassie heads toward the kitchen and pushes bread into the toaster. Crumbs scatter to the floor but she doesn't seem to notice. She flicks the kettle to boil.

'Coffee?'

'Why can't we open this week?' I insist.

'Don't pressure me, Amber. Why do you have to do that? Every time you come down here, you complain that I'm not doing anything.'

'I haven't complained.'

'You have by implication, look at you, you always want to make me feel bad.'

'I want to help.'

'It's my café. I'll do things when I am ready. I was going to lay out the cups there and stack the plates over there.' She points using her mug. 'But you come in and take over.'

'Cassie, there were cobwebs hanging from the lights. The place was a mess—'

'Here you go again…'

'I thought you wanted my help.'

'Not like this.'

'Then what do you want me to do? I can't just sit around at the weekend. Each day the café is closed we aren't earning any money and there are bills to pay.'

'Oh, here we go, it's all back to money.' She tosses her hair over her shoulder.

'It's not all about money. It's about business.'

'So you keep telling me.'

'No, you told me. How many times did I hear that you were fed up with auditioning and that you wanted a café near the sea? How many weekends did we go scouring the country for the ideal spot? How long did you spend each night persuading me to leave London? You told me this would make you happy. This is what would fulfil you.' I face her and add softly, 'You wanted this and I agreed to finance it. But I can't live like this. It's been nearly four months, Cassie, and the café is *still* not open. It's been painted and decorated, you've ordered all the stock, everything is here.' I cast my arms wide. 'What more do you need?'

'I can't run this place on my own.'

'You've been interviewing for weeks.'

'Everyone has let me down. Even Liz went to the supermarket—'

'There must be lots of people—'

'Well, Marion did mention someone she knew was looking for work – maybe I'll pop around and see her—'

'Can't you just phone her? Then you can help me put things where you want them.'

'I can do that next week when you are at work. It will give me something to do.'

'You could open this week, maybe on Wednesday. What else do you need? Come on, let's make a list together, Cassie.'

'Stop pushing me, Amber,' she shouts. 'Why can't you just let me do things at my own pace?'

'I just want to help.'

'Then do it all yourself. I'm going to see Marion. I can't put up with this all day.' Cassie heads for the stairs at the back of the café that lead up to our flat.

'Don't go, Cassie. Please stay and let's do this together. I only want to help you.'

'You don't, Amber. You take over and you have no regard for me at all. You don't know how hard this has all been and how much energy I've put into this. It really is stressful and when you come home, you swan around down here and make out I've done nothing all week. I need some air. I'm going out.'

'Cassie—' I plead.

But she is gone.

Chapter 2

'You have got to be joking?' I stare at Martin, my friend, colleague and mentor for the past ten years, aware that my mouth has fallen open. His lanky frame is leaning against the window, his opaque eyes watching me carefully. We're taking social distancing seriously. He shakes his head solemnly.

'I'm sorry, Amber. But the time is right.'

'But you can't! You can't leave.'

Martin has been my guiding light. He has nurtured my career and pushed me to take on bigger and more important legal cases. Now, after marrying his second, much younger wife and her falling pregnant, he is moving with her back to her native country.

I cannot disguise my disappointment. 'I will not let you resign,' I say sulkily.

He smiles sadly but there is a gleam in his eye. 'I'll miss you,' he says.

'But Australia is so far away,' I moan.

'Anita wants to go back to Perth. She's adamant, and now the borders are opening up and with the baby on the way, she's determined. She misses her mum and her family. And it makes sense that we go now before the baby is born. You'll have to come and visit us.'

12

'How will I manage without you?'

'You'll be fine and, besides, with me out of the way I'm sure they'll make you a partner next year.'

But it isn't just about the law firm, I want to argue. Martin's advice has been invaluable. He has a way of seeing a situation unfold before it's even happened. Last year he had said to me, 'think carefully about this investment, Amber. Buying a café for Cassie is a big step. You have a lovely apartment in Islington and you've only known Cassie for eighteen months. What if your relationship doesn't work out? It's a huge risk considering Cassie has never run her own business.'

'I'll miss you,' I add quietly and he grins.

'We can FaceTime and, you can visit.'

'It's not the same.'

'How are things at the café?'

'Awful.'

'Not working out?'

'Not really.'

'Well, you'll have to face up to the decision you made.' Martin nods gravely, as if he suspected it wouldn't work out, then he checks his watch and hurries off to a meeting and I am left alone.

I'm reviewing documents for a commercial business; an employee wants to sue the leaseholder of the factory, but I can't focus. I'm distracted. My mind is wandering and I gaze out of the window at the sullen April sky and London Eye on the Embankment.

Face up to the decision I made.

By mid-afternoon I need reassurance and I reach for my mobile but Cassie doesn't pick up.

* * *

The front door to our flat above the café is hidden down a narrow alleyway that we share with the property next door – the Indian. I push past the bins, wiping rain from my face. The air hangs heavy with a salty sea breeze and the smell of spicy curry. It's locked so I fumble for my key in the dark and when the door sticks I kick it with the toe of my boot.

Inside, on my left, the café is illuminated by the yellow glow of the street lamplights through the double-fronted windows. It looks soulless and the café kitchen is deserted so I flick on the stair lights leading up to our flat. The stained beige carpet reeks of rotting damp, and mildew covers the stairway.

'Cassie?' I shout.

I open the door and I'm greeted by a small soft thud and a tiny miaow.

'Hello, Scruff-bucket,' I whisper, tickling the ears of the purring silver tabby. 'Where's Mummy?'

But there's no reply.

I sling my work bag onto the rickety dining table and wrinkle my nose at the familiar smell of damp that I hadn't noticed when we bought the place, and I crack open the sash window and pause to gaze down into Harbour Street.

The shopfronts are an array of colours that had looked vibrant and sea-themed last summer but now, in the persistent rain, the deserted street looks forlorn and tired. To my left, the square lies at the end of the street and on my right the sixteenth-century clock tower straddles the road like Colossus. It's a grand entrance to the small fishing harbour and the clock chimes the hour with nine soulful dongs.

There's a handwritten note on the table and I scan read it as

Scruff-bucket pushes insistently against me, her tail flicking and curling round my wrist, her purring increasing.

'Have you eaten, sweetie? Because this mummy is starving.'

I don't wait for an answer, instead I fill her bowl and I'm rewarded with her bottom pushed toward my face.

'Thanks, Scruff-bucket.'

I grab my mobile, head downstairs, and lock the door behind me. Harbour Street is pedestrianised right under the clock tower until you get to the pretty harbour, south of the town. The only eyesore is the building opposite the café – a boarded-up travel agents – the name of which has been scrubbed off, and navy paint is peeling off the square-framed windows.

The Ship, I have long since realised, is Cassie's local and where she likes to hang out with Marion, owner of the Très Chic Boutique on the other side of the travel agents. She's Cassie's new best friend. One pub door is on Harbour Street and the other opens onto the square with its small fountain. The town parking is to the north, at the far side of the square, with the bigger chain stores, retail shops and the new builds. Everyone walks through the square and down Harbour Street to the little fishing port where there's a popular fish and chip shop.

The church lies in darkness but it chimes just as I step inside the busy and noisy pub. I zigzag between the rickety tables searching for Cassie. It's a well ventilated, open-spaced seaside pub with wooden tables, and in the winter a fire roars in the grate. Tonight, there's no fire and strangers don't bother to stare back at me. Only one man with a heavy scowl, nursing a pint, pays me any attention. I feel his angry eyes on me as I walk through the bar to the patio at the back where small groups sit together under large heated garden umbrellas.

Freddie Mercury blares from speakers – 'We Are The Champions.'

'Cassie?'

'Oh hi, Amber. You found me.' Cassie's Edinburgh accent is soft and she speaks quickly. She's wearing her thick coat but it's fallen open like velvet curtains on a stage revealing tight leggings and a white blouse. She flicks her red hair over her shoulders and giggles. She's obviously not on her first drink.

'I did call you,' I say above the music. 'You didn't answer.'

'My phone's off,' she replies.

'Why?' I ask, glancing at the empty beer glasses on the table.

'Celebrating.' She raises her pint of local ale. 'And you're just in time to buy a round.'

Marion raises her glass at me and when I nod back I'm rewarded with her fluttering fingers and a wide lipsticked smile that doesn't reach her eyes.

'I'm not staying, Cassie. I haven't eaten all day and I've an early start tomorrow.' I try not to think of my alarm going off at five-thirty and my daily commute to London in the morning.

'For heaven's sake, Amber, lighten up and enjoy the music.'

Marion leans across the table and while she speaks to Cassie, she nods at me. 'Have you told her about Karl?'

'Karl?' I ask.

'He's going to work in the café,' Cassie says to me.

Marion calls out to the landlady and waves her empty glass. Her miniskirt barely covers her bum and her red lipstick is smeared as if she has been snogging enthusiastically for the past hour.

'JJ, we need another round over here,' she calls.

'Are you coming home?' I ask Cassie. 'Martin is leaving the

16

company and going back to Australia and I'm really—'

'I told you, I'm celebrating.' Cassie leans precariously on her seat. 'JJ – you know Amber Hendrix, don't you?'

JJ places two fresh beers on the table and I take Cassie's arm to steady her balance but she shrugs me away.

'Hello, Amber.' JJ has long dark hair that settles on her shoulders and she wears a low-cut navy t-shirt that reveals a deep cleavage. Her eyes are heavily made up with black eyeliner like Cleopatra. 'Are you having a drink? The girls have a tab running.'

'No, I'm fine, thanks.'

JJ takes the empty glasses and turns away. She's already lost interest in me.

An old chap is waving and I am relegated to being a spectator as Cassie ignores me and banters with him across the patio. I wait until she's finished, my head thumping.

'Cassie—' I lean toward her as the music swells and Freddie Mercury blasts out a long note. 'Cassie, I—'

'You should tell her,' Marion slurs, leaning between us. 'About employing Karl?'

I reply, 'Who is Karl?'

Marion laughs. 'We're celebrating, aren't we, Cas?' She throws her arm over Cassie's shoulder and they giggle, then Cassie pouts dramatically.

'Amber hasn't even asked what we're celebrating. It just goes to show how interested she is in me. It's all about her.'

'What do you mean?' I pause and stare at the lopsided smile on Cassie's face. 'It's all about me?'

'Well, she'll miss you.' Marion staggers forward and Cassie grabs her arm, laughing.

'Miss you?' I gaze at Cassie.

'I've got a job,' Cassie says.

'Yes, I know. You've got the café.'

'I'm going to be assistant stage manager at the theatre in the Barbican.'

I stand staring at her.

'Yay.' Marion lifts Cassie's arm and she squeals with delight, punching the air as if she's the prize fighter in the boxing ring

'Close your mouth – you might catch something.' Cassie laughs at me.

'The Barbican? How?'

'I went for an interview.'

'What? When?'

'Last week.'

'What about the café?'

'Karl's going to run it.'

'I don't even know Karl.' I rub my forehead my mind is racing. 'It's not his—'

'She's changed her mind,' Marion interrupts drunkenly. 'It's a free country, Amber. She's allowed to do that.'

'We have to speak, Cassie,' I say urgently and I reach for her hand. 'Come home and let's talk ab—'

'There's nothing to say.' Marion speaks excitedly. 'Cassie's got a brilliant job and we're all pleased for her. Let's have another drink – JJ!' she bellows.

'Please, Cassie, come home. Let's talk about this.'

'I don't want you to be angry, Amber.'

'I'm not angry.' I lean closer toward her. 'I'm just confused and seriously pissed off. You dragged me down here to live when I was perfectly happy in London and now you're going back to work in the Barbican.'

Marion joins in the chorus with the rest of the crowd singing drunkenly at the table along to Mick Jagger. 'I can't get no… satisfaction…'

'Please don't have any more to drink. We need to speak, Cassie—'

Marion slaps me on the shoulder.

'We're partying, Amber. That's what people do when they celebrate. It's about time you got a life and started to enjoy yourself.'

She's at least ten years older than me, probably late forties and Cassie has told me she's on her third divorce. She hadn't worked for twenty years, always relying on payouts from her wealthy exes but just before the last lockdown she opened the boutique opposite the café, selling high-end fashion. It's one of those shops that is minimalist and very expensive.

Marion laughs and throws her arm companionably around Cassie, and I am suddenly filled with incredible sadness. I know, in this precise moment, that there has been a seismic shift in my life and that things will never be the same.

I'm happy that Cassie has Marion for a friend, someone to support her since I've returned to the office in London; someone to give her good advice but now I'm filled with a sense of betrayal. Resentment begins to grow in me, taking root, causing my hands to shake and my body to tremble.

I cannot speak.

Marion throws her arm over my shoulder but I push her away and the ale in her pint glass flies gracefully and, as if in slow-motion, through the air and spills down the front of her dress.

She gasps and pulls the wet dress away from her skin.

'You stupid cow!' she shouts.

But I've already turned away and, as I leave, all I hear behind

19

me are the wild shrieks of the crowd applauding.

* * *

I throw my bag onto the seat near the window and slide in beside it just as the train pulls out of St Pancras. My meeting was delayed and it means I won't arrive home until past nine o'clock – again.

I pull a file from my bag, determined to finish my day's work on the way home. I blot out the sounds around me, and concentrate on the paperwork in my hand.

It's an hour later when I yawn and reach into my bag for my mobile.

Sitting at the table opposite me a young mum struggles to soothe her baby and its raw wailing rips along the silent carriage, piercing my brain, sending shooting pains through my already throbbing head.

The man across the aisle glances up above his Covid-protected masked face and raises his eyes to the ceiling expecting a response from me. I ignore him and scroll to find Cassie's number. I slump back in my seat and let my head rest against the cool glass window.

Cassie doesn't answer her phone and I'm reminded of our conversation only last week. I'd been on the train back to Westbay and I'd called her mobile and we'd had the same old conversation we'd been having for the past few months.

Her words echo now in my head.

'Amber? Where the hell are you?' Her Scottish accent was crisp. 'You were supposed to be here two hours ago. We'll be late now,' she complained.

'I've had the day from hell, Cassie.'

My voice was muffled and I'd paused but there was no answer so I added lamely, 'Perhaps we could meet up with your friends tomorrow night instead.'

'Oh for heaven's sake, Amber, you're not the only one who works. JJ's birthday party has been arranged for ages. Besides, my day has been no better than yours. I haven't stopped all day. It's been hell. The coffee company hasn't delivered. I can't work their stupid bloody machine plus the catering company said they won't deliver on a Thursday which means I'll have to go all the way into Canterbury and collect it all myself and – as usual – you're not even home early to help me, as you promised.' She emphasises the last three words.

Opposite me the young mum is now checking her phone while the baby gurgles quietly in her arms. The train passes through a tunnel and the yellow carriage lights glow softly. In the reflection of the window my face looks gaunt, my cheeks hollow and my eyes wide. I run my hand through my unruly curly hair that rests on my shoulder and exhale slowly.

The memory comes flooding back.

'Cassie, I agreed to set you up in this business. You have to open the café.'

'But you're never here.'

'You know that my job is in London. You've always known—'

'Oh here we go again—' Cassie had shouted in my ear. 'It's bad enough I couldn't open for months because of this bloody pandemic and you said last week you'd be home early and—'

'I said I'd try,' I said quietly. 'All you talked about was opening a coffee shop in Harbour Street. You said there was nowhere like it with the pretty clock tower and the harbour. You said you would die if you didn't live there. You couldn't

21

wait to leave London—'

'I knew you'd throw it all back at me.'

'I'm not throwing it back at you. I'm saying that I have my job and you have the café. We have to work it out, Cassie. That's what happens when you're in a relationship and you run your own business. We have to talk this through and find a solution. It's what people do—'

'But you're not even interested—'

'I am interested,' I'd whispered, 'Can we talk when I get home – over dinner?'

'I had tapas at lunchtime so I'm not hungry.'

'Tapas?'

'Yeah, Marion and I huddled on the beach behind a break-water.'

The baby opposite me starts howling and the young mum ignores him. She's engrossed in her phone and the baby squeals. The woman looks up at me and our eyes meet then she opens her shirt and takes out her swollen breast. With its eyes closed the baby finds her nipple and sucks greedily. It's finally silent and I turn away.

Outside the carriage, Rochester Castle and the cathedral are illuminated and they flash past until the train glides to a stop at the station. I feel the eyes of the man across the aisle regarding me in the dark reflection of the window.

The memory of Cassie's voice rings in my ear.

'You leave home every day before six in the morning and you're never home before nine, and at the weekend you're always tired. You're not interested in the business—'

The man across the aisle stands up. On his way off the train he gives me a quick wink and I shake my head irritably at him.

'You should give up your job and work with me,' Cassie

22

whined.

'For heaven's sake, Cassie. I work for one of the top lawyers in London – that's what I want to do. I've already sold my flat in London so that we can live by the sea and you can have your dream. I'm even happy to commute every day but you must sort your life out and your business.'

'I want to spend more time with you.'

'Then you should have opened a café in London.'

'You're missing the point as usual,' Cassie said dryly. 'But it's up to you, Amber. Commuting is your choice. I think you should quit your job. We could run the café and be together every day. You don't realise how much I want to be with you. I sometimes wonder if you love me at all…'

Same old conversation, only this time, tonight – Cassie hadn't picked up the phone.

* * *

I'm greeted by the smell of the Indian takeaway and it reminds me that I haven't eaten since this morning. The front door is stuck so I kick it open.

The café is closed. There are no lights on, just the yellow streetlights illuminating the empty premises.

Upstairs, the flat smells of damp and tonight there's an air of emptiness.

'Scruff-bucket?' I call softly but there's no dull thud and no purring.

In the bedroom the empty wardrobe stands like a toothless smile – a mouth's dark cavern.

I open the sash window; opposite me, the travel agency is the only shop that is closed and boarded up permanently, and

23

it looks so out of character in the pretty street. Beside it, there are lights on in the art gallery but Marion's boutique on the left side lies in darkness.

I find Cassie's note sellotaped to the fridge.

Hi Amber,

Karl starts in a few weeks (not sure of the date). He has lots of people skills and will probably make more of a success of it than I could.

Things haven't been working out between us and I think this is for the best for both of us.

I never realised that I would miss London. Now that this pandemic is over (hopefully) I can return to my true love – the theatre.

Marion said she will keep an eye on you and help out if you need her.

I hope that we will stay friends.

Love Cassie xx

P.s. Please don't think badly of me.

I sit at our small bistro table in the flat staring down into Harbour Street and eventually, just after ten o'clock, Cassie finally answers her mobile.

'How can you just walk out like this?' I ask quietly.

'I had to. Believe me, it wasn't an easy decision.'

'But we never even discussed anything.'

She doesn't answer me.

'Cassie, why didn't you talk to me, confide in me, tell me you wanted to go back to London? I never even knew you went for an interview at the Barbican.'

'I couldn't.'

'Why?'

She answers sullenly, 'I've let you down.'

'We could have talked it through.'

She begins sobbing and I can hear her sniffing.

I say, 'I wish you'd told me that you didn't want this life and that this was just another whim of yours. It would have saved me a lot of money,' I say gently.

'You'll survive, Amber. It's only a café,' she replies, and I hear her blowing her nose.

'It's only a café?' I repeat slowly. 'Only a café.'

'I miss London, Amber. It's alright for you – you were coming back here every day but I was stuck down there.'

'*You* said you loved it here and that you never wanted to live anywhere else. I took out a massive mortgage—'

'Only because I couldn't get one in my name.'

'That's not the point.'

'I made a mistake, Amber.'

'I sold my flat.'

'I know. I'm sorry.'

'I would never have thought of moving here, Cassie. My life and my career are in London.' I stare down into the street below. A young couple wrapped in scarves and thick coats are carrying fish and chips and walking quickly, huddled against the wind.

'You can sell it, Amber. I don't want it.'

'What?' I reply.

'Sell the café. You can move back here. You could buy a flat in the Barbican and we could be together,' she says.

I don't answer.

'Well?'

'Well what?' I ask.

25

'Do you still love me?'

'Not at this present moment – no.'

'Don't be too hard on me, Amber. Please try and see it from my point of view.'

'I'm trying very hard to do that.'

'So, what will you do?'

'I don't know, Cassie. I have no idea.'

Chapter 3

Martin's leaving party is at the end of the month and, as I'm taking over his share of our litigation clients, I spend most of the weekend going through his files and making notes. Finally, on Sunday I have a few hours to go down to the café and I know I can't put off the inevitable.

I hang three large prints of Italian cities on the walls; stone houses, pretty cobbled streets and colourful flowers that all remind me of my grandma's home in the hills outside Milan and the happy times I've spent there. I check the stock and to my amazement there's one cupboard in the kitchen that is filled with enough ingredients to bake cakes and bread for the whole year. Again, this was just another job that Cassie never got around to doing.

I find a screwed up, old note hidden behind the toaster.

'Electrician – wiring for coffee maker. Plumber – dishwasher and leaking downstairs toilet tap, phone company for Wi-Fi installation...' I mumble aloud. 'Carpenter – shelves. Check flat roof – looks like a leak in the bathroom.'

I hear Cassie's voice in my head. Snatches of conversations are a regular occurrence; sometimes welcome but sometimes upsetting:

'I'll need money for advertising.'

'A couple of thousand.'

'There's a glossy local magazine that all the wealthy local people read—'

'This is Harbour Street. This is *the* street. It's the most expensive and upmarket street in the town. It has the expensive boutique, as well as all the independent retailers. These are local, *wealthy*, shopkeepers and I will *not* be their poor relation.'

I sigh and shake my head. Where did those memories come from?

What has she been doing every day?

There's a heavy rapping on the front window. A man with a heavy frown and dark beard presses his face against the glass. I recognise him as the man sitting alone in the pub the night Cassie and Marion were celebrating. He has a brown and black dog on a lead that sits patiently at his feet.

'Are you open?' he shouts.

I shake my head. 'Not yet.'

He's scowling as he raps hard on the window again and I think he might break the glass so I unlock the door and fling it open.

'What do you mean, not yet? It's past lunchtime.'

'Well, we're not open.'

'Well, what time are you open then?' His tone is angry and aggressive.

I say aloud and with polite firmness, 'We are *not* open – at all.' I point at the closed sign hanging on the door.

His eyes are blazing with anger. 'What's the point of having a café if you don't open it and sell coffee?'

'We are going to – I am opening it. I—'

'It's all a waste of bloody time. Useless woman.' He turns

quickly away and his dog follows and I slam the door on his back.

* * *

Martin's client, who is now my client, has paid more than he ought to have done for a lease on a commercial business in Clerkenwell. He has also agreed, illegally, to sublet the property, giving the renter the right to run a business in the property for twelve months.

It takes me a few hours to read all the legal clauses and I cannot believe the mess that people create for themselves. I'm so engrossed with the paperwork that it's seven o'clock by the time I leave my office and arrive at St Pancras.

It's been a difficult day and my head is throbbing. Given half the chance I would stay over in London for the night but since Cassie left I've still kept the routine of going home to a musky smelling flat and getting up again early for my commute.

Keeping busy.

It's under ten minutes to walk from Westbay train station and I yawn as I push open the gated door to the alleyway and the entrance to our flat – my flat.

The smell of curry is enticing and tonight it is stronger than the sea air. The front door appears unlocked but it's still stuck. Puzzled, I kick it open.

'Cassie?' I call.

A young black guy with a patchy beard and a nose stud looks around the kitchen door. He wears a turquoise shirt and yellow jeans. He holds a tea towel and waves. 'Hi.'

'What the—'

'I'm Karl – Karl with a K not Karl with a C. You must be

Amber. Cassie's left me in charge. I'm the new manager.'

'Manager?' I glance around and I'm relieved to see that the café looks neater. The chairs and tables have been set up and the cardboard packaging has disappeared.

'Is Cassie here?' I ask.

'She's gone, hasn't she?' he replies with a frown. 'Back to London?'

I nod and he continues, 'So I'm all organised for the morning.'

'The morning?'

'We're opening tomorrow, aren't we?'

'Are you the friend of Marion's? Did she recommend you?'

'Who? I don't know anyone called Marion. Cassie gave me the job. I walked past here a few weeks ago and it looked like the café was going to open up and the guy in the art gallery across the road found me the phone number. So, I called and Cassie gave me the job but I couldn't start until today. I did tell her. Didn't she tell you?'

'How did you get in?'

'She gave me a key.'

'A key? Have you worked in a café before?' I sling my bag onto the counter.

'No, but it's hardly rocket science is it?'

'Umm, no, I suppose not. Do you have any retail experience?'

'I used to be a vet's receptionist then I worked for an undertaker, and my last job was cleaning a pet shop.'

'What a varied career,' I mumble.

Karl begins to wipe the counter. He's light on his feet and he appears to dance as he moves quickly around and I'm irritated, he seems so much at home. He's taller than me, and

30

on closer inspection I see he has tattoos on his arms and studs around his ears. This stranger also has complete access to our personal space upstairs – to my flat. We've never locked the door between the café and the flat. Cassie didn't even know this guy and yet she gave him a key.

I take my mobile from my bag and dial Cassie's number. It rings then clicks to her answerphone.

'Cassie, call me when you get this message,' I say, then I turn my attention back to Karl.

I need time to think. I need space.

'You've worked hard, thank you, Karl, but you can't stay this late if you're opening in the morning. It will be an early start for you. Did Cassie say what time you were opening?'

'She said around eleven.'

'Eleven?'

'Yes. She said there was no hurry and you can give me some money to buy the stuff we need first thing. I'll go to the supermarket.'

'You will miss all the breakfast trade,' I say.

He looks at me blankly, so I continue, 'Cassie and I had talked about a special opening with all the local retailers in the area, like a soft opening, did she mention it to you?'

He frowns and shakes his head. 'No. I don't think so.'

He must see the disappointment on my face so he adds with a bright smile, 'But it is something I can do. I've done it before.'

'At the undertakers?' I grin.

'Oh no, at the pet shop actually but to be honest not many people turned up.'

'Here in town?'

'No I was living in Wales then. In a tiny village. I hated it.'

'And where do you live now?'

31

'Just up the road. I've rented a caravan,' he says proudly. 'I want to impress my girlfriend.'

* * *

The next morning I'm reluctant to leave for work but I make sure I lock the adjoining door between the flat and the café. Afterwards, I stand for a minute in Harbour Street to stare at the front of the café. There is still no painted sign, no café name, hanging above the door. Cassie was organising a signwriter but like most things it never happened.

Although we had worked companionably last night until past ten o'clock, I walk up the street toward the train station reluctant to leave Karl alone. He's opening the café today, on his own, for takeaways. He's prepared to heat part-baked rolls and frozen croissants and he's coming in early to make sandwiches.

When I get to my office, instead of researching for my next litigation case, I spend hours Googling recipes for cupcakes and various types of bread. I place an order online for same day delivery and phone Karl mid-morning to tell him my plans.

'You'll cook?' he says.

'Bake. Tonight when I get home. There's enough ingredients to fill a supermarket. And you can sell them in the café. At least you can offer something for people to eat. Even if the menu is limited, it will be different.' I don't tell him my budget is limited and I have little access to money now because I'm maxed out on my credit card. I'm also determined not to waste the stock in the kitchen.

'But what about breakfast?'

'We will have to stick to croissants, toast and filled rolls. Nothing too complicated. You can't be in the kitchen and serving tea and coffee and clearing up. You'll need help. I've phoned the job centre.'

'Will I interview them?' he says excitedly. 'I am the manager.'

'No, I will arrange to meet them in the evening.'

'Oh? But what if we don't get on? What if I don't like them?'

'I'm confident you will, Karl. You are so lovely you will get on with anyone,' I say truthfully.

I spend the next few hours with a client then afterwards I telephone Karl. There is no answer.

I imagine going home and my flat is ransacked, all the boxes gone and it's completely empty but then my phone rings and it's my litigation client and all thoughts of Karl and the café leave my head.

On the train going home I read through cupcake recipes and icing methods and when I walk home from the station, I'm imagining an evening of baking ahead of me.

The café is in darkness.

There is no Karl and no note but the supplies I ordered are packed neatly away, so I tie an apron around my waist.

I measure ingredients, mix thoroughly, and separate paper casings in the baking tray. I throw one lot in after another, cool them, leave them to stand and prepare the icing. By midnight I am exhausted. The sponge cakes are still too warm to decorate so I fall into bed setting the alarm at four o'clock so I can ice them before I leave. I've never baked before. I'm a savoury person and the sweetness of the flavours makes me feel quite ill.

I'm at my office desk in London when I phone Karl.

'Are the cakes okay?' I ask.

'For a mothers' meeting or for a charity fundraising they're fine but not for a five-star café in Harbour Street. They're simply awful.'

'What?'

'They're lopsided and they look like a child of five decorated them.' He laughs.

'Can you sell them?'

'Couldn't give them away.'

My heart sinks. All that effort and still so many baking ingredients in the cupboard. 'I'll do something else tonight.'

'Like what?'

'Maybe a chocolate cake?'

'Choose something that doesn't need much imagination or decoration, Amber,' he replies before adding quickly, 'Oops! Busy! Customer's here – have to go.'

* * *

That night when I get home there are receipts from credit card payments and a note from Karl.

You need to buy a safe for the cash. A girl turned up from the job centre but she wasn't suitable. K.

There's also an envelope with twenty-three pounds in cash.

I spend the evening baking then fall into bed and set the alarm early so that in the morning I can heat up fresh croissants and bread rolls for Karl.

It's a busy day in the office but with the promise of lockdown easing I leave work early and once I'm home I head into the café where I rearrange the furniture, disinfect the tables and sweep the floor, which Karl must have forgotten to do.

I check the space between the tables and bake fresh bread; rolls with aniseed, and trays of rolls with chopped Brazil and hazelnuts, and other rolls with grated orange peel.

The next morning Karl phones me.

'What is wrong with you?' he asks. 'Where do you get your recipes from – Mars? Is this what aliens eat?'

'Are they popular?'

'No. Stop even trying, Amber. Concentrate on what you do best. The clients want quality. Must dash – here's a customer. Hello, Ben, how are y—' He hangs up.

He leaves me hanging on the line with my mouth open. Later in the afternoon I have the opportunity to phone the job centre for the third time.

'But we've sent three people around to you already,' the lady says, checking her computer.

'I asked you to phone me,' I reply testily.

'We did phone but there was no answer so we sent the applicants around to the shop.'

'Café.'

'Yes. There.'

I sigh and hang up. Between clients, I dial the number for a sign-writer and I'm pleased to get through on the first ring. I explain what I want and he tells me it will be at least a month until he can get around to it.

By Friday afternoon I'm exhausted. A month I think, another month without a sign or a name for the café. I take a quick look at staff uniforms before meeting my last client of the week and that's when my boss arrives in my office.

Ralph Stewart is dressed in his customary Savile Row pinstripe suit and he looks every inch the successful lawyer with receding pepper-grey hair and a firm jawline. Based on his looks alone and his charming smile you would trust him; you'd probably even want to marry him.

'Amber, how are you?' His tone is soft and his voice caring and I feel my eyes welling up at his concern. It's been a long time since anyone took an interest or even cared about me. He continues, 'You've been taking on most of Martin's work and I wondered how it's all going?'

He perches on my desk, leaving me to lean back in my chair and look up at him.

'Fine. All under control.'

He gazes at me and smiles.

'You look exhausted. You also look… a mess.'

I nod. I don't trust myself to speak. I have been averaging four hours sleep a night for almost four weeks.

'At least it's Friday, so perhaps you can have a proper break and get plenty of sleep this weekend?' he suggests.

I manage a grin.

'Are you enjoying life beside the sea?'

He was not a supporter of my move to the coast.

'It's different,' I reply, hiding a heavy sigh and biting down heavily on my bottom lip.

'A long commute,' he agrees. 'You need to think about what you want out of life and where you need to be. You clearly can't continue like this, Amber, you'll be ill.'

Chapter 4

I try to get into some sort of routine and on Saturdays I work companionably with Karl all day. Jean, a middle-aged woman with two sons in their early twenties who still live at home, has joined us. She is happy to be in the kitchen preparing breakfasts and lunches.

'It's like feeding my tribe at home,' she says good-naturedly. She's small and overweight and she's lived in Westbay all her life and, in her words, has worked just about everywhere at one time or another. An extra pair of hands is welcome and she's amenable and efficient. She and Karl chat away like old friends.

We managed to get through Easter and the weather is warming up and encouraging visitors to the coast. Today is busy with young families and couples ambling down to the harbour.

Karl is efficient and polite with the customers, he's also fast at serving and he keeps me on my toes. Now that I'm buying in cakes and scones it's easier but I am still exhausted. We run out of bread twice and I go to the supermarket across the square to replenish the stock. At the end of the day Karl laughs and high-fives my hand.

'Well, we survived another Saturday.'

'Thank you.' I grin.

'Day off tomorrow.' He leans on the counter. 'Are you going out tonight?'

I grin. 'I can barely stand or even keep my eyes open, Karl.'

'Just a hot bath and a glass of wine then. Have fun, Amber. I'm meeting my girlfriend in Canterbury. Molly has agreed to move in with me.'

'Have you known her long?'

'We met at the undertakers, she was a receptionist.'

'Dying to fall in love?' I tease.

He grins. 'Dead gorgeous and she's very special, Amber.' He dances as he moves, wiggling his hips salsa style and then he stops and says seriously. 'But she also suffers from depression. She's very anxious but we're good for each other. You know when you just meet – the one.'

No, I didn't or maybe I thought I did.

'Well, have a lovely evening both of you,' I reply. 'She's a lucky girl.'

'I'm taking her to Nando's.' He beams.

'Lovely.'

I turn quickly away as my eyes fill with tears of self-pity, a lump forms in my throat and my heart burns. I'm so tired and I think of another takeaway, alone upstairs and the bathroom full of damp. Carrie had promised she'd paint it and make this flat our first proper home together. She'd even said she felt guilty about bringing me here from my luxury London apartment – but obviously not guilty enough to do anything to make it like a proper home.

After Karl leaves I'm about to lock up when the café door opens.

JJ looks vibrant, fresh, happy and she's smiling. Her makeup is immaculate and her fingers are adorned in an assortment of unusual chunky rings; a skull, cross-keys, and a shiny fake diamond.

'Hi, Amber, I just want to welcome you properly to Harbour Street. I see that you're open now and oh wow, it looks lovely in here. I love the pictures on the wall – all very Italian – little Italy.' She giggles.

'Thank you.'

'We haven't had a chance to chat properly and, as a business-woman like you, I know how lonely it can be in the beginning – it's all very overwhelming. I remember what it felt like when I came here.'

'Really?' I mumble, surprised at her friendliness.

She leans her hip against the table and looks around. 'I understand how hard it must be for you, coping with the café and trying to commute backwards and forwards to London. You must be exhausted. You look tired.'

I turn away so she doesn't see tears of self-pity in my eyes and she continues.

'But you've done so well, this place looks really amazing. Did you paint it yourself?'

'Yes, does it look like it?'

'No.' She pauses and the lie hangs between us as she looks around with interest and delight.

'I love the chalk board. It's a great way to get your specials known. Much better than grubby paper menus. Oh, I see you have those too.'

'They're easily wipeable.'

'You've got plastic covers on them, wonderful.'

'It's all down to Karl, he's been brilliant.'

'Have you got a name for the café yet?'

39

'I'm still working on that one.'

'I'm sure you'll come up with something; Ground Beans or Café Aroma, Amber's Place or something original like that.'

I smile.

'And of course, I suppose you'll be getting an awning like all the other shops in the street, but choose your colour wisely so it won't clash.' She laughs. 'I don't think the turquoise Kingdom Pets shop goes with the olive green Mobile2Go shop. To be honest, I think they must be colour-blind. Anyway, I'm here to help if you need any pointers, help or advice.'

'Thank you.'

'Well, that's what you need, Amber. It's what we all need. Support. And, I just want to let you know that we are all here for you. If there's anything you need, you only have to ask.' She grins. 'I'm only on the corner and I know what it's like running a business.'

'It can't be easy, running a pub,' I reply.

'Oh, I'm used to it.'

'Have you always been in hospitality?'

'Goodness, no.'

'Have you had it long?'

'I bought it about ten years ago and there's nothing I haven't been through.' Her laughter is bright and easy, her tone friendly and engaging. 'But you know what people are like, Amber. There are easy ones and difficult ones. Fortunately, I like to think I've cultivated the right sort of people who come in the pub. There's always a friendly atmosphere and the banter is healthy – it's welcoming.'

'You sound like you enjoy it.'

'It's hard work. It's alright if you have the right staff but of course when they let you down it's awful. You must come and have a drink. I'm sure you need to relax and unwind. I hope to have the live bands playing outside again soon.'

I nod but don't reply. My back aches and I want to sleep.

'Have you met all the other Harbour Street owners yet?'

This time I shake my head.

'Well, I'm surprised Frances hasn't been around. She's the vicar. She keeps the peace around here. I think she puts the fear of God into everyone, literally! Some people say I'm not really in Harbour Street, that the pub is really in the square but as I have a side entrance, I do count. We have a Harbour Street committee and I'm normally the one who organises everything. We're a very friendly bunch. There's Derek the butcher and Ian the grocer, they have been here for donkey's years so if there's anything you want to know just ask them – or me of course.' She smiles. Her black eyeliner and straight nose give her a regal appearance.

'It's a shame about that building opposite.' I nod at the boarded-up travel agents.

'Yes, that's an eyesore. They closed because of the pandemic during the first lockdown and everyone stopped travelling abroad. I'm not surprised it's closed. Most people book online now anyway. Well no one will want it now. Only an idiot would open a new business here what with everything we've all been though in the past few years. Things have been bad for everyone in the country. It's a shame as Harbour Street was just taking off.'

'Where did you move from, JJ?'

'I moved from Devon and it's the best thing I've ever done. I love it here. This is home now. It probably doesn't feel that way for you yet but it will do soon, Amber. Things will pick up and when it does you'll feel much happier.'

I shake my head and smile.

Home?

She hasn't seen the flat upstairs.

She grins. 'Well, why don't you pop over for a drink one night – maybe during the week? It's quieter then and we can have a catch up and I can fill you in and introduce you to everyone. Most of them drink in there – and it's a great way to meet the locals and socialise with everyone. Marion is a loyal friend and she misses Cassie. It would be great for you to get to know her.'

'I might just do that.'

JJ smiles. 'Please do. It will do you the world of good. Come and have a drink on me.'

* * *

After JJ has gone, I'm about to go upstairs when there's a rap on the windowpane. I sigh. I don't want to speak to anyone else but the thought of going upstairs is equally unappealing.

A petite blonde girl is standing with a bouquet of flowers.

It must be a delivery – who would send me flowers?

'Hello?' I open the door.

'Hello, I am Eva. I am originally from Poland but I have been here twenty years,' she says in a clipped tone. Her voice is heavily accented and her face serious. She thrusts the flowers at me. 'These are for you. Welcome. Happy opening.'

'Er, thank you. I'm Amber. They're beautiful, Eva,' I say truthfully. 'I love sunflowers.'

'Me too.' She beams but her smile is short-lived and she points across the road. 'I'm from the flower shop; Darling Buds and Blooms. These are left over and, as I don't open on

Sundays until next month, by Monday they will be past their best.'

'I know how they feel,' I reply.

'You are ill?' She frowns.

'No, just exhausted. It's been a busy day.'

She tilts her head to one side and I realise then that she is not as young as I originally thought. She has crow's feet each side of her blue eyes and she's probably even older than me; mid-forties.

'Well, have a good rest tomorrow and take care of yourself.'

'Thank you, Eva.'

She turns to walk away and I call out, 'Eva, do you ever drink in The Ship?'

She frowns and shakes her head. 'No, never. That woman JJ served my children alcohol last year. They were seventeen and underage and I am not happy with her.'

I nod. 'She seems to think it's a place where all the locals go.'

Eva shrugs. 'Not for me or Sanjay in the Indian, and not him either – Ben Taylor.' She points to Taylor's Art Gallery beside her shop. 'They hate each other.'

'Is that the man with a black and brown dog?' I say, referring to the angry man with the beard who rapped on the café door. I've seen him a few times in the art gallery and now, as we speak, he's changing the display in the window. He ignores us, his wide shoulders look cramped in the pretty double-fronted window space and I realise it's been a long time, before we moved here, since I've actually walked through Harbour Street and looked in the shop windows.

Eva continues, 'He's angry at the whole world. But Ben's very clever with his hands. He makes amazing chess sets, have you seen them?'

I shake my head. I don't tell her I've hardly ventured out of my own flat except to go to work in London.

'Well,' she says decisively. 'Have a look sometime, they are incredible but don't go near him because he's always very angry. He hates everyone. Although my shop is next door to his I don't have much to do with him. He often just scowls at everyone, not like Ozan and Yusef, do you know them?'

I shake my head.

'They have the Turkish barbers on the far side of Ben's gallery. They're really funny. Do you know anyone in Harbour Street?' she asks.

'I haven't really had time—'

'I know, wasn't your girlfriend Cassie running the café?'

'She was going to but—'

She holds up her hand. 'I know. James, my husband, left me eighteen months ago for his secretary. You couldn't make it up – that old cliché. A younger model of me.' She reaches out and touches my hand and her eyes fill up with tears. 'But it still hurts. The kids have never forgiven him – or me. Nick and Emma are twins and they've just done their A levels and it's all been a mess for them with this education process at the moment, but they're going off to uni in September. They can't wait to leave. I think they just want to get away from me.'

'I'm sure they love you but it's natural progression for them to want to move on—'

'James can't wait for them to go. He thinks they'll come around to his way of thinking and he'll have more access to them. He will buy them, you know, offer them luxury holidays and expensive gifts and I will lose them. I may lose them for good. He's very persuasive and he's often not kind. He's a bully. You have to hold the same opinion of everyone that he has, or he thinks you're being deliberately disloyal.' Her eyes are dark and worried and I realise I'm not the only one in the street who has problems.

'That's tough, Eva. At least Cassie only took Scruff-bucket.'

'Who?'

'The cat,' I explain.

Eva looks at me and tilts her head wondering if I'm joking but I'm tired and I give her an apologetic smile.

She brightens. 'Sanjay is lovely. His chicken curry is good too.'

'Sanjay is the only person I've really spoken to, he keeps me trying his new dishes, I've been living off takeaways,' I explain.

'I tell him my Polish food is better than his Indian recipes but he doesn't believe me,' she says, touching her nose and laughing self-consciously. It suits her and it's the first sign of her sense of humour.

I think of Sanjay's greying hair and handsome smile. 'Then maybe you should cook him dinner,' I tease.

She shakes her head angrily and turns away. 'I'm not like that,' she replies tersely.

I want to call out to her, I'm sorry, forgive me and thank you for the flowers but she's already crossing the street, tottering on high heels, and I'm left feeling much lonelier than I could have possibly imagined.

Chapter 5

'Are you finding it too much to cope with, Amber?' JJ asks, sliding a gin and tonic across the counter for me.

Coming to The Ship for a drink had seemed like a good idea in the loneliness of the flat but now, in the pub with couples and families all drinking and laughing around me, the jovial atmosphere and gentle banter, I feel even more isolated.

'You'll soon get the hang of it,' she says.

I smile at her optimism rather than her practicality. Outside the rain lashes against the window. 'I don't think I'm cut out for this,' I say.

There's a flicker of interest on her face, and a quick frown causes small wrinkles on her carefully made-up face that remind me of tiny ripples on a smooth pond.

'You'll be fine.'

In the far corner, Ben – the man from the art gallery with the thick beard and heavy scowl – is seated at the same table as the night Cassie and Marion were drunk. He nurses a pint and stares back at us as if he hates everyone.

'Take no notice of him,' JJ says, following my glance. 'He's a weirdo. Stay away – give him a body swerve.'

She moves away effortlessly and elegantly, gliding with familiarity between the bottles, chatting across the bar and greeting customers with ease.

I run my fingers along the bar counter. 'I'll be fine.' My voice is hoarse and my throat tight as if trapped in a nervous seizure like it was when I had spoken to my mother last weekend. She had phoned me from Grandma's home near Milan and she had sounded worried.

'Fly over at the weekend. Come and visit us, Amber,' she insisted. I imagined her fingers gripping the telephone and my father standing at her shoulder, both of them gazing out across the garden to the hills beyond.

'I can't. I've too much to do,' I'd stated flatly.

'I do worry about you,' she said.

'I'm fine,' I had lied.

'Amber?' JJ stands in front of me and I blink, suddenly remembering where I am.

'Sorry,' I grin. 'I was miles away. I think I need a coffee. A quick dose of caffeine and I'll be as right as rain.'

I grab my bag. I suddenly can't wait to get out. I have never felt claustrophobic before, especially in a pub. It would be laughable if I didn't feel so sad.

'You haven't finished your drink,' JJ calls after me.

'Next time,' I mumble.

Outside, the rain has stopped and there's a burst of bright evening sunlight. It fills the street. A woman is shaking rainwater from a brolly with determination and a bright smile. She waves and I think she might want to speak to me but I put my head down, ignore her and head back to the safe space of my flat.

* * *

Ralph Stewart is waiting for me in the office, but instead of his usual jovial confident smile his face has a weary and sad look.

'What's wrong?' I ask.

His lips form a tight line before he takes a deep breath. 'I know that you were hoping for a partnership in the firm, Amber, but I'm really sorry, it's not going to happen.'

My knees buckle and I slide into the chair opposite him. 'Why?'

He spreads his arms wide and smiles sadly. 'I have to be honest. You're killing yourself with this commute and trying to run the café at the weekends.'

'It hasn't affected my work,' I argue.

He sighs. 'Not affected, no, but you can't give it the same amount of time.'

'I do,' I protest but he holds up his hand.

'Look, Amber, I want – no, I need someone who will give me everything. I need more than a hundred percent, you know what this business is like—'

'You'll get it. I just need a bit more time.'

He raises his neatly trimmed eyebrows. 'More time?'

'Yes, the café is up for sale and I'm moving back to London.'

He shakes his head. 'And how long will it take you to sell the place?'

I shrug.

'Realistically, Amber, it's May now and you will not sell it this side of Christmas.'

'You don't know that.'

He smiles. 'Look, I'm really sorry. Martin told me what happened with you and Cassie. It's just really bad luck that you invested in that café and moved away.'

48

'I can manage.'

'Have you looked in the mirror? Have you seen the state of yourself? You have shadows all around your eyes and, I saw you napping in the meeting yesterday morning—'

I open my mouth.

'You even snored.'

I giggle nervously. 'It was an accident.'

Ralph smiles. 'You were dribbling.'

I wipe my mouth with my fingertip, cursing myself for not painting my nails. At one time I would be groomed to within an inch of my life, smelling of expensive perfume, my hair styled, and I'd be relaxed after an expensive massage. I stare out of the window at the familiar site of the Embankment and the London Eye and bite my thumbnail.

'Why don't you take a sabbatical?' he suggests. 'I wouldn't offer it to anyone else but I value the ten years you've been with us.'

'Martin thought I'd get a partnership,' I wail, hating the sound of my voice.

'Martin's not here anymore and things change, Amber. People move on. Circumstances change.' Ralph's tight understanding smile disappears as he checks his watch. 'Sorry, Amber, I have another meeting. Clear your workload by the end of the month.'

'You're firing me?'

'I'm offering you a sabbatical.'

'Paid?'

Ralph shakes his head. 'I'm sorry, no.'

I stand up and tug down the hem of my skirt. 'Call it what you like, Ralph. You're firing me.'

* * *

Never underestimate the power of the perfect spring sky, the shape of hazy fluffy clouds, their wispy format textured like white candyfloss and the soft rustle under the shade of the trees. It's Sunday morning and I walk with determined strides with my hands tucked deep into my jacket pocket and my chin wedged inside the collar.

Dog walkers let their pets run free. A brindle boxer darts between the rows of beach huts sniffing excitedly, probably at the scent of a fox and a small terrier chases a tumbling feather while a man hurls a tennis ball for an excited spaniel.

I have decisions to make.

Ralph is right. I can't continue commuting and trying to run the café. I'm exhausted and as hard as I try to block out my responsibility for the café, I'm financially bound to this weighted anchor around my neck. It's drowning me.

I have already listed the café and the flat for sale with the local estate agents but they don't hold out much hope I'll even get what I paid for the property. Business is slow, they said.

It turns out that not only have I overpaid for the property, with the work needed to repair the flat it will end up costing far more than its market value.

Without the income from my job in London, I will have no money to pay off the mortgage on the property or to invest in the business.

I'm no longer angry with Cassie.

I've turned the anger on myself. I'm furious at my own stupidity. How could I have been so naive as to think Cassie would want to spend her life with me?

She had been my only friend – apart from Martin who is

now in Australia. I can't believe he's told Ralph about my situation with Cassie and about the café. He had been my rock yet he's let me down. He had no right to discuss my life with my boss.

My life has always been my work, the law firm and I was on the verge of a partnership – even Martin had acknowledged that but then he went and jeopardised it. I'd been trying to hide my situation but Martin had told Ralph.

I lean on the wall and gaze out at the sea.

Cassie had given my job the kiss of death.

In the beginning she had brought sunshine and excitement to my life. When we met at a corporate musical event, she was full of life and passion. She was excited and I'd been caught up in her dreams. She'd been on the stage then, in her last major role in *Hairspray* in the West End but then Covid had struck and although Cassie and I hadn't been ill, everything changed. Theatres closed and it was as if a light in her died too. She said she wanted stability and that she would welcome routine and that she needed a challenge, a business and a forever home.

She wanted me.

I couldn't believe my luck. Cassie a gorgeous, glamorous actress – wanted me.

The café was never my dream, nor was Westbay and certainly not Harbour Street but where does that leave me now?

I think back to my last phone conversation with my parents. Now they've retired early, they spend most of their time at their home near the Italian lakes, near the home of my maternal grandma and, although I spend holidays there, London has been my home for years.

'I hate the city,' Mama had said. 'Milan, London, Rome –

they're all the same. Lovely buildings but faceless people.'

'Come and see us,' Papa had said. 'Now the lockdown is over, come and rescue me from these mad Italian women.'

They had liked Cassie. They enjoyed the theatre. They only wanted me to be happy – and well fed but I still hadn't the heart to tell them. Each time we FaceTime I pretend that I'm happy and all is well – I'm too ashamed to tell them the truth; that I followed my heart and not my head.

They would be very disappointed in me.

Looking around me now, after months of restraint and intermittent lockdowns the May bank holiday is busy. Couples stroll in leisurely fashion, children run wildly on the beach and dogs pull on their leashes. Optimistic families are even having picnics on the beach, and lighting small barbecues.

To my right, a broad-shouldered man stands at the shore edge staring out to sea. He's wearing shorts, wellingtons and a colourful, striped tank-top, his beard is thick and ragged and when he turns to look in my direction his grey eyes are sad and thoughtful.

He wipes his eyes. Is he crying?

It's Ben Taylor, the grumpy owner of the art gallery across from the café. He appears to stare at me so I raise my hand in greeting but he ignores me and turns abruptly away.

Feeling ridiculously rejected I dodge back through the narrow alleyways to the harbour, and I spend a while watching the fishing boats before turning back to Harbour Street. Under the old stone clock tower the sun comes out and it's suddenly hot, and I'm aware of the atmosphere and how the street is beginning to get busy.

Perhaps I should open the café on Sundays. I need the income.

I stroll along, looking in the windows, absorbed in the luxury of this pretty, quaint street with its uneven roofs, and quirky shopfronts. Each property is unique, some with bay windows and others modern and sleek. There's a blend of artistic and historic influences; each shop caring for its outside space with flowers and exotic plant pots, colourful awnings and a variety of outdoor furniture.

Only cars or lorries delivering have access down the narrow road to the harbour, which is invariably at the beginning or end of the day. If it happens at any other time it becomes an event to watch the driver negotiate the narrow route between the stone legs of Colossus, the clock tower.

Jean has filled me in on most of the shop owners. She's given me a brief resume on their names and a rundown of the characters in the street and now I consider the businesses; the double-fronted window of the Turkish barber's, Eva's friends, has an expensive circular logo stencilled on the window.

The Grooming Room – Esquires of Westbay.

I shade my eyes and peer through the glass.

Ozan and Yusef, obviously brothers, are dressed in black trousers and neatly ironed immaculate white shirts. Their salon is busy and neither of them looks up. It's a classic male grooming shop, luxuriously fitted with three steel and black leather grooming chairs in front of wall-sized-mirrors. There's an expensive array of wet shaving sets, and an assortment of colourful beard brushes all with their well-crafted logo. In the window are gift sets; a skull armour wet shaving set, marble effect razors, boxes of unique cufflinks, spotted bowties, lapel pins and belts. There's also a variety of creams, gels and sprays. Outside on a wooden bench a queue of young men is already forming.

Next to them, on my right, is Taylor's Gallery with a navy awning, then Eva's, Darling Buds and Blooms with its bay window and beautiful floral displays in grey wheelbarrows, and on wooden shelves are a variety of flower pots and watering cans. All very tasteful and well-presented. It's a sea of colour, beautiful, and the aromas of the fresh flowers fill my senses. Eva is now open on Sundays and she's busy inside and doesn't look up.

The boarded-up travel agents looks out of place.

On the far side the wooden-framed windows of Marion's Très Chic Boutique holds two bald dummies draped in expensive red and white dresses with matching accessories; bags, scarves and summer jackets. The price tags have been hidden.

On the left, Jane's Jewellery shop with a cream awning is opening up. She wears colourful trousers and pink lipstick. Her shop window displays rings, necklaces and earrings on soft colourful cushions that are minimalist and expensive. The sign in the window says that everything is bespoke and hand-made and commissions are undertaken, and again, all the price tags have been turned away from curious eyes of the window-shoppers.

In From The Heart Gift Shop, Kit and Jenna are busy hanging out a mixture of beach items from crab lines and buckets to sunglasses and beach hats. Colourful bunting hangs in the window along with pictures of ice creams. They don't look up as they work but I realise they will be busy today and, if I want to make money to pay the bills, I will have to open the café at the weekends. It's the busiest time of the week.

As I walk past Ian in the grocers, he smiles vaguely at me and I wonder if I should wave back. My café is closed and I'm aware that it's still without a name.

The owner of the Step Ahead beauty salon, Tracey, often pops in for a takeout coffee. She gets along with Jean and they often chat together.

Yesterday Jean had told me about Harbour Street.

'This street was very undesirable up until five years ago. When people first came to Westbay they headed for the main square where they would sit around the fountain. You see, Harbour Street is where all the fishermen lived and they reckoned for years that the whole place still reeked of fish. They said the stench was in the walls, the floorboards and even in the stone. So, some of the owners like Ian and Derek bought their shops for nothing. They think they're the big entrepreneurs.' She laughed.

'And people like me,' Tracey said, 'who have only been here for a couple of years have paid the new market prices but then it all ended in lockdown – and financial disaster.'

'Tell me about it,' I'd replied quietly.

Sanjay's takeaway Indian is closed. And on the corner the courtyard of The Ship is fenced off with trellis and pretty flowers. The last three shops beside the travel agents are; Kingdom Pets shop, Mobile2Go phone shop and the Harbour Butchers.

I don't venture into the square with the newer shops and the church but I focus on a small dog tied up outside the butchers.

Derek the butcher is chatting to the dog's owner and I'm reminded of Scruff-bucket. I miss her and so impulsively I cross the road to Kingdom Pets run by Mario and Luke; they always chat away with Karl when they come in for coffee and seem very pleasant.

I stare in the window but they don't sell pets and there's

no sign of any kittens. I turn away and walk quickly past the closed travel agents that is ripe for development. Marion's Très Chic Boutique is closed, I haven't seen much of her recently and I haven't spoken to her since Cassie left.

I pause outside Taylor's Art Gallery and stare in the window; displayed on a cabinet with three tiers are the most beautiful chess sets, elegantly carved, in fine olive, mahogany, walnut and rosewood: Lord of the Rings, Harry Potter, Alice in Wonderland, US War of Independence, famous London landmarks, local landmarks including Canterbury Cathedral and a beautifully intricate set of Chinese figures.

The attention to detail is so impressive that I find myself crouching down for a better inspection. I'm absorbed. I often played chess with Papa and I'm wondering which one he would like – is it too early to think of Christmas? There's a medieval chess set, an animal one, a sports one and even a literary one with well-known, instantly recognisable fictional detectives like Agatha Christie and Sherlock Holmes.

'Hi.'

I jump up quickly. 'Oh, hi, JJ.' I smile self-consciously. I'd been so totally lost in the beauty and craftsmanship. 'Have you seen these?' I ask, pointing in the window.

She waves her hand dismissively. 'Don't be too impressed. Ben doesn't actually make them. He pretends he does but…' She leans forward to whisper and her eyes darken. 'You can't believe a word he says.'

'Really?'

She leans closer to me. 'He's a bit special, you know, damaged. He's crazy.' She twirls the tip of her finger at her temple. 'He's also very aggressive so be careful. He's spread some awful lies in the past.'

I nod. 'Oh?'

'Yes, about his uncle, but Ben was the one who brokered the deal for me to buy the garage. He persuaded his uncle to sell his garage to me.'

I turn away. Across the street Kit optimistically hangs out some fishing nets and crab lines.

'So, how are you really getting on, Amber? I see you have Jean in the kitchen making the sandwiches and helping Karl out, is she okay?'

'She seems fine.'

'Not opening today?'

'No.'

'Well, I believe you have it up for sale anyway. Charlie, the estate agent, tells me things are very slow moving. Nothing is selling.'

'Yes, that's true.'

'Are you getting back with Cassie and going back to London?'

'Er, I'm going back to London, yes…' I answer truthfully. I don't tell her I haven't spoken to Cassie since the day she left me.

JJ rubs my arm in a reassuring fashion. 'Look, Amber, so long as you know we are all here to help you. We want to keep Harbour Street special. But it would be nice if you got a sign above the café and perhaps an awning?'

She waits expectantly and we both look across to the café.

'It's on my to-do list.' I grin.

'I understand, but we do want to keep this street up to scratch. It's bad enough that the travel agents looks so awful. They went out of business in the first lockdown and couldn't afford the rent or the rates. The property is an eyesore.

There's really no reason not to develop it into something unique.'

I follow her gaze to the boarded shop window and murmur my agreement.

'You'll probably find it hard to sell the café, Amber. You overpaid on it and I believe the flat is in a terrible state – full of damp.'

'How do you know?'

'Oh, Cassie told us in the pub one night. She said it wasn't even fit for her cat.'

I stare at JJ wondering what else Cassie had told her, but before I can ask JJ says, 'I'll see you later at the meeting then. Bye.'

'What meeting?' I ask but JJ has already disappeared. She's ducked into Darling Buds and Blooms and she's already cornered Eva.

Chapter 6

The promise of blue sky and May sunshine has encouraged crowds down from London for the day and I'm sitting inside the closed café staring morosely out at the busy street. I have a cold cup of coffee on the table in front of me and the closed sign is hung inside the door.

I stand up, take a look around the café and head into the kitchen with my dirty cup, drained of emotion and at a loss for what to do.

I lock the café door behind me and venture into the warm sunshine and head toward the beach where I sit against a breakwater, out of the wind, my face turned up toward the sunshine. I've dried my tears of self-pity and I concentrate on all the beautiful nature that continues to live and breathe around me.

There is a quiet time. It's the moment between the wave breaking and the gulls squawking, and I watch the sea flow in and out, deciding on my options and my choices, tossing pebbles into the ebbing tide.

I can keep the property on the market and return to London and pretend this incident never happened or I can continue to live here, fight for my job and put in a manager – Karl?

Do I want a café?

Bored, tired, frustrated, I wander back to Harbour Street and stop at the flower shop thinking I may buy something pretty to cheer up the flat. I am hidden behind the flower display but outside the art gallery a man and a woman appear to be arguing.

'We have to do something,' she's saying, 'and if I'm the only one to stand up to JJ, then so be it. You're all cowards.'

'It's not like that—'

'It's exactly like that, Ben Taylor. You say you're not happy and then when I propose we do something, you don't want to back me.'

'It's not easy,' he replies.

'I thought you wanted justice.'

I peer between the plants on the wooden shelf display. The woman has a strong profile and I recognise her as the woman shaking her umbrella the night I ran out of The Ship.

'I do, it's just that—'

'You're a businessman, Ben. What will this do for you, for all the businesses in town?'

'It will bring employment.'

'There's enough employment. You're making excuses so you don't have to do anything,' she says dismissively. 'Where's your spirit?'

'It's not easy.'

Frances turns to look down the street. She is wearing a vicar's collar and she doesn't notice that I'm standing listening to them.

She turns back and faces Ben. 'Look, I know you're upset. I know you lost Bumble.'

'It's difficult without her.'

'You helped your neighbours and rescued her. You gave her

a good life.'

I remember Ben banging on the window of the café with a beautiful black and brown hound at his feet. He had been furious at me for not serving coffee. He must have lost his dog and having lost Scruff-bucket I understand how sad he must feel.

'It's not easy, Frances,' he repeats, scratching his unkempt beard.

'Nothing is easy. Life isn't easy as you well know,' she hisses angrily, 'but I thought there was more to you than this. It's about moving forward, Ben, in a positive and meaningful way. It isn't enough to be angry with everyone without being active and taking responsibility.'

He raises his voice. 'Don't talk to me about responsibility—'

'I'm sorry, I know, Ben.' Her tone mellows. 'It's just that every vote counts and I need you on my side tonight.'

'Look, Frances, ask the others. I can't promise...' Ben's voice fades and he's moved to stand inside the gallery. He's wearing Bermuda shorts and his legs are firm and tanned.

Frances follows him inside and, knowing I won't hear any more and my desire to buy flowers has diminished, I cross the road and return to my flat.

The boxes are still stacked up and I pick up a jumper and straighten my shoes. That's the problem of living alone – everything is always exactly where you left it. I fold the local newspaper and glance at the headline that highlights the dispute between the Harbour Street shopkeepers and the local councillor.

JJ – Jackie Johnson's smiling face is on the cover and the reporter seems in favour of the travel agency turning into a penny arcade, or as she calls it an amusement arcade like the ones further along the coast in the bigger towns.

I'm surprised Frances, the vicar, is involved and is so vehemently against it. But that's what new plans can do to people and to a place. I've seen it all before in London. They call it business development, progress, moving with the times but mostly it's often about money, power and certainly always greed.

Thinking of money, I've spent my savings on the café and I'm mortgaged up to my neck. I open my laptop and check my financial spreadsheet. I painted the interior of the café and hired an electrician but my living quarters remain untouched and rose-patterned paper peels off the bedroom wall and black mildew in the bathroom smells rank. My entire savings are invested into these two floors of real estate in a pretty coastal town, along with a crippling mortgage that I had assumed Cassie would help pay with the profits from the café. And, as if that isn't bad enough, I'm miles away from my parents in Italy and the few people I knew from work.

I sigh, close my laptop and throw myself onto the couch, lying on my back, staring up at the nicotine-stained ceiling and spider's nest in the corner of the room.

Cassie hadn't bothered with anything.

What had she done every day?

Exhausted and unable to sleep for the past few nights, I yawn loudly, feeling suddenly weary and very alone. I close my eyes, blotting out my problems, hoping sleep rather than tears will finally claim me and that when I wake up it will all have been a bad dream and Cassie will be downstairs working in the busy café.

It's dark and I wake with a start.

There's a bang, or was it a thud?

I sit up and tilt my head listening. It's coming from downstairs.

Cassie?

I move quickly, treading gingerly down the stained carpet staircase and to the back of the café and I pick up a broom handle, just in case, to defend myself.

'Cassie?' I whisper, ready to strike. 'Is that you?'

A light is on.

'Hi.'

I scream and spin around.

Karl with a K is standing behind me.

'Sorry, did I scare you?' His laugh is a deep rumble. 'You look frightened.'

'What are you doing here?'

'I was just putting the bins out, they were overflowing and I thought you might forget in the morning. I'm getting ready for tomorrow.'

Karl walks past me, picks up a cloth and begins wiping the surfaces. He wears skinny black tight jeans and a bright red t-shirt. He's well-muscled and his waist is skinny, he's shaped like a long piece of spaghetti.

'When am I getting the uniform?' he asks.

'Uniform?'

'Yes – Cassie, she promised me one.'

I watch him tidy, clean and organise the chairs neatly against the tables. He looks up at me and when he smiles his whole face lights up and his eyes sparkle. He knows I'm watching him, so he minces around theatrically, waving his arms with a flourish as he straightens tables and putting chairs neatly beside them. He obviously likes an audience and the irony is not lost on me.

63

'There. That looks much better, doesn't it? Are you going to help or just stand there gawping at me?'

'Do you really want to work here?'

'Yes. I need the money to pay my bills.'

I push my unruly hair from my face.

He continues, 'I have to pay for my caravan. The rent is due next week.' He covers his face with his hands and sinks dramatically into a chair, holding his face in his hands. His fingers are long and slim and his nails well-kept. 'This café is a life-line for me. You can't imagine how tough things are right now. My girlfriend – Molly – has depression.'

I stare at him.

He continues, 'You have no idea what it's like trying to get a job. It's impossible. This lockdown has been unbearable. Now everyone wants experience. They want a professional and pay minimum wage and I say to them, if you pay peanuts you'll get a monkey. I'm worth far more and that other girl, Cassie, she knew it. She promised me an extra two pounds an hour after the first month.'

'An extra two pounds?'

'Yes. She said I was worth it.'

'Well, let's get one thing straight. Cassie is not the owner, I am, and anyway she's gone.'

He shrugs. 'She trusted me. She had faith.'

'Well, it wasn't her money. It's mine and she's gone and I'm here. And, if you want to continue in this job you'll have to earn it. I'll pay you minimum wage but I will come to an agreement with you about profit share, so each month I will give you a percentage of the till takings, and we can review your situation in three months. How's that?'

He stands up and flashes me a smile, the sad look instantly

disappearing. 'What percentage?'

'Give me a few days to work it out.'

'What about the tips?'

'They're yours or whoever works here. You'll have to share them equally.'

'And, do I get a uniform?'

'Yes.'

'Deal.' He holds out a hand but then remembers not to shake hands, so he waves and gives a little jump in the air and spins around. 'Wow, my very own café. At last.'

I sigh heavily and shake my head. I've heard all that before.

'Stop your daydreaming, Karl, and let's get to work, there's lots to do if we're going to be organised for tomorrow.'

* * *

I use the side entrance. The back door sticks so I lean against it and shove hard with my shoulder, making a mental note to add it to my list of jobs. Inside, the air is cooler and a welcome relief from the summer heat.

I make my way into the back of the café and listen to Karl serving the customers inside.

'Coffee, tea or me…' he sings theatrically, and someone laughs, but I make a mental note to ask him to be more professional.

I place the shopping on the counter, bread, eggs, milk, and Jean looks up and smiles. With her colourful bright red mask, she is busy preparing quiche and salad and when I attempt to help her, she nudges me quickly away and whispers, 'You look exhausted, Amber. I'm so pleased you've quit that job in London. It wasn't doing you any good. You couldn't continue to commute like that every day.'

'I know,' I reply, conscious that it is turning into a long day in the café and an even longer working week and that I can't bring myself to tell her I've been fired.

A sabbatical, Ralph called it.

He followed up our chat with a confirmation email and shortly after that a farewell dinner at the end of the month for a handful of staff – all bonhomie and promises that my job would always be open to me – once I sold the café and returned to live in London.

It had all ended so quickly that I still can't quite believe it. On the plus side I have been paid three months' salary which has given me the finances to sort out the café name and branding.

'How long could you have continued working two jobs?' Jean insists.

I lean on the counter realising I haven't eaten breakfast yet and it's past midday.

'Something was going to have to give, Amber. You couldn't keep up that pace; working in London all week and in the café at the weekend.'

'I guess it's for the best.'

'Well, you've sorted the awning and it looks absolutely lovely, it makes it cooler in the café now the summer is here and Karl is very pleased with his uniform.'

I grin.

'It suits him. It suits us all.' She smooths the front of her long maroon bistro apron. 'You were very kind to include him in the decision-making. It's very classy.'

Our new uniform with the new name Harbour Street Café sewn on in large beige letters matches the maroon and beige awning outside. I know the branding is important for the sale of the café and the flat upstairs.

I make an attempt to put away the shopping; more coffee, more tea; Earl Grey, green tea, white tea, breakfast tea, and I try desperately to think of a solution to sort out this café, get it sold, and get my job back next year.

I'm only grateful that Jean is such a good worker and she keeps me up to date with everything that's going on. She is as solid as she is sturdy. She has a stout figure and she is as reliable as her warm smile. She is a godsend, happy to make breakfasts and sandwiches, and her practicality balances the scales of Karl's creative impetuosity.

Jean has lived in Westbay all her life. She knows everyone and she tells me everything that's going on in the whole street. For example, I know that Freddy in the mobile shop is depressed since his daughter moved away, that Tracey and her boyfriend Des are trying desperately for a baby, that the lease on Jane's Jewellery shop is overdue by seven months, and that Eva, the Polish florist, was married to James Rochester, the senior partner of a prestigious accountancy firm in Canterbury.

I rub my temples as Jean tells me about the travel agency going into liquidation.

'There's just no demand for travel. Now it's all this staycation business which is great for Westbay if you rely on the tourists for your business like holiday homes and Airbnb, and places like that but some folk around here aren't happy. They think they can live with just the local people supporting their businesses.'

I place the milk in the fridge and Jean reaches past me for another lump of cheddar.

She calls out, 'Karl, table two, sandwiches,' then says to me, 'I mean, Frances is determined to bring the town together. I've never met anyone more Christian than her, she's a very determined woman, Amber. We need more people like her in the town. She's spirited.'

Karl reaches for the plate of sandwiches.

'I like her,' he says. 'Besides, she is the local vicar so she must have some powerful people on her side.' He winks at me and raises his eyes to the heavens. 'Including Him up there.'

'You missed the meeting, Amber. JJ was very insistent. She doesn't seem to understand.' Jean spreads egg mayonnaise on sliced brown bread. 'We don't want an amusement arcade where the travel agents used to be, do we?'

I frown.

'You know we have to do something,' Karl says, joining us. 'We can't let JJ persuade the whole town into agreeing with her.'

Fortunately there's a sudden influx of customers and I'm able to ignore them both and help Ingrid, the Saturday student, clear the tables. She gives me a guarded smile and watches me from the corner of her eye to see if I am carrying everything correctly. Presumably, Ingrid has been waiting tables in her father's restaurant since she was eight.

By the end of the afternoon my back aches from carrying stock from the makeshift storeroom into the café.

Mrs Richards sits outside with her black poodle, Bertie, tucked under her chair. She wears a decorative floppy hat, baggy red trousers and a yellow and blue striped shirt. I stop for a chat knowing that I will probably be the only person she speaks to all day.

'They'll ruin Harbour Street if they turn it into a penny

arcade,' she says.

'There's a lot of opposition,' I reply, thinking of Jean and Karl.

'Don't you believe it. JJ is very determined and she always gets her own way.'

Across the road Eva smiles and I wave back.

Normally at the weekend, I like to let Jean, Karl and Ingrid go home at five and I try to close up by five thirty. After that, I go through the accounts and write up the books for the day, checking stock and placing orders for the following week.

'That's it then for today.' Jean's round jolly face never fails to make me smile. She unties the apron from her ample waist, folds it neatly and places it on the counter. Her arms are thick and her gold watch is lost in the wrinkles of her skin. She is carefully made up with good foundation and she looks younger than her sixty years. She has been my rock in the past few months.

'Are you off home?' I envy her going home to her small, busy terraced house where I know she will spend the next few hours in the kitchen lovingly preparing dinner for her husband and two sons who, although in their twenties, still live with her and seemingly have the appetite of a whole army.

'My boys will be hungry,' she says as if reading my thoughts. 'Don't you stay down here all night. You look like you need a decent night's sleep. And, stop worrying! You're bound to find a buyer soon.'

I shake my head. 'I hope so.'

'She's got a cheek, that Cassie. When I think of the mess she's left you in. That flat upstairs isn't fit for purpose, there are damp stains all over the ceiling and the bathroom looks infested. You said she was here for months while you went up to London, I don't know what she could have been doing.'

'Nor me.'

'You'll have to get it sorted. You can't live like that.'

I don't tell Jean that I'm not earning enough money for me to repair the flat, plus pay the heavy mortgage on the property as well as pay staff and afford stock – or even that I've been sacked from my proper job and I can barely cover the costs each week.

'Maybe I'll do something tomorrow.' I shrug. 'I guess I could give it a lick of paint.'

'It'll need more than that. You need a professional in.' Jean leans forward and embraces me in a tight bear hug and I smell cheap perfume. Her grip is strong and her body is comfortingly soft and squelchy. It's a protective mother's hug.

'I'd love you to come and stay in our house but what with Andrew and Devlin and their girlfriends – there's barely enough room for Johnny and me.'

I laugh. None of them are small people and I know the size of Jean's terraced house and I wonder how they all manage living together.

Jean, Karl and Ingrid leave and I fuss around them, seeing them to the door and waving them off as if they are my friends and I've had them over for a successful dinner party. I turn the closed sign on the glass and lock the door.

I make myself a latte and sit in the window of the café and open my laptop. I check the receipts in front of me and plan the orders for the following week. The more I can get delivered to the café the better.

Harbour Street grows quiet. That calm time between afternoon and evening. A woman clutching a child's hand hurries out of From The Heart Gift Shop, the little boy carrying a fishing rod and a red plastic bucket.

Across the road, Eva is bringing in her lovely flower displays and in the harbour I imagine queues are forming at the fish and chip shop. But my attention then focuses on the table and the pieces of paper in front of me and I work methodically as the sun dips behind the boarded-up building opposite and Harbour Street lies in half shadow like a lifeless forgotten ghost town.

I yawn and rub my eyes. I don't feel like going upstairs. The flat still feels empty without Cassie, it's as if the soul has flown away. She phoned me last week and left a message. She said she wanted to tell me first, and she didn't want me to hear it from anyone else. She didn't take the job as stage manager at the Barbican. She's accepted a part in the chorus of a new musical in the West End. She said acting was her life. She wasn't coming back – oh, and could I package up the rest of her things as she wouldn't have time to collect them. There were a few jumpers in a box under the bed.

Why hadn't I seen the signs?

It had been Cassie's idea to come here.

I had been born and raised in Brighton, and I holidayed in Italy. I had spent most of my years in London. It was Cassie who had been sick of London, tired of auditioning, convinced she'd get nowhere. When we met she said she was beyond her prime at thirty-five. She had wanted security, a business – and a wife. She had talked me into a new life here in Westbay.

I glance into the street. I don't dislike Harbour Street, there is something honest and reliable about the place but – it's just not me.

My life is in London.

Marion and Pamela from the Très Chic Boutique are locking up. Pamela looks positively uncomfortable. She has a sad face but I guess that comes from working with Marion. They both stare at me sitting in the window and I feel like I'm in a brothel in Amsterdam's red light district.

They turn and walk away. The older woman with the pinched face is hunched whereas Marion seems to inhale the whole essence of the street. She walks in her high heels with a confident strut and I know I would break my neck wearing those shoes.

Taylor's Art Gallery stays open. Ben seems to be in there most of the time. Last night, I'd looked at the paintings. I'd stood at the window and it dawned on me that the pictures weren't his but they were painted by other local artists. Apparently, he was just the front man and I realise that I've never actually seen anyone leave the gallery with a painting or even a chess set.

How does he make money?

I shuffle through the till receipts and place the orders online until I am tired enough to go upstairs to my empty and abandoned flat, feeling very alone and extremely depressed.

Chapter 7

After I check the locks and climb the stairs to the flat, I'm wondering if Cassie is already on stage in London. I've seen her in musicals a few times but I wasn't to know how good her acting skills really were in real life.

She had been the first to say, I love you.

Upstairs, I kick off my shoes and wiggle my toes. I throw myself onto the sofa realising how sparse and soulless it all is.

A worn red sofa that Cassie just had to have, a double bed and a flat screen television. There is enough cutlery and crockery to feed four people from my flat in London, pots and pans in the kitchen, but my prized possession is my herb collection on the kitchen counter.

In another life I would have cooked with them but tonight I'm not hungry. Having spent the day serving food I am too tired to eat. I stretch out on the sofa then, unable to settle, so I wander into the bathroom and run cool bath water. Swimming in the sea beside a busy beach wasn't an option this evening.

I lift my polo shirt over my head and dump my trousers on the floor, then my bra and my pants. Although there is mildew on the ceiling, a bath is my ritual and sometimes my saviour. I find my special relaxing spa soak oil, an old Christmas gift and something I now can't afford, and pour it into the running water watching it cloud and develop an oily sheen.

While I'm waiting, I clean my face with cleanser and then tonic, breathing in the calming spa fragrance, all left over from the days when I had money, a decent job and a manageable sized mortgage. I sit on the edge of the bath, and the cold ceramic seeps into my thigh bones. I wait until the bath is at the perfect temperature then I ease my body under the water sighing contentedly and lie my head back, allowing my neck to rest against the bath. I close my eyes and my head begins to clear and my aching shoulders relax.

As the water cools I submerge my head under the water. My hair is cut short now and I duck under the water again before picking up the flannel. I begin to soap my body with slow relaxed, comforting strokes until my eyelids grow heavy.

I climb out of the bath and dry my body slowly. I trace the tattoo on the underside of my right arm with methodical care. It had hurt like hell at the time and, fifteen years ago, it had seemed like a good idea.

'Still waters run deep', is tattooed in Japanese letters around the bicep on my arm.

I had been eighteen and Akimo had been my first true love. We went to San Francisco on holiday. A mini-honeymoon we called it and the love for my Japanese waitress had lasted until three weeks after we returned to London. It had been a mini-honeymoon alright but the tattoo was for life. Cassie had never liked it.

That was before my engagement to Steve. He'd broken my heart.

Maybe I was destined to be alone forever.

* * *

A few days later, I'm sitting at the bistro table upstairs in the flat eating dinner, Sanjay's spicy chicken curry, and studying menus of popular cafés when the doorbell rings.

When I go downstairs I'm surprised to see the local vicar on my doorstep.

Frances smiles. 'Hello, Amber, I'm not canvassing for the church,' she says.

I don't know what to say but I grin back, liking her and her blond highlights and twinkling eyes immediately.

'I'm here because of JJ's proposal for the travel agent premises.'

I nod and try to look interested.

'Karl spoke up at the meeting. He was against the idea of the amusement arcade. Are you?'

'Erm, I haven't given it a great deal of thought.'

'Right.' She appears confused. 'You couldn't come to the meeting?'

'I was in London,' I lie and to cover my guilt, I add, 'And, there wasn't much point anyway.'

'Why?'

'I'm selling the café.'

'You're selling the café?'

'Yes.'

'So soon?'

'It's a long story.'

'Well, you'll be able to tell the new owner what's going on then.'

I sigh. 'Maybe. If I ever get organised and have a set of business accounts and find the right person who will buy it and…'

'I thought you were doing well, it always looks busy and you've a great reputation.'

'Have we?'

Frances laughs. 'Don't look so surprised.'

'It's hard to know, Frances. I've been working in London most of the time. Karl is doing a great job and I've been working here too but I know nothing about coffee, well, I mean, I like coffee but a café is a whole new ball game. It's a balance, you know with food and everything and it's hard enough managing this place but when staff leave and we get so busy and—' I'm babbling. I know I'm talking too quickly but who else is there?

'Would you like a coffee and a chat?' she asks.

'We're closed but you can come up to the flat but it's a mess. Cassie even took Scruff-bucket, and I miss her so much and—'

'Come to my house. I can pop the kettle on.'

'Erm—'

'It's alright, but it sounds like you need someone to talk to, Amber.'

I open the door with tears welling in my eyes. 'Come in, Frances, we can sit in the garden patio at the back.'

* * *

Garden patio might be an overstatement. It's a tiny scruffy concrete area that I've tried to tidy up but is used as a dumping ground for a few rickety chairs, cardboard boxes and tins of empty paint from the café all lined up to go to the local tip.

We stand staring at it all and I can sense her disapproval as I drag two chairs together. It's a warm evening and I haven't realised how pleasant it is outside.

'The patio's on my list of jobs. It's a mess, I'm sorry.'

'Don't apologise.' Frances sits down and leans forward, resting her elbows on her knees. 'Have you finished working in London?'

'Yes but I haven't got organised yet.'

'That's understandable. Everything takes time to grow including us.'

'I have sorted the uniform and branding though.'

'I like the name Harbour Street Café and, the maroon and beige awning looks lovely. Very in keeping with the rest of the street.'

'That's good. I'm pleased you like it.' I frown. 'Coffee?'

She nods. 'If it's no trouble. I'll come with you.'

She follows me inside, and seems relaxed as we speak about Harbour Street and how fast the summer is upon us.

'It's taking me ages to get organised,' I confess, carrying our coffee back into the warm air in the patio area. 'I should have cleaned up here. It would be a nice space for our customers.'

'Everything has a place and a time.'

'I know but the schools will be finished soon and then we'll be really busy.'

I sit with my face turned up to the sunshine relishing the warmth on my face. Frances is a good listener and it's been a while since I've been able to speak openly but once I start I can't stop. Everything comes flooding out, about Cassie, our dream, my investment and how I'm trying to find a balance in my life between the sabbatical from my job and working in a café that I know nothing about.

'Sabbatical?' Frances wrinkles her nose.

'Yes, you know, a year or so and then I can go back.'

'So, you'll sell this place and go back to London?'

'That's the plan but I obviously want the café to be a success. I intend to get it off the ground and put some proper accounts in place. The estate agents reckons I'll get more for a thriving business.'

'You look like you're succeeding but it must be exhausting,' Frances says encouragingly. 'Have you made any friends here?'

'I'm not having much of a social life but it doesn't matter. I'm so tired anyway...' My voice trails off and I clear my throat to get rid of the lump lodged firmly in place, and hope my business acumen disguises the talent I have for not making any friends.

'It must be hard for you?'

I keep my eyes firmly closed and pinch the nails of my fingers into my palm. 'It's how life is.'

Frances smiles. 'I'm lucky I have Greg, my husband. We've been married twenty years. He's such a rock. I don't know how I would manage without him. We all need friends, Amber.'

'That's what JJ said to me,' I reply.

'Well, be careful. That's all I'll say.'

Frances speaks about her husband and the life they lead in the town and their friends in the community. 'We're so lucky to live here and I love this town and I do honestly feel that the amusement arcade would be a mistake. It would encourage a lot of undesirable behaviour. At the moment the pubs and restaurants – even the cafés do well. But an amusement arcade would seriously affect the type of people we get to the town. You've seen all the independent businesses, they thrive because Harbour Street is so pretty and so unique.'

I nod. 'It's why Cassie and I wanted to live here. That's the charm. It was the only place for us.'

'Exactly.' Frances smiles enthusiastically.

'So, how can you stop JJ?' I ask, thinking of the conversation I overheard between her and Ben Taylor outside his art gallery.

She frowns. 'It's difficult because she's so popular. JJ's business allows her to cultivate people and change opinions. While they're sipping a pint she has their ear. People like her. They want to please her and she is a good businesswoman but this is one step too far. I can't turn away. Not this time.'

'What do you mean this time?'

She hesitates before saying, 'When JJ bought The Ship, there was a small garage at the back of the pub. William owned it. He was a mechanic and the business had been in his family for years. He sold it to JJ for a snip of what it was worth. Well under market value. Everyone thought that JJ would keep it as a garage for storage but once the deal was done, she flattened the lot, and extended the pub patio garden. It was prime town real estate.'

'And that's made her popular?'

'The town is divided. Some people don't care, others believe JJ did the right thing as the garage was an eyesore, and then there are the others who…' She pauses. 'There are lots of rumours and bad feelings still about it today.'

'Others?'

'There are one or two who believed something was wrong with the whole situation. There were consequences and people paid for their mistakes but it was years ago now and the whole town has to move on.'

I remember Frances arguing with Ben.

'Does this have anything to do with Ben Taylor?'

'He was involved yes. William was his uncle. Now he wants

nothing to do with her. There was a big fallout and he wants nothing to do with anyone at all. He won't get involved in anything.'

I sit mulling over Frances's words. I'd assumed that in Harbour Street everyone was living happy lives never realising the undercurrents, the politics and the emotions that tie everyone together. As well as their own personal problems, there's a community at stake. At least London life is easier than this community, you can go home from work and forget about everyone. I need to go back to the city.

'We need your support,' Frances says earnestly.

I remember the earlier email from the estate agents about a viewing in the morning and I'm hoping it's more successful than the one a week ago when the prospective buyers practically ran out of the flat and into the street.

'Can I count on your support, Amber? It would be great to know that least one shop owner will support me in this. I'm not giving up. JJ isn't going to get away with it again.'

* * *

It's early morning and the sun is just rising when I wake. It was a warm and stuffy night and although all the windows are open there is no cool air circulating in the flat. I feel claustrophobic so I check the Tide app on my mobile and to my relief it's high-tide.

I pull on my swimming costume, slip into flip-flops and pull on a baggy shirt. With a towel tucked under my arm I'm feeling light-headed and excited. It will be my first swim of the year – it's like being on holiday.

The last time I went swimming was with Cassie. In between

lockdowns last year we'd managed a week in Westbay. We'd both decided it was better than the hassle of airports and a Mediterranean holiday. We had fallen in love with this place immediately. We knew we had to be within commuting distance of London for my job which would keep us going financially until the café began making money. We had been excited, full of plans, passion and energy but now it all seems a long time ago.

I've changed. This country and even the world has changed.

The beach is deserted and I throw my towel on the pebbles. A swim had seemed a good idea in the flat but now there's a cool sea breeze and when my toe touches the water I yelp involuntarily. It's freezing and I shiver.

'It's not that cold.'

I spin around at the sound of a voice, lose my footing and end up toppling forward and splashing ungraciously under the water. When I emerge and spit out salty water, Ben Taylor is in the sea a few metres away. I hadn't noticed him. I'm annoyed and self-conscious in my swimsuit – and I want to be alone.

'I nearly drowned,' I shout at him.

'Don't be silly. It's not that deep.'

'It's freezing,' I say, gasping, trying to regain my dignity as well as my breath.

'It's colder out there on the beach. The wind is rising with the turning tide.'

Not knowing what to do I splash clumsily in a crawl and just before my head is submerged I'm sure I hear him laughing at me.

I recover with a gasp. The water is cold and refreshing but I don't want to share my morning swim with him and he hasn't swum away. Annoyingly he's treading water and watching me. His hair is plastered to his scalp, his grey beard looks matted, but his shoulders are broad and tanned.

'Are you alright?' he asks.

'Fine.'

'You look like a dolphin.'

'You probably mean a walrus.'

'No, they're attractive.' He laughs. 'Besides, they are very graceful in water and can swim at an average speed of seven kilometres an hour.'

'Well, I can't and besides, I want to swim alone.'

He moves away swimming with his head in the water, breathing properly as his arm comes up and over his ear; strong, easy and natural strokes. I turn away and float on my back, relishing the warmth of the sun on my face, then I roll over onto my stomach and practise my breast-stroke, dipping my head in the water and breathing rhythmically.

I want to say that I'm sorry for the loss of his dog and that I know how he feels because I feel so alone without Scruff-bucket, but I don't say anything. Instead, I think of our beautiful cat and wonder if she's settling in or if she's missing me in her new London home.

I break into a fast crawl and I feel the strength of my arms in the water. I turn on my back, gasping for breath and pleased with myself, and that's when I look to see if Ben is following me but he's already climbing out of the water. His clothes are in the breakwater next to mine. I didn't see them when I came to the beach.

I'm disappointed.

I was rude to him but I can't be responsible for him. I only want a quiet swim alone before heading into the café to work, but as I breast-stroke alongside the beach I can't shake the feeling that I've upset Ben and that in my own clumsy way I've let him down.

Chapter 8

It's a frantically busy day. The hot weather has encouraged everyone to leave their homes in the city and head to the beach. The town is crowded and there are queues in the square as well as in Harbour Street for the restaurants, cafés and takeaways. We're open later than anticipated and by the time I've sent the staff home and I'm closing up, I've decided I'll make amends with Ben.

I cross the road to Taylor's Art Gallery and I'm surprised when I walk inside at the coolness of the interior; air conditioning. It's a blessing after the hot and busy café and it's an idea I could consider – it might be an incentive for potential buyers and help me sell the café.

There are several people milling around inside admiring paintings and Ben is chatting to a couple about a landscape of the beach, so I take my time and enjoy the artwork. There's also a new chess display, a chess set of dragons, it's intricate and beautiful and I can't believe he makes them by hand.

Does he?

I love visiting art galleries and museums in London and this evening it makes a pleasant change for half an hour, and I lose myself for a while until I realise Ben is alone at the counter and there's no one else in the gallery.

'I've come to apologise,' I say by way of greeting.

'There's no need,' he replies dismissively.

He's wearing an open-necked white shirt and his body is tanned and taut as if he works out. There are several tattoos on his chest, and on his fingers there are letters written in Greek.

'I'm Amber, I have the café across the road.'

'I know who you are, I've been in there. You should train your staff better.'

'Why?'

'Coffee, tea or me?' He mimics Karl's falsetto voice but there is irony in his tone and he hides a smile.

'That's Karl's idea to relive the boredom sometimes. I'm sorry if it offended you.'

'It did the first time but I'm used to him now.'

'Good. He doesn't mean any harm. I think he gets bored.'

'I like him.' Ben moves to the corner of the gallery where there's a workshop area and he picks up a wooden frame. He ignores me so I follow him.

'Do you paint?' I ask.

'Sometimes.'

'Do you have any on show?'

'No.'

'Why?'

He turns to face me and his eyes are dark and wary. 'Well, why should I?'

'I don't know, I thought it would be nice—'

'So that people can patronise my work?'

'No—'

'So that strangers who have no idea about art can say they don't like them?'

85

'No—'

'Then why?'

'Look, I'm sorry, I seem to have offended you – again. I actually came to apologise about this morning on the beach. I thought I had been rude—'

'There's no need. I'm used to it.'

'Not from me.'

He glances up and glares. 'It makes no difference.'

I try frantically to think of something to say. Something original and engaging. Something that we have in common.

'Frances has been asking for my help. What do you think of the plan for the amusement arcade?'

His eyes darken and his mouth turns down and he pauses before finally answering. 'I told her and I'll tell you, I'm not interested. I don't want to know.'

I wait and then reply slowly, 'Me neither.'

He returns his attention to the picture frame in his hands and I move away to look at the paintings. Some of them are really lovely. Had they been cheaper and I had a nicer home, I would have bought one but they are way beyond my budget. There's nothing left to say but at the door I pause and look back.

'Bye,' I call.

Ben doesn't look up and he doesn't acknowledge me. And I'm left wondering if the chill in the room is from the air conditioning at all.

* * *

'Hi, I'm Amber Hendrix.'

'I know who you are. I'm Pamela.' She smiles.

I know Marion isn't working in the boutique but I have to be quick so I can get back to the café and more importantly, I don't want to bump into her. I haven't spoken to her since Cassie left.

'I'm looking for a birthday present but I have to be quick.'

I'm sure Pamela can tell I'm not a proper shopper. Perhaps she thinks this shop is out of my price range.

'What sort of present?'

I see her looking at me wondering if I have a new girlfriend. I'm sure Marion has told her all about Cassie being a very pretty actress.

'I don't know.'

'Who is it for?'

'It's for Jean, the lady that works with me, the one with the pretty face-masks. It's her birthday tomorrow and she adores this shop but I have no idea what she would like.'

I gaze around the room. 'I'm not very good with things like this. I'm not a very good shopper. I mostly order online to save any embarrassing situations like this.' I smile.

'What does Jean normally wear? I've only ever seen her in your uniform.'

'She likes bright colours.'

Pamela reaches out and picks up a pink candy-coloured blouse.

I flinch. 'That's a little too...bright,' I say gently. 'How about something like this?'

I hold up a conservative navy blouse with a pretty ruffle at the neck. 'It would be a flattering colour for her.'

'It's a bit boring,' Pamela grins. 'How about a lovely leather handbag or a belt? Do you have a budget?'

I move around the shop lifting up unsuitable bags and

matching belts.

'How about this?' Pamela holds up a red silk blouse. 'It is definitely sexy and probably not at all suitable.'

I find it hard to disagree.

'It's something Jean would never buy for herself,' I agree.

'If she doesn't like it, you can always get her to pop over here and change it,' she says.

'That's kind. Thank you.'

The blouse is overpriced and very expensive. A department store in London or Canterbury would have something similar for half the price. Pamela wraps it carefully in tissue paper and reaches for a gift bag from under the counter.

'What do you think about the plans for the amusement arcade?' I ask. 'Do you think it will affect the boutique?'

'I suppose it will mean more people coming here.'

'Is that a good thing?'

'I suppose so.'

'Have you had your coffee this morning?' I say.

'I'm on my own in the shop. I haven't been able to get out yet. There's always been someone in here.'

On cue the doorbell tinkles.

'Keep the receipt and tell Jean she can change it if she doesn't like it,' Pamela says.

We smile and she hands me the neatly packaged gift.

'I'll ask Karl to bring you over a coffee. Do you want your usual?'

'That would be great, thanks, Amber.'

Back in the café, I ask Karl to take over Pamela's regular order and he smiles happily, always eager to oblige.

'Service with a smile,' he announces grandly, placing a steaming cup of coffee and an almond croissant on a tray to carry across the road.

'Tell her there's no charge,' I say.

'Okay, I'll say it's a gift from Amber.' He skips to the door. 'But if you carry on giving everything away we'll make no money at all and I won't be able to afford the rent on my caravan.'

* * *

The following day, Jean opens her present. 'I've always wanted a red silk blouse. Thank you, Amber.' She holds it against her chest. 'It's so beautiful. Johnny would never think to buy me something as pretty as this.'

I smile. I'm happy but I'm not sure if she's just saying that to please me. 'You can change it if you like.'

'You are joking! I'm going to wear it tonight. He's taking me out for dinner in town and it will be lovely to have something new to put on.'

I return her smile and then ask quietly, 'What do you know about Ben Taylor?'

Jean's face clouds over. 'I don't gossip.'

'But—?' I probe.

'He's been in prison and he's a very angry young man.'

'Prison?'

'Yes.'

'Is he young?' I query, wondering how prison life can age a person.

'Probably forty.'

'He looks older,' I say and I wonder if that's been from the effect of time spent inside.

'It's that awful beard. He doesn't look after himself like he used to.'

'Why?'

Jean turns away. 'Life takes its toll sometimes.'

'So, he's had a difficult life?'

'He hasn't made it easy for himself. He's been away for years and he only came back last year and he bought the art gallery. Then we've been in lockdown so no one has really seen him or spoken to him. Besides, he isn't that friendly either now. He seems changed – angry and not at all like he used to be. He came back with a dog but I think it must have died. I haven't seen him with it—'

'The dog died – it was old,' Karl interrupts.

'You spoke with him about it?' I ask.

'He was angry with me once.' Karl looks sheepish.

'Why?' I ask, surprised.

'It was early on and I was bored so when he walked in I said, coffee, tea or me and I thought he was going to punch me.' Karl laughs.

Today his long hair is beaded and wound around his head. His maroon apron makes his figure look lean and sharp.

'He wasn't happy. Now he just comes in and I know what he wants. He barely even grunts but he's not a bad man – well, I don't think he is. I like him.'

I look out of the window toward Taylor's Art Gallery and notice the busy street. If I was in London I would be going out for lunch or planning dinner in an expensive restaurant.

Will I ever sell this place?

The feedback from Charlie in the estate agents from the last viewers was that it's overpriced even though I have it on the market for less than I paid for it.

'We need to make more money,' I mumble.

'If we had a proper chef we could do cooked breakfasts and lunches,' Karl says. 'We'd make tonnes more money – probably even a real profit at last.'

'I'll think about it,' I reply, knowing I can't afford another person in the café. I'm making very little money as it is and I already need to arrange another loan from the bank.

'Karl's right,' Jean says. 'And, if you're interested, I know just the person. Lucas is a friend of my son's. He has been let go from a restaurant in Canterbury and now the furlough is over he needs work. He has a new baby and he's desperate for work. He would be ideal.'

'I'll think about it.'

'It will mean more profit share for me,' Karl smiles.

'It will mean more outlay for me,' I smile back sarcastically.

'Only temporarily, once you've bought the stock and sold food, you'll soon make money. Give it three months,' Karl says persuasively.

'I'll think about it.'

Karl smiles. 'Well, while you're thinking so hard, give some thought to getting a drinks licence too then we can sell wine with the meals.'

'You're so funny,' I tell him and I walk away with my mind already whirling. He's probably right. With a bar licence and more income then it will be much easier to sell this place and I can get back to London.

* * *

Later that afternoon Eva comes into the café with her twins. 'Emma and Nick,' she introduces us.

'They're spending a couple of weeks with James before going

91

off to live in halls of residence at different universities,' she explains, as I clear the tables beside where they are sitting.

I smile at them all.

'Take a seat and I'll come and take your order.'

'Mum, can you get my black dress from the dry cleaners for me?' Emma's dark eyes are like her mother's but she wears clothes like a dated hippy; mismatched, misshapen and miscoloured.

'I won't have time, darling. I'm not going into Canterbury. I'm working and—'

'Well, if you don't get it today when will you get it? We're leaving tomorrow and I'll need it in Manchester.'

'Can't you pick it up yourself?' Eva studies the menu.

'I'm having lunch with Amy.'

'Where?'

'Abode.'

'That's not far from the cleaners,' Eva replies.

'I don't want to carry it on the bus,' Emma wails. 'And besides, it's a special leaving lunch. It reminds me of Dad and when we used to go there – when we were all happy.'

I risk a glance to look at Eva.

Could her daughter really be that hurtful?

Emma continues, 'I probably won't see Amy now until Christmas. I probably won't come home during term time. I mean, this isn't like home anymore, is it? It's not like our family home.'

Eva's face remains passive and she concentrates on the menu in her hands.

'What would you like to eat?' she asks calmly.

'It's the only home you've got,' Nick says, shuffling his long legs under the table and looking up from his phone. 'This is it.'

Nick's hair is tied back in a ponytail. He's wearing baggy jeans and, although it's warm outside, a hooded sweatshirt.

They have Eva's thick dark blond hair and small nose but they have big brown eyes and long black eyelashes and wide lips that I assume is from their father's gene pool.

The twins look almost identical and I feel a sudden surge of envy, as the thought of a family is suddenly overwhelming. I miss Mama and Papa and I have a longing to see my younger brother Roberto, who's working in Rome.

I busy myself straightening chairs at a nearby table, unashamedly eavesdropping, wishing I was part of their family.

'I don't need to be reminded, thank you. I know perfectly well why we're living here.' Emma smacks her brother's arm. 'Mum, I don't know why you bother with the shop. Why don't go back to work in what you trained in?' Emma pouts. She has this annoyingly pretty way of hanging her bottom lip down and looking distraught like a helpless child.

'Studying history of art twenty years ago is not going to help me earn money,' Eva says flatly.

'You could get a job in one of the museums, or one of the colleges or even in the cathedral,' Emma adds helpfully. 'That's why Daddy fell in love with you. You knew lots then.'

'Well, I have to make a living and the flower shop is the best thing for me, besides I enjoy it.'

'I wouldn't want to be on my feet every day.'

'You have an answer and a solution for everything,' Nick mumbles to Emma. He's already scrolling his phone. 'I'll collect your dress for you. I'm going into town later.'

Emma looks triumphant.

'Problem solved,' Eva says. 'Thanks, Nick. Now what do you guys want to order?'

'Just a coffee. I'm meeting the lads in town to look at some new software later and we'll grab something to eat.' Nick nods seriously.

'And, I've got plans tonight. I told you,' Emma whines. 'Don't you ever listen to me, Mum?'

'Oh, right, of course I remember,' Eva replies and I recognise instantly the lonely disappointment in her voice.

* * *

Now I've left the law practice, I seem to have more time in the day. Not having the commute alone saves me at least three hours and although I still wake early now I have time to walk on the beach or have an early swim depending on the tide. I haven't seen Ben on the beach since our last meeting.

The café is going well and I realise the importance of the summer trade as well as getting to know the locals. Karl is better at PR than I had realised and I notice how he greets each customer by name and he remembers their orders, their likes and dislikes.

At Jean's insistence, I've interviewed Lucas and subsequently employed him. He's very professional in the kitchen and he gets on well with Jean and Karl. I feel blessed that he's so amenable, talented and enthusiastic.

He was born in Croatia but his family moved here when he was five. As well as the café's favourites, he has good ideas for other dishes and new recipes. We talk about changing the menu and about adding new lunch dishes but initially we keep it simple with a variety of English breakfast choices and eggs in multiple different ways, salads, cheeses and cold meats then soups and stews in the winter.

We agree to review the situation in a few weeks after he has an idea of our customers and demand.

At five-thirty the café is empty and I'm feeling optimistic. With a new chef, I can build a solid reputation which will help sell the café and I can return to London.

Michael Bublé sings, 'I Just Haven't Met You Yet' and I'm singing loudly from behind the counter when a voice calls out.

'Hi, Amber, Karl didn't take any money from me this morning for the coffee and panini.' Eva's smile is warm and friendly. I stop singing. 'I was busy and he couldn't wait.'

I tut dramatically. 'Can't get the staff these days – they'd give everything away.'

'Your coffee really perks me up. It's often the best part of my day.'

'Well, if the coffee is that good and your day was that bad – I can make you another one now if you like? Have you closed up?'

Eva's shoulders appear to relax and she attempts a warm smile and sighs. 'Yes. And, do you know what? That sounds great. It will fortify me before I get home.'

I busy myself making the coffee, flicking switches and tipping milk into a jug to froth it loudly with the steam spout.

'How much do you need fortifying, Eva? I've a lovely piece of cheesecake left if you'd like some.'

Her laugh is warm and friendly.

'I need enough strength to see off two difficult teenagers to university tomorrow.'

'You don't look old enough but I saw you with them the

other day, so I believe you. Which university?'

'One to Manchester and one to London.'

I place a large piece of lemon cheesecake on a plate and slide it towards her.

She looks at it and says, 'Only if I can pay.'

'We're closed,' I reply.

'I'll get fat!'

'Who cares?'

We both grin.

'Come and sit over here and be fortified. Tell me, what are your children studying?'

She follows me to the window seat.

'You often sit here, don't you, Amber?'

I smile. 'It's the best seat in the house.'

She sits opposite me. 'They're twins,' she explains. 'Nick is studying computer programming and wants to be the next Bill Gates and Emma is studying art, and I think she wants to be the next—'

'Tracey Emin?'

'No, Banksy.'

We both laugh and Eva spends the next half hour telling me how difficult it has been raising two children alone, after James left.

'We divorced last year but if I'm truthful he left me years ago. I thought he was having an affair but when you have a lovely home and two children I thought it best to ignore it. To pretend that the late nights were work or that the long weekends away were really important business trips.'

'It must have been difficult.'

'It's worse now, I think. Because I sheltered them. I've never told them the truth or explained my heartache. I've never

96

criticised him. I never told them about his affairs. I think they thought that this last one has only happened recently and they blame me. It's all my fault.'

'Why haven't you told them?'

'I suppose I wanted to shelter them from him, from our marriage – from what the real world is really like. It would only upset them and, I don't want to turn them against him either. How can you explain to your children how badly their father has treated you? It's embarrassing and to be honest, I feel ashamed I didn't kick him out but I love my children.'

'You'll miss them when they go,' I say.

'I will. But part of me is ready to move on with my life. I feel that I can have some time for me and find out what I want to do with my life. Does that make sense or does it make me sound selfish?'

'It sounds like you have devoted yourself to them for the past eighteen years and now you need a break. You're a good mother, Eva. So you must be kind to yourself. It's your turn now or it will be – after tomorrow.'

'I hope so and what about you, Amber? Is there no one since Cassie?'

'I'm far too busy to have friends let alone a relationship.' I smile, hoping she can't see through the fake veneer of my confidence and false cheerfulness. 'It's all about trust,' I add.

'Marriage is also like friendship,' Eva says. 'It's about being valued.'

As she delves into the cake, I manage to change the subject, deflecting attention from my lonely life, and instead I speak about my parents in Italy and Roberto, my brother.

'He's a teacher,' I say, 'we try and meet up each summer but this is the first time I haven't been back to see them.'

We spend an hour talking companionably, and by the time she leaves I feel as though a burden has been lifted from me. It reminds me of those unexpected moments when you talk or share secrets with a complete stranger on a train or plane and then never see them again. More than anything, it was fun and pleasant. It was cathartic.

Chapter 9

I arrive at Frances's house beside the little church just after eight o'clock.

'Come in, Amber.' Her smile is welcoming and I follow Frances into a small dark sitting room. It's neat with chintz sofas and lots of books and reminds me of an old-fashioned house from an Agatha Christie movie. She looks far too young and modern to have such a dark and gloomy home.

Her husband Graham has grey hair and a neat goatee. He appears to be at least twenty years older than her. 'Would you like some wine, Amber?'

'Thank you,' I reply but I am distracted by the number of books lined along one wall.

He laughs. 'I was a theology professor. I keep the books for reference when Frances and I get into discussions.'

'Who wins?' I ask.

His eyes twinkle. 'We agree to differ.'

We chat a little longer before Graham is distracted and I sit beside Sanjay from the Indian.

'You will have to try the biriani,' he whispers. 'I think it's the only thing you haven't yet eaten, Amber.'

'You'll have to start adding some new dishes or I'll get bored and have to transfer my allegiance to another Indian,' I tease.

Kit and Jenna, the owners of From The Heart Gift Shop are both tall, slim and blond. They have two adopted children, now almost teenagers, who, Kit says smilingly, 'spend more time playing on the computer than doing their school work.'

'My cousin's children are the same,' Sanjay admits.

Mario and Luke, owners of Kingdom Pets, are seated on the sofa. Luke has a deep rumbling laugh and Mario wears round glasses that make him look both studious and interesting.

'I call him Super Mario,' Luke says, 'he spends more time gaming than with me.'

'Not true.' Mario punches his partner's arm good-naturedly. 'Apart from being Super Mario, of course.'

'Sit down and help yourself to a glass of wine.' Frances nods at the table but Graham already has a bottle in his hand and he's pouring a glass of chilled white for me.

'You're very welcome, Amber. Great to have you on board,' he says. His accent is from the north of England.

Frances places a hand on her husband's sleeve and chides him. 'Don't presume, Graham. We hope she's on board but we have to persuade her tonight.'

The doorbell chimes and Frances disappears.

'Sorry I'm late.' Eva arrives wearing a pretty red and beige floral, patterned dress.

'Come in, Eva. Thanks for joining us. I'm hoping Ben will join us as well.'

'That would be good, I haven't seen Ben for ages. We need him on our side after what happened—' Sanjay is silenced by a frown from Frances and then she looks around the room to make eye contact with everyone before beginning.

'Now we're all here, we'll make a start. I want to know who will support me against the development of the travel agency into an amusement arcade. JJ is stepping up her game and it seems that she has a surprising amount of support in the town, so I want to know how you all feel.'

'That's because JJ's holding regular meetings in The Ship. She's persuading everyone that it's the best idea, and it's all she talks about,' Kit says. 'We went in there last night and she was holding court with everyone.'

Sanjay rubs the greying hair at his temple. 'I can't see why they're falling for her old tricks again.'

'That was a long time ago,' Luke says. 'Not everyone remembers. Besides Marion is banging the drum, supporting her friend too. She's a firm supporter of the plans.'

Frances looks at me. 'Marion is one of JJ's biggest campaigners. Did you know that?'

I'm suddenly self-conscious when everyone looks at me.

Do they know that I blame Marion for the way Carrie behaved and that I can't bring myself to speak to her?

'I'm not surprised,' I reply eventually.

'Well, I'm pleased we had our chat the other night.' Frances smiles. 'It just goes to show, you never know what side people are on, unless you ask them.' She glances around the room. 'Now, I'm trying to make a list of people that we can start canvassing. We need to get the residents to vote and we need to create a stir of opposition. We have to stop JJ and this ridiculous idea of hers.'

'Someone needs to stop her this time,' Kit agrees. 'It's a shame Ben hasn't shown up, we need him on our side.'

'Ben won't get involved,' Luke says. 'I spoke to him and he's got his head buried in the sand.'

'In the past,' agrees Mario.

'We can't rely on one person,' insists Frances. 'It's a numbers game and I'm sure when the time comes Ben will help. Now, in the meantime, let's draw up a list…'

We spend the next hour running through names of the Harbour Street owners but I remain quiet. I don't know any of them well and so I don't speak up. The sparkling, confident, fiery, righteous-fighting lawyer, well, that was another person, another life. It's easier fighting someone else's battles.

This is me. This is the real me. Café owner and exhausted mortgage owner who owes a fortune to the bank and who is too tired to care about a Harbour Street development.

'So,' says Frances, looking at the list in her hands. 'We are exactly matched. 'The main deciders will be the ones sitting on the fence; Derek the butcher, Ian the grocer and Tracey from the beauty salon.'

'And, don't forget Ozan and Yusef from the Turkish barbers.' Eva is leaning intently over Frances's shoulder, looking at the list. 'If we get them, then we'll get the others.'

'How do you know?' asks Sanjay, smiling at her.

'Because Derek and Ian can't believe how well those boys are doing with their business. It's so upmarket and unique, they are the most successful in the whole street. There are queues outside every day and I think they're actually quite jealous. They want to be a part of whatever those brothers say and do.'

Sanjay smiles admiringly at Eva. 'It's amazing what you find out when you own a flower shop.'

* * *

The sign now hangs proudly above my shop: Harbour Street Café. The terrace tables outside the two big glass windows on either side of the door are full. Mrs Richards and Bertie her black poodle take shelter from the sun at one of the bistro tables under the maroon and beige awning, and on another one a group of Asian students chat excitedly, taking pictures on their iPhones.

Karl with his Rastafarian dreadlocks is dressed in our new uniform; a long maroon apron and white t-shirt. He serves coffee professionally from a silver tray to a couple sitting inside beside the window.

From my vantage point outside Eva's Darling Buds and Blooms, it's interesting to see how the café looks and I feel a surge of pride. I imagine the taste of the rich dark coffee and I can feel the smooth flavour of it on the back of my tongue.

I study the wheelbarrow displays that hold a selection of fresh plants, wondering what flower arrangement would be pretty on the café tables and as I move behind the far side of the stepladder that's overflowing with luscious plants I hear a voice.

'Don't go over there. Amber's not nice.' Marion's voice is a loud whisper. She is standing outside the Très Chic Boutique on the other side of the art gallery. She can't see me but she lowers her voice.

'We don't buy our coffee from there.'

'Why?' It's a woman's voice.

'Well, aside from being awful coffee and overpriced, I don't talk to her. She treated her girlfriend very badly. Poor Cassie. She's an actor now on the London stage.'

'Really?'

'Amber's even flirted with me. You couldn't trust her an inch.'

'Oh.'

103

Marion continues, 'I met Cassie just after they moved here, She was lovely – is lovely. She was great fun. Larger than life and we hit if off right away but her girlfriend Amber is awful. Some hot-shot lawyer with no sense of humour. She expected Cassie to do everything. She didn't lift a finger and Cassie was left to sort everything out. It was Cassie who found that waiter – him – that one with the silver tray in his hand, Karl. So that Amber could open the café.'

'It seems to be doing well. It always looks busy.'

I move nearer the wall to see if I know the other person. Tracey, the beautician who has the salon beside me, is a young girl with light makeup and a ready smile.

Marion says, 'It's all thanks to Cassie it's a success. She did all the hard work.'

'But then she left?'

'Yes, the poor love. She missed the stage, the theatre. It's in her blood, so she went back to London. She's offered me tickets anytime. We could go up one weekend if you like? She would give us a couple of tickets. You'd really like her, Tracey.'

'Okay, but I'll have to ask Des. He can be a bit funny about things like that. He hates not knowing where I am.'

'Well, it will be good to have something to look forward to in the autumn.'

'Sounds exciting.'

'Well, don't go to that café any more. Pop along to Gourmet Kitchen in the square, Tracey. They're on our side in this war.'

'What do you mean, our side?'

'Well, you know about the arcade and all that. You must know JJ had her proposal turned down. She's furious. There seems to be more people against her plans than she thought. She wants as many people on her side as possible and she's holding a meeting next week in the church. She thinks Frances is the one behind the negative campaign and she's going to tackle her head on.'

'Frances the vicar?' Tracey seems surprised.

'Yes, presumably she thinks it will bring down the tone of the town. What do you think?'

'I don't like amusement arcades.'

'Well, don't tell JJ that. Think of all the new business it will bring to your beauty salon. While the men and kids gamble, the women will be over in your place getting massages and their nails done. Now, go to the Gourmet Kitchen. Their coffee is much better. Stay away from them over there.' The boutique door closes firmly behind Marion's retreating back.

Across the road, Karl lingers with Mrs Richards at the table. They laugh when her dog jumps up at his apron, and he gently pushes him away. There is an easy familiarity between them and his smile is warm and welcoming, just like the late September sunshine that greets me as I step back into the street.

* * *

After Lucas and I have gone over the menus for the following week and I've worked out the stock we will need, I check the till receipts and call it a day. I close the shop. Now that I have more staff I've found more freedom to enjoy the late summer with sometimes the occasional swim or walk around the harbour.

Sometimes I wander over to the beach and on my way back I pause to look in the shop windows in Harbour Street and in particular at the displays in Taylor's Art Gallery. Ben changes them regularly and I'm often amazed at the talent on display. I also notice that he often works late. There's a light on in the art gallery as I turn off the lights in my flat at night.

Today, as I pass by his shop, Ben's just inside the door balancing on a stepladder. He's altering the direction of the spotlights pointing at a painting on the wall. As the light catches the harbour, I pause at the door, mesmerised by the transformation of colour highlighted and the instant impact it has on the scene.

Ben beckons to me to go inside.

'Just give me a hand,' he orders, 'Is this better or this?' He adjusts the spotlight and I stand back and look closely before giving my opinion.

'That one,' I say decisively. 'It shines more on the fishing boats, giving them energy and bringing them to life.'

He moves the spotlights accordingly and then jumps down from the ladder with agility, making him seem younger than he looks.

'You've just closed up then?'

'Yes,' I reply.

'Busy day.'

'As always.'

'Do you want to go for a drink or do you want to go to the beach on your own like you normally do?' he asks gruffly.

'I'm flattered you noticed.'

'Don't be.' He folds the stepladder and places it at the back of the workshop. 'Well?'

'You can buy me a gin and tonic, if you like.'

'Just the one and you'll have to make it last. Sip it slowly.'

'Why?'

He stares at me. 'I might tell you when we're in there.'

* * *

The Ship isn't busy. It's early evening and the windows and doors are open, and instead of heading outside to the patio Ben ushers me to a seat in the far corner of the room.

'Why this table?' I ask.

'I always sit here,' he replies.

'You could be more adventurous and we could sit at a smaller table or even outside.'

'It's deliberate. I want to sit here.'

He puts his pint on the table and my double gin and tonic in front of me. He moves his chair and sits deliberately facing the bar.

'JJ isn't here,' I say conversationally.

'She's probably hiding out the back.'

'She did say, at the beginning of the summer, that I should come over and get to know the locals in Harbour Street.'

'And have you met anyone in here?'

'I've been too busy and besides...' I pause and he waits with his glass halfway to his mouth and I'm thinking of the afternoon I found Cassie drunk with Marion and I add, 'I came in once and I don't have great memories of that afternoon.'

'Why?'

'My girlfriend Cassie had been drinking all afternoon, she was celebrating her new job in London that I knew nothing about.'

'I heard rumours.' Ben stares over my shoulder at the bar and scratches his beard.

'Then you'll know I bought the café for Cassie and then she upped and left. The café was her dream.'

'Had you known her long?'

'Eighteen months.'

'Do you miss her?'

'I did at first but then I was angry. I'd sold everything in London to buy this for her but then she said she didn't want this dream anymore. I didn't realise she was so fickle. I was upset and angry but even worse – she took Scruff-bucket.'

'A dog?'

'Cat.'

'Um, pets can break our hearts.'

'I'm sorry about your dog. I saw you with him once.'

'Thanks.' He scratches his beard but won't look at me. 'He was old but I wanted him to have a happy ending.'

'That's kind.'

His eyes narrow. 'Do you miss London?'

'I was a lawyer and they were about to make me a partner in the law firm.'

'That's tough.' He wipes beer from his lips with the back of his hand.

'It was awful,' I say.

He takes another sip of his beer and doesn't look at me.

To gain his attention I ask, 'How long have you lived here?'

He smacks his lips. 'The first time, since I was a child, my parents moved down from London, when I was six.'

'First time?' I repeat.

'I left here ten years ago and I came back last year.'

'Where did you go?'

'Travelling mostly; South America, Africa, Vietnam.'

He cups his beer glass in his hands and I'm aware of the tattoos on his fingers.

'Greek letters? What do they mean?' I ask.

He glances at his hands. 'They're numbers.'

'What do they represent?'

He doesn't answer; instead he watches JJ who has appeared behind the bar. She's wearing a low-cut top and heavy makeup, and her dark hair is rich and curly. I smile at her and wave but she ignores me.

It makes Ben laugh.

'She won't acknowledge you if you're with me.'

'Why? I thought she wanted me to meet the locals. It doesn't make sense.'

'We've got history.'

'You and JJ?' I say, surprised.

'Don't tell me you didn't know.' His laugh is full of irony and I shake my head. 'There must be rumours, especially in this street.'

I shrug.

'You can't trust JJ. She's evil. Don't ever make her your friend.'

'I haven't any friends.'

'I was working in here ten years ago when she bought the pub. I wanted to go away but Mum had just been diagnosed with cancer. I felt bad leaving her and Dad, so I got a job in here.' I follow his gaze to the bar and imagine him ten years younger working behind the bar with JJ.

'She hit on me. I thought it was my natural charm...'

'But?' I prompt.

'My uncle William had a garage out back where the pub patio is now and she said she wanted to buy it for storage. She got him to sell it to her for much less than the market value.'

'How?'

'She got him all loved-up. He fell for her.'

'Not nice.' I sip my gin.

'It gets worse. He was thirty years older than her.'

'True love then,' I mutter.

'You see, Uncle William wanted to change his mind the next day but she wouldn't sell it back to him. She'd already submitted plans to have the pub patio extended. Uncle William had always been special. He had depression and very often anxiety but he was happy as a mechanic. He tinkered with a few cars, made enough money to spend in the pub, but she talked him into retiring.'

'And spending more time with her?'

His eyes narrow. 'How do you know?'

'It's a guess.'

'I was furious. I worked here and it created an atmosphere between us but I wouldn't leave. She wanted to sack me but she couldn't. I was good at what I did but she didn't want me here, so she framed me.'

I see the hurt in his eyes. His voice is low.

'She took cash from the till that I had touched and an old envelope which had my fingerprints and she hid it in my car and called the police. She said I'd been stealing from her.

'Of course they believed her. She can be very charming and believable. She also told them I'd been creating trouble because of William's land and basically she lied and lied.'

'And the police believed her.'

'Worse, a few nights later she arranged to meet me and after a big argument she set light to the pub. There wasn't much damage but enough to be classed as arson. She was very clever. There were witnesses who saw us arguing and she stashed the matches she used in my apartment and tipped the police off. I think she was dating one of the police officers by then, anyway.'

'That's convenient. How did she get into your car and apartment? Don't tell me she had a key?'

'You're sounding like a lawyer.' He rubs his chin. 'The truth is I never locked anything and she knew that.'

'So what happened?'

'I got sentenced to four years in total and I served eighteen months.'

'That must have been—'

He looks up at me. 'Hell on earth,' he says quietly. 'Mum died while I was inside. I think the shock of me going to prison made her cancer worse and sadly my dad passed away a few months later. He was broken-hearted. He'd lost us both.'

'That's terrible.' I reach over and take Ben's hand and he lets me hold his fingers.

'When I got out I was in a terrible state. I couldn't face coming back here so I travelled – I went anywhere and everywhere, picking up work but never settling. There's nowhere like here anywhere in the world.'

'You wanted to come back?'

'This has always been my home and it always will be. The numbers on here...' he raises his fingers, 'Represent the eighteen months she robbed from me and, since I've come back, I sit here every night for an hour to remind her of what she did. She's turned the town against me; people like Derek and Ian don't even look at me, but worse than anything she killed my parents and I will never forgive her.'

'And Uncle William?'

'He killed himself after I went to prison.'

Chapter 10

I stand at the bar and order two more drinks from a young boy who barely looks eighteen. I watch him work, thinking of a younger Ben and how he would have performed the same duties.

I'm suddenly aware that Marion and Pamela are standing at the far side of the counter behind the column but they haven't yet seen me.

When I glance over at Ben, he's looking down at the table lost in thought and staring at his hands. I know he's telling me the truth and now I'm aware of the tragedy of his life, I feel even more annoyed at JJ – and Marion. The lies people tell and get away with – it's these type of injustices that make me angry. It propels me forward, galvanises me into action, finding justice in the world and I know now that I must return to being a lawyer. I must go back to London.

I pull out my credit card and, from across the bar, I hear Marion saying, 'Cassie went back to London – thank goodness. She was a terrible influence on me. She used to get wasted most days.'

'Really?' Pamela doesn't sound interested.

Marion continues, 'I mean being gay. Why do they have to broadcast it? Who cares? I don't want to see it. I mean, let's be honest, it's not natural, is it?'

Pamela lifts her glass and looks over her shoulder toward the pub patio.

'You think it's funny, Pamela? You wouldn't if one of your children came home with someone of the same sex, would you? You wouldn't think it funny then.'

'This is the twenty-first century, Marion. We don't live in some parochial narrow-minded Middle Eastern country. For heaven's sake, isn't it time we all learned to live in harmony together, regardless of race, creed or sexuality? Hasn't that been the root of so much trouble for years?' Pamela replies.

'That's not the point. There's no excuse. I wouldn't want them in my house. And I'm very tolerant, Pamela. I'm no judge of character. But I just don't like people flaunting their peculiar habits trying to influence and persuade everyone. I don't mind what people do or who they sleep with so long as I don't have to know about it and it's done behind closed doors. I don't want my nose rubbed into their sordid little lives.'

'It's not sordid. There are lots of gay people in the world,' Pamela adds mildly. 'Besides I thought Cassie was your friend?'

'Well, she was but I never approved of their relationship. That's why I don't get coffee from *that* café.' Marion raises her glass. 'Cheers.'

'Well, I think you'll be safe,' Pamela jokes. 'You're hardly this summer's catch.'

Marion ignores her. 'Ben's over there again. He's got a face like thunder. You wouldn't want to get on the wrong side of him. He looks like a murderer.'

'I know Ben. He's not all bad.'

'You do?'

'He was a popular boy at school,' Pamela says, glancing out of the window. 'I know lots of people who knew him.'

'Well, he's not popular anymore. No one wants his art gallery in Harbour Street. He's got such a cheek coming back after being in prison.'

'Don't be ridiculous Marion. It's his home.'

* * *

I place the drinks on the table and Ben looks up at me. He looks haunted by sadness and I see how some people may interpret his intense frown as anger. All I see is internal torment, angst and frustration.

'That's kind of you, Amber. Thank you.'

I slide into my seat beside him. 'Marion and Pamela are on the other side of the bar.'

He rubs his forehead. 'Oh no, save me.' He grins.

'Marion doesn't like gay people, presumably,' I say.

'So, you won't be getting a Christmas card,' he quips.

'I don't consider myself gay.'

He looks surprised. 'Really?'

'I was engaged once – to a guy. I'd just finished uni and I'd broken up with a Japanese waitress, and then I met Steve.'

Ben sits up. 'What happened?'

'He was lovely, a really kind and decent guy. We were together four years.'

'And?'

'He went to a party one night and slept with another girl and couldn't understand why I got upset.'

'You must have been hurt.'

'I was but you get over it, it didn't work out. Some

114

relationships don't, do they?'

Ben nods in agreement.

I add, 'We met too young. It wasn't his fault. I was working long hours.'

'So, are you bisexual?'

I sip my gin. 'I never categorise myself like that. It's all about who you fall in love with. It's about the person and it has nothing to do with labels, male or female. It's about who makes me happy.'

Ben sips his beer.

'Do you understand?' I ask.

'I guess so, but to be honest...' he smiles. 'I've never been attracted to a man.'

I shrug. 'Maybe it's different for men.'

'Do your parents know?'

'Yes. They're really cool with it all. They just want me to be happy. I guess that's what always shocks me, you know, when your parents are so normal and understanding then you meet a complete stranger who's homophobic or racist, or whatever.'

'I don't know what would have happened if I'd brought a man home to my parents. We never discussed things like that. But they were never racist or homophobic.'

'Well, your experience with JJ didn't put you off women?' I laugh.

Ben frowns. 'We never had a relationship. I just worked here. I didn't have enough money for her. I had nothing she wanted – except bar experience. She had no idea about running a pub.'

'So why did she buy one?'

'I think she inherited money or something from an uncle or someone. She'd been a carer before but she said she wanted a change. She wanted to work with the living and not the dying.'

'So, it's just as well you weren't in a relationship with her.'

'She's not my type.'

'Who's your type?'

'I had relationships before I left and then while I was travelling I hooked up with an Australian girl for a few years but she didn't want to come back to England and I didn't want to go to Australia, so we broke up and I came home.' He shrugs. 'It was for the best. I wasn't in a great place and I didn't realise how hard things would hit me when I got back here. I missed this place, I missed the sea, and my—'

'Parents?'

'Yes. I had to face that shock and, in a way, grieve for them all over again. I had to sort out their house and there were lots of memories. I was overwhelmed. We were in partial lockdown and I'd come back to a very strange place – it was all so different.'

'What about your friends?'

'Most of them went off to uni and never came back, there were a couple of people but they moved on. And, since I've come home, because of lockdown I haven't bothered. It's all been very unusual and then a neighbour had a dog, Bumble. He was in a kennel and they were stuck in Spain. Bumble was old and ill and so I agreed to take him home with me, to look after him at the end, as they couldn't get back. It's been a strange world.'

'Do you live above the art gallery?'

He shakes his head. 'No, that's more of a storeroom, I inherited my parents' house but I never came back before I went travelling. So, in the past year, I've been sorting everything out. Bless them. They hadn't done much work on it. Dad was an office worker and he was never very good with his hands. He was always surprised when I wanted to be a carpenter.'

'Well, you're home now.' I smile. 'And you have Taylor's Art Gallery.'

'It's crazy, I'm still getting used to it all.'

'It will take time to settle back in.'

'Oh, it's not that.' He nods over to JJ behind the bar. 'I sit here for an hour every evening wondering how to get even with her. I sit here imagining what she would be feeling if she'd been locked away for something she didn't do, and if her parents had died while she was in prison.'

'That's not healthy, Ben. It's not good for you. Sometimes bad things happen but you have to let it go.'

'I can't.'

'You must or it will eat away inside you and then she will win all over again. She will poison your mind and that's not right.'

He leans across the table and says through gritted teeth, 'Well, what would you do, smartarse?'

'I don't know, Ben. I can't begin to imagine how you must be feeling and what you've gone through. It's simply horrendous.'

'Exactly,' he hisses. 'You have no idea.'

I lean toward him, emboldened by the double gins. 'But I will tell you one thing. I wouldn't give her the satisfaction of seeing me sitting in hcr pub every night and giving her my money.'

Ben raises his eyebrows in surprise.

'And,' I continue, 'I certainly wouldn't be walking around town like I'm a dropout and a dirty tramp with a filthy beard and no friends.'

He drains the rest of his pint and slaps the glass on the table.

'My mother wrote to me in prison.' His voice is trembling. 'And, do you know what? I can't even read her letter. Not then and not now. I haven't even opened it.'

'Why?'

'Because I can't win, Amber. It's Catch 22, she'll either be very angry with me or very forgiving but either way it will break my heart. Can't you see? I wasn't even here when she died.'

'Then maybe you should read it. You can't keep hiding, Ben. Sometimes you just have to face up to the fact that crap has smacked you in the face and you have to wipe it off and get up on your feet again because if you don't, life will just get even more miserable and unbearab—'

Ben stands up. He's red-faced and angry. He grips his fists tightly at his side. 'Thanks for the sympathy.'

'I am sympathetic, Ben. But I'm also practical.' I look up at him. 'Please don't be angry with everyone. Get smart. Get even. Move on with your life or get JJ to wish she'd never done what she did.'

* * *

The next morning, I'm first one inside the Turkish barbers – The Grooming Room. It smells of scented aftershave that is both relaxing and arousing. A big sign on the wall in fancy writing says,

Our gifts for men are thoughtful, unique, and will bring him joy. We have the perfect presents for him. Bespoke, handmade or precious, our collection of gifts are original ideas for men.

Two brothers, late twenties, in crisp white shirts, black trousers and trimmed beards welcome me with wide smiles.

'Hello, beautiful, what can we do for you? Facial massage? Hot towel shave?'

'Yusef, stop teasing the young lady.' The smaller of the two men holds out his hand. 'I'm Ozan and this is my brother, Yusef. You're the lovely lady from the café.'

I grin and shake his hand. 'Amber, and I like the young lady, thank you. Are you twins?'

Ozan smiles. 'Brothers but not twins. I'm the eldest.'

'And I'm the better looking.' Yusef grins. 'And the funniest.'

I laugh. Their humour is infectious.

He continues, 'You see, bro, she likes me. She can't resist my charm.' Yusef is light on his feet and, as he talks, he continually checks his reflection in the mirror and strokes his smooth, manicured beard.

'How can we help?' Ozan asks.

'I'd like a voucher. It's for Ben, your neighbour in the—'

Yusef interrupts, 'Hey, bro, that's Ben from the art gallery. We love Ben. He's our main man and boy, does he need a trim. We've been tellin' him for a year. We've said, hey Ben, get yourself a trim, man. How you gonna meet the ladies looking that rough? Haven't we, bro?'

Ozan smiles at me. 'He is in need of our services.'

'Man, we tell him all the time, don't we, bro? But it's good you're talking to him, Ambie baby. He don't have many friends. I don't think he has any – apart from us. You tell Ben he needs us. He needs sculpting, that guy. He's a great man but he needs looking after, he needs a massage to sooth his facial skin. He's a sad soul, we tell him that, don't we, bro?'

Ozan smiles and passes me a variety of cards. 'If it's a gift voucher perhaps—'

'Is it Ben's birthday, or something?' Yusef interrupts. 'We can do something for him, can't we, bro? You know, trim the beard, his ears, the nape of his hair.' He presses the back of his neck where Yusef's own hair is neatly shaved. 'We can show off his dreamy eyes and make him look cool.'

I grin. 'Please let him choose what he wants but if he comes in here, can you just give him what he needs and I'm happy to pay any extra costs.'

'I know what you're doing.' Yusef sidles up to me. 'You're tidyin' the man up. You can see potential in him, isn't that right? I've bin sayin' that to Ozan. I said, hey, bro, check out that Ben. He's seriously cool, man and he's got some great tatts.'

'How much would you like the voucher for?' Ozan asks me, ignoring his bro.

I shrug. 'What's normal? Would fifty pounds be okay?'

'Aw, man,' cries Yusef. 'You're lovely. I'll tell him. I'll say, Ben, she's a seriously lovely lady, man. Get yourself together and take that beautiful woman on a date.'

I hold up my hand. 'I don't want a date.'

'No date? With that cool dude? Are you serious?'

I smile. 'Very serious.'

'He needs a friend.' Ozan takes my credit card and while I wait I'm distracted by the array of shaving brushes on display and just how relaxed I feel in this environment.

'You've some lovely things in here. Beautiful gifts.'

Yusef is beside me, looking over my shoulder, and I can smell his intoxicating, pungent spicy aftershave. 'Anything you want, baby, we have it right here. All the gifts for everyone. The Grooming Room is the best.'

'I'll bear that in mind, thank you.' I smile at Ozan who gives me the receipt and the voucher, but I hesitate.

'Perhaps you'd give Ben the voucher?' I say, thinking of how angry Ben had been when he stormed out of The Ship last night.

Ozan frowns.

Yusef snatches it from his hand.

'Leave it to me, bro, I'm good at this stuff. I can smell romance at forty miles. I'll drop it into the cool guy and...' He waves the voucher and leans closer to whisper in my ear. 'I'll make sure I book him an appointment. This isn't going to be one of those vouchers he sticks in the kitchen drawer never to be seen again. This is serious, bro, isn't it? This is our op-por-tun-ity, to spice up the man's life – to make a change.'

Ozan nods and smiles. 'Ben does need looking after.'

'Thank you.'

Yusef opens the door for me and guides me outside. 'Come on, pretty lady, I'll escort you back across the road. I need to confirm Karl's appointment, pronto.'

'Karl? Does he come here?'

'All the time.'

'I thought he always looked well-groomed.'

Yusef grins. 'It's not just you ladies who have to take care of yourselves. We owe it to you, to look goooood. We've got to look hot for you beautiful wo-men.'

Chapter 11

I stand at the back of the church like I did with my family as a child. Although religion has not featured much in my life, we always attended Midnight Mass. It's still my favourite time of the year – the birth of Christ and I remember how our local vicar had always sounded reassuring and confident. His voice had filled me with a wonderful feeling of peace and tranquillity leaving me calm and contented.

But this evening it is very different.

It's October and all the pews are full and even the extra wooden seats laid out at the back are crowded. This is a big event for the community of Harbour Street and it appears, by the level of commotion and raised voices, that everyone has an opinion. The discussion has already begun and Frances calls the group to order. Her practised and measured voice rings across the vaulted ceiling and one by one the crowd fall silent.

'Hello, everyone, good evening and thank you for coming. Let's crack on, shall we? Prior to the submission of the planning and development of the old travel agents property in Harbour Street, JJ, who most of you know as the proprietor and landlady from The Ship, would like to say a few words.'

JJ, who until this moment has been sitting in the front pew, rises to her feet. She turns and faces the crowd. She's wearing a conservative two-piece beige and navy suit, looking every inch a businesswoman and not a barmaid.

She beams happily and confidently at everyone, laughing with practised ease at a comment from someone in the front row. Her manner is one of genial friendliness and goodwill. Anyone who knows JJ sees this as her public persona. After what Ben told me last week, I can see she's fooled many people. She is very popular.

She raises her hands in greeting and to silence the crowd.

'Thank you for turning out this evening. I welcome the opportunity to involve you in my plans for this incredible development opportunity. You are all a part of our wonderful community and it's important that you understand where I'm coming from,' she pauses.

Someone from the back shouts, 'Lining your own pockets.'

Although a few people around me laugh, JJ either doesn't hear them or she ignores them and she carries on speaking.

'This new attraction will bring vibrancy to our town that will offer visitors and locals an alternative entertainment venue other than the normal.' She lists them on her jewelled fingers. 'Shops, bars and restaurants. I will of course apply for the necessary gaming licenses and adhere to the government guidelines in keeping with the law, being a responsible patron for this premises. I will also make sure the necessary requirements for fire and safety, employment legislation and food safety are—'

'What machines will you have?' asks Sanjay. He's sitting near the front.

JJ pauses and then smiles reassuringly. 'They are multi-gaming machines, the latest ones; shooting, driving, dancing, flight simulation and driving, boxing—'

'And what about the gambling ones, what are the stakes?' asks Eva. She's sitting in the middle of the church at the end of the pew. Her face is one of cold apprehension.

'The gaming machines will vary from 5p to one pound with a maximum jackpot of five hundred pounds.'

'What about security?' asks Mario from Kingdom Pets.

JJ answers easily, 'It will be staffed and managed at all times. There will be heavy CCTV and robust ID checks to make sure people are over the age of eighteen.'

'So, it's not family entertainment?' Eva calls out.

'Provided you're with an adult, families are welcome—' JJ's smile has disappeared.

Frances moves forward and interrupts. 'I think perhaps we are missing the point. The question is, do we want an amusement arcade in the centre of our town?'

'No!'

'No!'

'It's not right.'

'This isn't the place.'

'Yes.'

'Why not?'

'Employment.'

'It will bring more people.'

'Tourists equals money.'

'Yes.'

Chaos ensues and Frances raises her hand. 'Is this the sort of business that we want in our town? Do we want an amusement arcade?'

Marion raises her hand and when Frances nods for her to speak, she stands and faces the audience. In a clear voice, she says, 'Like all of you here, I'm a local shop owner. You know I own the Très Chic Boutique. Like you, I've been here for many years, working hard and paying my bills and taxes. I've worked closely with the local shopkeepers like Derek and Ian, and more recently Tracey and Jane. And, I'd also like to say, I've worked with JJ for many years. If we're not all regulars at The Ship, I can bet that we've all had a drink in her pub at one time or another. JJ is the epitome of a successful woman who has the community and its progress and safety at her heart. And I for one am very happy that JJ is willing to turn that eyesore in the centre of Harbour Street into another successful business.'

It's a rehearsed speech and she gets cheering and applause as she sits down, as well as an appreciative, demure smile from JJ.

'Thank you, Marion.'

Frances looks around. 'Who else would like to speak?'

'It's an antisocial business for us walking our children up the road. It's not setting a very good example, is it?' says Tracey, from the beauty salon. She's young and well-dressed. 'It might encourage them to gamble.'

Some people laugh and Frances intervenes. 'Planning officers are not always concerned about the sensitive or moral perspectives of the business.'

'Well they should be,' she argues.

'Hear, hear,' cries another.

'Look, I'm one of you. I'm a shop-owner and I live in the community, among you all.' JJ lowers her voice so the crowd strain to listen. 'I want what's best for our community. We all want a better town and we have to be forward thinking and innovative. What happens when it rains and it's cold in the winter? All the visitors leave but now, with this business, they will have somewhere to go, in between showers.' She smiles. 'It will be an additional reason for them to visit Westbay.'

'What's wrong with the bars and restaurants and cafés?' Karl calls out. 'Not everyone wants to take their kids into a gambling den or has money to throw away. Gambling is a vice.'

I'm surprised Karl speaks up and I'm secretly proud of him. He's not fazed by the shop owners. He's sitting with a young intense looking girl with wide grey eyes that I assume must be his girlfriend Molly.

JJ shakes her head and laughs. 'Everyone loves a slot machine or a quiz machine. It's only a couple of quid – it's not Monte Carlo. Besides, this meeting is for residents and owners of properties to air their views – not employees,' she adds dismissively.

Karl's face clouds over and I see Molly reach out and squeeze his hand.

Derek the butcher jumps to his feet and faces us.

'I think it's a great idea. I'm right behind JJ. She's done a fabulous job with The Ship, that was a right dive ten years ago, and she's doing a lot for the town and she has even more plans—'

'Not now, Derek.' JJ holds up her hands. 'One thing at a time.'

The crowd begin to speak among themselves, voices are raised and I realise that it's JJ's friends and associates at the front, and the residents and the people who oppose JJ seem to be at the back of the church.

Ben Taylor is leaning against a pillar behind me with his arms folded. On the opposite side of the aisle Mario and

Luke from Kingdom Pets are chatting earnestly together, and beside them Kit and Jenna and their two adopted children Sia and Kanan have their heads bent together in discussion.

Jenna looks up and calls out. 'Kit wants to say something.'

Her husband rises to his feet. He's tall, skinny and very blond.

Frances raises her hand. 'Please, everyone, let Kit speak,' she calls over the noise of the congregation.

He clears his throat nervously. 'It may be of no surprise to any of you that I am opposed to the planning and the whole idea of an amusement arcade in our town. It is completely inappropriate and it's against the historic and aesthetic beauty of the image we have created for the town. Years ago, they couldn't give away the property in Harbour Street for the smell of rotting fish. Now, it's one of the most prestigious streets in the town. All of us, as residents, tradespeople and shop owners, have worked hard to create individuality and independence. We have fought off and resisted the investment of big chain stores and cafés in Harbour Street. We are independent and proud and, I believe, we should stay that way. Any cheap gimmicks or inferior businesses that don't sit well within the community will lower the tone of what we all stand for.'

He sits down suddenly and there's a round of applause.

'Hear, hear.'

'Rubbish! What's wrong with progress?'

'Well said.'

'Things change.'

'Places change.'

Frances says, 'Kit is right. If this planning application was made for example in Windsor or Bath or any other beautiful

127

historical English town it would be denied. This is an historic street and it should be treated accordingly.'

'Think of the clock tower,' Sanjay says. 'That's the heritage of our street, not a cheap amusement arcade.'

'I don't want an amusement arcade near my flower shop,' Eva adds.

JJ raises her arm. 'All I want is the best for us all and for our town. I will listen to all of you but thank you for the opportunity that you've given me to explain my plans before I submit my proposal. One final question, is the Harbour Street Shop Owners Community still happy for me to arrange our annual Halloween street party on the 31st?'

There's a pause then with the attention of the public deflected; there is general consensus of opinion in agreement with Halloween. But as the meeting draws to a close some people are still focused on the amusement arcade, and as the crowd begins to disperse I'm the first person out of the church, conscious that Ben is only a few paces behind me. Like him, I've said nothing in the meeting.

I've always avoided personal conflict and that's probably why my life is now such a mess. The development in this town is the last thing I need. I'm not staying here and hopefully I'll have sold the café by the time the planning permission goes through. It's nothing to do with me.

* * *

'Why didn't you speak up in there?'

I turn around and as everyone spills out of the church Eva is chasing after me in high heels. There's no sign of Ben, he must have ducked down one of the alleyways. He's probably avoiding me after our drink in the pub.

'Because it's nothing to do with me,' I reply.

'Of course it is, you're a shop owner,' Eva insists.

'Yes, but I'm not staying here. The café is for sale, remember?'

'Does that mean you don't care or you don't have an opinion?'

I shrug. 'Well, if I was staying. I don't think it's a good idea.'

'Then why didn't you speak up?' Eva is annoyed, and having upset Ben, I'm suddenly aware I must tread carefully.

'I'm – I don't know, Eva. I'm sorry.'

'Frances was counting on you. Even Karl spoke up and JJ dismissed him as an employee. She's so rude.'

'I know. Look, I'm sorry. It's been a long day.'

We're standing outside Sanjay's takeaway, so I say, 'I'm getting a curry, would you like to have dinner with me and we can eat it in the café?'

Eva tilts her head and sighs. 'Well, I have no one to rush home to now Nick and Emma have gone.'

'I know how you feel, come on, a bit of company will do us both good.' It's an olive branch and Eva has made me feel guilty, as though I should care about Harbour Street.

Inside the takeaway, Eva knows all of Sanjay's cousins, and although I've seen some of them she introduces me to them all as if memorising their names; Vinjay and Umar, then in the kitchen Sujan and Devika.

'Harini is having a night off,' she explains to me.

When Sanjay returns from the church he moves quickly behind the counter to take over. 'Hello, ladies,' he says, 'what a farce that meeting was, JJ will get her own way.'

'This is what I'm worried about.' Eva glances up from the

menu.

'Have you ordered?' Sanjay asks.

'Yes, Umar served us and I've said hello to everyone.' Eva smiles at him. 'I'm pleased you spoke up at the meeting, Sanjay. We need more people like you.'

He smiles back and nods approvingly. 'But how are we going to stop JJ? There was little opposition in the church. It's crazy.'

'Kit spoke up but people don't care,' Eva moans. 'They think more people coming to Harbour Street equals more money in their pockets.'

'It's the quality of the people coming here,' Sanjay says. 'And how they behave.'

'I agree.' Eva sighs.

'I think it was split, not everyone agreed with JJ,' I say.

'Not everyone spoke up.' Sanjay frowns at me and continues, 'Even Ben said nothing. I'd have thought he'd have said something under the circumstances.'

I think of my conversation with Ben and I wonder how much of the truth Sanjay and Eva know. Do they know that JJ framed him?

Sanjay continues, 'Ozan and Yusef didn't come tonight either. We must do something to get them on our side. We need to be a stronger group.'

'I agree,' says Eva earnestly and then Sanjay takes an order over the phone. When our food arrives, we wave at Sanjay and carry the bags back to the café.

* * *

I switch on some music, one of the classical albums that Karl enjoys, and open a bottle of red wine. Eva organises the food and plates and I give her serviettes.

'I want to buy some pots and plants for the back patio for the autumn,' I say.

'Okay, I'll sort out something nice for you.'

'Something that isn't a lot of work.'

She grins. 'I know just the thing.'

'How are things at home?' I ask.

'Quiet.'

'In a good way?'

'It's just so strange without them,' she says, picking up her serviette and opening it on her lap. 'They weren't at home much but I knew they were coming in, or they'd text or phone but now since they've left, I've hardly heard from them.'

'I imagine they're settling in. Life has changed so much since the pandemic I'm sure they want to be free—'

'Did you feel like that?'

I sit opposite her, snap a poppadom and help myself to rice and chicken curry.

'Well, university was a long time ago.'

'But the quietness...' Her voice is filled with despair. 'After Cassie left.'

'In the beginning I thought Cassie and I were perfectly happy but when she left there was a part of me that felt relief from the constant bickering and accusations. Now it's Scruff-bucket, my cat, I miss.'

'Emma is so contentious, she'd start a fight in an empty field.'

I laugh.

'But I even miss that.' Eva chews slowly. 'Nick's quiet but it's just knowing he's there, even if he is on his phone most of the time.'

Pavarotti is singing 'Caruso' and it echoes in the empty café. Outside the streets are still busy with people heading out for dinner, drinks or for a walk in the harbour.

'Do you miss working in London, Amber?'

I barely pause before answering. 'Yes, but it's not far away. If I want to go up to town and see a show or go out for dinner I can always get the last train home.'

I don't tell her that I haven't the energy to go out at night or that I don't have money for the train fare. I don't mention that Cassie has left a huge gap in my life and that I have no friends. I'm not forthcoming like Cassie. By now she would have dragged Eva to the pub and told her the joys of being a lesbian. But I'm not like that.

Eva eats slowly. 'You've done well with the café, it seems very successful and I think you're a good businesswoman, Amber. Maybe it's good to live someone else's dream.'

'No. It isn't! Believe me, I'm happier in London.' I top up our wine glasses. 'But I have a good team now; Lucas is excellent in the kitchen. He has lots of experience and he's well-travelled and has some great ideas. Jean is always supportive, and Karl, well, he's just a natural; always so upbeat and positive and it's infectious. It's hard not to be in a good mood with him around. Even Ingrid is developing a sense of humour.' I grin. 'I'm lucky.'

Eva regards me carefully. 'You have a good team because they like you. They respect you and they enjoy working for you.'

I mull over her words as I think of the jobs I have yet to finish tonight. I have the till to sort out and the rest of the stock to stack for the morning but now I'm not in any hurry.

It's good to have company. I have nowhere to go, I certainly don't want to be alone upstairs in my damp flat and it's great to be able to sit and chat and not serve in the café. It's also interesting to see someone else's perspective on my life and business.

Eva says, 'There's always a happy atmosphere in here, Amber. It's relaxing and fun.'

'To be honest, I'm surprised sometimes that I actually enjoy it myself.' I grin.

'Well, maybe you won't sell the café then after all.'

I smile. 'I'm definitely selling it, Eva. I belong in London.'

Eva says, 'Nick loves London too. He said he might have to come home next week and get the car. I really don't want him to take it. I know he doesn't drink and drive, he's very sensible, but you know how it is when all the young ones get together and try to impress each other.'

'He won't need a car in London. It's expensive and there's nowhere to park. Cassie doesn't drive and I never had a car and I only bought the van when I came here so I could buy stock.'

I suddenly don't want to talk about Cassie so I ask, 'Do they like their uni courses? How are they both getting on?'

'Emma loves her course but Nick doesn't say much. The other day I told him I had collected his computer cable from his friend's house and he only sends me a smiley face – nothing more. He's obviously too busy!' She laughs ruefully. 'It was so strange when they left last week. I had always imagined that James would be with me to see them off to university. But he wasn't. It was surreal in a way. I can't really believe they've gone. All those years of school runs, sleepless nights, colds and flu, birthday parties, scraped knees and falling out with their

133

friends. Then the holidays we used to have in the Caribbean, skiing in the winter.' She pauses. 'We had a luxurious life. But, that was a long time ago.' She sips her wine. 'I have a new life now.'

'I know how you feel,' I say.

'The trouble is - is that it doesn't exactly fit me yet. My new life…'

She takes a deep breath and struggles to speak. Her eyes are contemplative and I might as well not be here. She just needs to talk. She needs to get it all out of her system and I feel sorry for her. Over twenty years of marriage and here she is, talking to a virtual stranger about her feelings. How depressing is that?

She looks at me.

Can she read my thoughts?

'You probably look at me and see a very spoilt woman, Amber.' She doesn't wait for me to answer. 'I was, in a way.' She lays down her fork. 'I used to go for massages every week, the hairdressers every Friday. I shopped daily and I even took golf lessons. But I had to do all that for James. I had to look my best to entertain for him. His accountancy firm is one of the biggest. He has important wealthy clients and he would rely on me to look and act the part. The ideal wife of the successful accountant. I was the best hostess. I was the best cook, the best conversationalist and I was an asset to his business. The perfect accessory. Sometimes he would phone at nine o'clock at night and I was expected to host six people for a late supper or suddenly at the weekend I was expected to act as a tour guide around Canterbury to the wife of an important client.'

'Did you mind?'

'I didn't think about it. I was his wife and I loved him.'

'You must miss him,' I say quietly.

'I was angry at first. You know, for leaving me for the younger woman and all that but what can you do? I miss everything,' she says. 'I miss my family and the life I had. How it all used to be but nothing stays the same, does it? To be honest, I think I'm miserable because I'm just hankering after my youth and a past that I can never have again…'

Tears are brimming in her eyes and I know exactly how she feels.

I reach across the table and take her hand. I know what it's like to be so utterly, utterly, lonely. How many nights have I sat upstairs feeling exactly the same?

As Eva grips my hand in return, I look up and Ben Taylor is staring at us through the window. He pauses before scowling and then he turns and walks away.

Chapter 12

The following morning Karl's usual good humour is absent and when I ask him if he's alright he's monosyllabic. The café is busy but I notice that he's not cheerful with the customers and he barely looks at Jean or Ingrid. He doesn't even speak to Lucas.

I have a few minutes just after the lunchtime rush and I whisper to Jean.

'Is Karl okay? He seems very quiet.'

'He's upset.'

'Is there anything I can do?'

'Talk to him.' She doesn't look at me but continues making sandwiches and I wonder if I've done something to upset her.

Later in the afternoon, I mess up with an order at a big table with crying children. I've got a headache and my shoulders ache and I wish I hadn't had the third glass of red wine last night. I'm running out of patience. I head to the counter, away from the shrieks and banging tables.

'Karl, I'm sorry. I think I've messed up table nine.'

'Can't you sort it?' he asks angrily.

'Okay but hold back on the milkshakes, that's where I've gone wrong.'

'Hurry up! There are other people waiting,' he hisses under

his breath.

No sooner have I delivered the right drinks to the right table than Ben Taylor arrives. I try to catch his eye and smile but he ignores me and heads straight to Karl at the counter.

'Your usual, Ben?'

'Please, Karl.'

Karl smiles but when he sees me coming over he scowls.

'Hello, Ben, how are you?' I ask.

He takes a deep breath and replies coolly, 'I'm fine.'

'Good.'

I'm about to walk away but he says, 'You didn't need to do that.'

'What?'

'The voucher. It wasn't necessary.'

I lean closer to him. 'It's my way of making an apology for the other night. I don't want to upset you again.'

'I'm not upset. Your opinion isn't important to me.'

'Oh.'

'Why should it be?'

I shrug. 'I just thought we might be… friends.'

He shakes his head. 'You have to be a friend to have a friend.' He raises his voice and takes the recyclable cup. 'Thanks, Karl.'

'You're welcome, Ben.'

That's the most cheerful I've seen Karl all day and just before closing time, I corner him in the kitchen.

'Are you okay, Karl?'

He stares at me. 'No.'

'What's wrong? Can I help?'

He unties his apron and folds it up. 'I don't think you'd know how to.'

'Try me.'

He leans back against the counter.

'Well, tell me how you'd feel if you were a complete failure at everything you've ever done, and then you finally found a job that you love. You actually find a job where you're respected and valued, and you've got a pretty good salary with a profit share, and a girlfriend who loves you, and even though you're living in a pokey caravan there's hope. Hope.' He folds his arms. 'For the first time in your life you feel like you belong. That you're wanted and you have a purpose and, you might actually have a future but more importantly, you're worth something. You mean something—'

'You mean a lot, Karl, you're amazing and—'

He holds up his palm. 'Wait! Then, it turns out that near where you work they're about to build something you don't believe in, and you feel as though you have to say something. So, it takes you a tremendous amount of courage to speak in public, in front of strangers, and tell them very politely that it's a bad idea. You don't tell them that your dad was a gambler and that he used to beat you when he didn't win, or he'd get drunk when he lost and hit your mother. You keep that inside. But you do say, you're against the idea. But then, you're told to shut up because you're not the owner of the business. You're only an employee and you have no voice. You're a nobody.'

His eyes are sad and I want to reach out to him.

'Karl, I'm so sorry. JJ had no right to—'

'This isn't about JJ.'

'Isn't it?'

'No. It's about you.'

'Me?'

'Yes, you're the owner of this café. You should have spoken up. You should have been fighting for the integrity of Harbour

138

Street Café instead poor Kit was the only one saying no to her.'

'But the café is for sale. It's nothing to do with me.'

He leans in my face. 'This is everything to do with you, Amber. While you're here and you're the owner, you must do what's best for this business and for this street. You have a duty to protect your staff, to think of our future rather than thinking of how much profit you're going to make and how fast you can get back to London.'

'Karl, I'm sorry—'

'If you're sorry then do something, Amber. Otherwise it means nothing. It's a fake apology that gets you off the hook to make *you* feel better – not me. I'm going home now because I have a girlfriend who actually cares about me and understands what this place means to me, even if you don't.'

* * *

After Karl storms out, I lock the café behind him, turn off the music and stand in the kitchen alone, Karl's words still reverberating around the walls and echoing in my head. I guess the staff all knew that Karl would speak to me; Jean, Lucas and Ingrid left with barely a goodbye. Gone are the days when I would wave them goodbye after work as if they were leaving my dinner party. Gone is the good humour and banter and relaxed atmosphere that Eva noticed.

They're all angry with me.

I'd had the perfect team. The perfect staff, and now they all think I've let them down.

'But it's not my fault,' I say aloud. I shout, '*This is not my bloody dream!* I never wanted a café!'

I'm fed up with everything and everyone. I've given up my career for this café and it's hard work. I live in a dump upstairs that stinks and I haven't the time or money or energy to do anything for myself. I've put this business first; Karl, Jean, Lucas and Ingrid, and I pay their salaries, order stock and support them – or I thought I did.

I go outside to the patio that's now adorned with pretty pots and growing perennials and I sit in the cold, hugging my arms around my waist trying to make sense of everything.

Poor Karl.

He's another person in Harbour Street struggling with his own demons and fighting his past to survive in the future.

I shiver.

The drops of rain turn to a shower, then it's raining hard, faster and faster. I go back inside, pick up my keys and head back out into the fading light, along Harbour Street to The Ship. As I pause in the doorway, there's a crack of thunder nearby and suddenly torrential rain is falling onto the pavement and bouncing back up, dancing in the gutter. There's another rumbling rolling crash of thunder followed by an incredible flash of lightning and the road is quickly flooded. Drains are blocked and massive puddles stretch across the road and the streets are suddenly awash. My feet are soaking.

I need a drink.

* * *

It looks like lots of people have escaped the rain and taken refuge in the pub. It's busy with people shaking jackets and wet hair, laughing at the sudden downpour, and there's a damp smell to the pub now that reminds me of my flat.

140

JJ is serving. She pulls a pint while she jokes with Ian the grocer, who leans on the bar. I wait to be served, standing away from other people; a young family, a couple having a heated discussion and a couple of guys playing dominos.

It's a wet evening and the storm has caught people unawares. They come flooding in grabbing seats, gathering them around tables and getting settled.

'What can I get you?' JJ asks coolly.

'A gin and tonic, please.'

I watch her deftly place the ice and lemon in the glass but she doesn't make small talk with me or attempt to be friendly.

When I give her my credit card she gets the machine and as she returns I ask, 'Do you think the meeting went well?'

'I'd like to think everyone understood the importance of getting rid of that eyesore.'

While I tap the machine, she looks up.

'Swapping one eyesore for another?' I reply.

She frowns and tears off my receipt.

I continue, 'I'd like to say, I don't care about the empty travel agency or what business goes in there, and the truth is – it's nothing to do with me. The café is up for sale. I can't wait to leave here and go back to London but I do care about how you treat Karl. He had every right to speak up at the meeting and he's entitled to his opinion.'

JJ hands me my card and receipt and she smiles as if we are friends.

I continue, 'You didn't have to be rude to him in front of everyone.'

'I wasn't.'

'You were. You deliberately put him down and it wasn't necessary.'

'I was right. I am right. He is not an owner. I only want owners' opinions.'

'I don't think you want anyone's opinion,' I say, suddenly conscious of a looming presence at my side. 'You're steam-rolling everyone into agreeing with you.'

'And what's wrong with that?' Marion is suddenly at my elbow. 'They're all very feeble in Harbour Street, you saw what they were like. Someone has to take the lead.' She grins at JJ. 'I'll have my usual, please, darling.'

'Everyone is allowed an opinion,' I argue. 'People are allowed to disagree.'

JJ laughs. 'No one will go against me. They've got no backbone, besides I do believe it's the best thing for Harbour Street. As I said, it will bring in the visitors, and they'll have something to do here other than stare at the sea and buy crap in the local souvenir shops.'

'Besides,' says Marion. 'It will create employment. JJ will be the biggest employer in the town and she'll probably even be the mayor soon.'

JJ pushes out her breasts, raises her shoulders and appears to stand taller. She smiles. 'Let's not get ahead of ourselves, Marion. It took God six days to create the world. One step at a time.'

'I know what you're like with your employees,' I say.

JJ continues to smile at me. 'I doubt it, Amber. You never speak to anyone and you've no friends.'

'Ben told me what you're like and what really happened. He told me what you did to him and his family.'

Beside me, Marion gasps and covers her mouth with her hand.

JJ leans across the counter and lowers her voice menacingly.

'He's lucky he's even allowed in here after what he did. I only let him in so I can take his money. He's a lowlife and an ex-con. And, if he's the only friend you have in town then I suggest you get out now.'

She picks up my gin and tonic and tips it down the sink then she slams the empty glass on the counter in front of me. 'Believe me, I've thrown out more important people than you,' she hisses.

* * *

It's still raining heavily and by the time I run back to my flat and I've kicked open the front door, I'm soaked through to my skin. My wet t-shirt clings to me, and my hair is plastered and flattened to my head. My hands are still shaking and my body quivering. I hate confrontation but worse still, I've never been thrown out of a pub.

What even possessed me to go in there?

I didn't even want a drink, did I?

I only wanted to stick up for Karl but I was even useless at that.

Spineless.

I should stick to the facts; paperwork and documents instead of getting emotional.

Upstairs in the flat there's a noise coming from the bathroom. I call out and take the stairs two at a time and push open the door.

Water is dripping through the ceiling from the flat roof outside. It looks like it's been leaking for a while. There's a massive puddle on the floor and I'm worried it will go through to the café. I find a bucket in the kitchen and realise the leak is spreading, there's a damp patch across the kitchen ceiling and the bedroom is worse. My bedding is sodden and I think the roof will collapse.

I call a 24-hour plumber and spend a few hours waiting for him and, after he arrives, listening to his tale of doom.

'Didn't you know that the boiler is in the attic?'

I shake my head. 'I thought that the boiler downstairs was for the flat and the café.'

He shakes his head. 'Two separate boilers. One for upstairs and one for down.'

'But the one downstairs in the café is okay.'

'Yes, but this one is on its last legs. It's springing water in three places and it's riddled with rust. But that's not your main problem. Most of this water is coming from the flat roof. You'll need a builder or roofer.'

I groan, thinking of the cost.

'Well,' he adds cheerfully. 'The good news is that the storm has stopped.'

I think he feels sorry for me, because he patches the hole the best he can but the damage is done. The brown watermark has spread, leaking through to the lounge and the whole flat seems sodden and smells damp. There's a chill in the air and I pull on a sweatshirt to stop myself from shivering while mentally calculating what it will cost me to get all this repaired. Now, without my lawyer's income, I have to pay the bills and the mortgage out of the profits of the café, which are minimal.

I check the till downstairs and I give the plumber what cash I have left.

My head is jumping all over the place and after he goes, I sit at the bistro table upstairs in the flat, poring over the accounts. If the figures stay the same and if business carries on like it has been then I may still be open at Christmas – if I'm lucky. Staff still have to be paid and stock purchased, plus now fixing the roof, let alone drying out the flat and waiting, is a logistical nightmare. I can't afford a hotel or even an Airbnb.

I look down into Harbour Street. The road is wet and the travel agents across from me looks boarded up and weather-beaten.

I know how it feels.

During the summer months we opened the coffee shop most days but now, as we move into the autumn, I've considered closing one day a week. We are all exhausted. The town is less busy but how can I guarantee the staff their salary?

I stand up and stretch my back and stare down at Taylor's Art Gallery and Eva's Darling Buds and Blooms across the road. I have to keep the business open. It's the only way I can make money. And it will be the only way that the business will sell. I must show a profit. I look at the staff rota. Jean wants to take two weeks off before Christmas and Karl wants a week off next month. So, if I want to increase my earnings then I must invest in the business, not just in staff but more importantly, in new menus – new ideas.

Chapter 13

After I tell Jean what's happened, she takes no time in persuading Tracey from the beauty salon next door that it's urgent.

Tracey's boyfriend Des agrees to come to my flat after he's finished work later this evening, to see the damage.

Everyone agrees it was rotten luck that the torrential downpour happened, and reassures me that, luckily it's stopped now and the sun is shining again.

But it's not their flat, it's not their investment and it's not their life.

'You need to get some proper rest,' Jean says. 'You've dark circles under your eyes and you look exhausted.'

'It will be easier once Des starts work,' I reply. 'I need to get it fixed.'

Jean shakes her head.

'You work too hard. You need a break now and again, Amber. You'll have to start getting out and meeting new people. You need friends and a social life.'

'I don't want to meet anyone.'

'I don't mean fall in love. I mean meet people like as in a hobby or a class or something…'

'You have got to be joking. I don't have time for hobbies or

146

classes.'

'You have to make time. Be strict with yourself and organise your day so that you have some free time.'

'I do have free time. I go for walks or sometimes I go swimming.'

'I know, but that was at a ridiculous time in the morning or the evening – it's not sociable and now it's getting cold—'

'I don't want to be sociable. I haven't anything to say to anyone.'

'Don't be silly. You chat away to everyone who comes in the café – you have a lovely smile, you're naturally friendly and you have a likeable manner.'

I grunt. 'It doesn't feel that way.'

'You could go to art classes or Latin American or ballroom—'

'I don't want to meet anyone, Jean. My life is busy enough.'

'What's really wrong, Amber?'

'Nothing.'

'Tell me.'

'My flat is full of mould and I'm worried about another leak if it rains. Oh, and – I'm thinking about selling my furniture to pay for the roof, and I'm not sure the café will make enough profit to get us through the winter.'

'What?'

'But it's fine.'

'Do you need money?'

'No. I need to make this business work.'

'So that you can sell it and go back to London.'

'That's the bloody plan,' I mumble. 'That's my dream.'

* * *

My day goes from bad to worse. I drop nearly everything I carry. I mess up orders and I forget to order the olive oil that Lucas specifically requested. He's not happy with the changes to the menu that I suggest, and he complains about the lack of space in the kitchen and he wants another hot plate installed.

At lunchtime, Jean asks if she can pop over to the boutique and I imagine her gossiping with Marion. An hour later Lucas receives a call on his mobile. He's flustered and worried. His wife, Aaliyah, isn't well and he needs to get home and help with their new-born baby immediately.

I have a terrible headache and all the muscles in my neck and shoulders are tense. I feel sick and wonder if I've caught a bug, the virus, and my low spirits fall even further.

Karl works on autopilot, serving, smiling and keeping busy but he's still angry with me and I haven't the energy to tell him about my confrontation with JJ and Marion. Besides, I didn't challenge JJ for him – I did it for me.

I can't wait to close the café and go upstairs but to what?

I have no money to go anywhere else.

Eventually, I turn the sign on the door and then my phone rings and Papa calls me from Italy.

He complains I hardly ever call them, and that I'm always busy and he asks if everything is alright.

'Everything is fine,' I lie. I won't ask for help.

'Roberto is coming for the weekend,' he says.

When Mama comes on the phone she does her Italian mama routine.

'I miss you, my darling. You should be here with us. The weather is beautiful and we went to the lake today and we went out on the boat…'

I imagine them happy and enjoying life but I can't tell them the truth.

I hide the lump in my throat by constantly swallowing, and then tell them I have another call to take, and I promise I'll ring them soon.

I stagger upstairs, flop down on the futon and look up at the damp ceiling. It will take ages to dry out. I can't seem to get the heating going to dry the flat and I feel too ill to move. I wish I had gone to the chemist for some paracetamol.

I curl onto my side feeling the hard mattress under my bones. I have lost weight. My trousers are loose and my stomach is flat. I'm barely eating and, working around food every day, I'm beginning to lose my appetite.

I lie with my arms over my head breathing deeply as Cassie had once taught me from her yoga days. Breath through your diaphragm, she ordered, so I do. I close my eyes, breathing slowly, blocking out the images of the damp patches over my head and the fact I'm mortgaged up to my neck and I have invested everything I have into a failing café, and if I don't return soon, my life as a lawyer in London will probably be over.

I'll also be bankrupt.

I fall asleep, and then sometime later I wake with a start.

When I check my watch it's three in the morning and I'm fully clothed and freezing cold. I change into pyjamas, find some socks and lie down again on the sofa but I can't sleep. I lie worrying, shivering and trying to keep warm. I'm too tired to move.

Finally it's daylight. I shower quickly and go downstairs but I'm still cold.

I squeeze fresh oranges, warm a croissant in the microwave and make strong coffee.

It's a bright morning and when I open the door the cold morning air rushes in around me. In my Harbour Street Café T-shirt I skip across the square to the chemist and I buy a Covid testing kit and then I shop in the supermarket to buy extra milk.

Back in the flat, I wait patiently for the test results which are negative and I breathe a sigh of relief.

Lucas appears.

'Sharon has the flu, so my mother-in-law is looking after the baby,' he explains. 'She's better today,' he adds then he frowns at me. 'You look terrible, Amber. You can't serve customers looking like that.'

'You should go back to bed,' agrees Karl. 'Maybe you have the virus.'

'I tested negative.'

I spend most of the morning at the coffee machine turning out macchiatos, lattes, cappuccinos, and flat whites.

By midday I've lost count of the teas and coffees I've prepared. I want to curl up and sleep. My limbs are heavy and my whole body aches as if I had been kicked and beaten in my sleep.

'Jean,' I say. 'Des didn't come round last night, should I ask Tracey again or try and find someone else?'

'You'll be lucky, builders have a few months' waiting list. They're in great demand since lockdown. Leave it with me and I'll speak to Tracey again. Des is a bit lazy so she probably needs to give him a bit of a nudge.'

* * *

The following evening, I've just finished cleaning and sweeping the patio at the back of the café, keeping busy and warm, when there's a tap on the window. I turn around and JJ has her nose pressed against the glass door. She indicates for me to open it.

I wipe my hands and flick back the lock.

'Hello.' She smiles, as if our last confrontation didn't happen.

'We're closed.'

'I know, I know. I just wanted to have a word.'

'About what?'

'Well, I want to clear the air. Sort things out.'

I'm surprised by her cheek. 'You threw me out of the pub.'

'I'm not here about that, Amber. I want to speak to you about the planning permission for the travel agents across the road. There are some residents who are against it, and I was hoping that I could speak to you and allay your fears, if you have any.' She laughs. 'And, we can discuss them before everything gets out of hand and, look, Amber, I don't want to fall out with you—'

'They blocked your planning application?'

JJ's eyes darken.

'Erm, yes, exactly.' She appraises me. 'You're a woman after my own heart, blunt and straight to the point, Amber. That's good. You see, my new business will create more footfall to the town. It will be busier and your little café will do well out of it. People always get hungry when they're gambling or playing computer games, and they're bound to come in here afterwards. And I've been thinking, perhaps we could do a deal or something and you could provide some of the catering inside the arcade. You know, like a takeaways or fresh sandwiches. You'd be our preferred café to do business with.'

I stare at her.

'Well, the thing is, they won't want all these fancy shops in Harbour Street. They won't want overpriced souvenirs, or expensive pet shops or stupid art galleries. These people are hard-working and they want value for money, good pub grub or café food, a sandwich or something simple.'

'We're changing our menu.'

'Great! Good, I can work with that.'

'We're going upmarket.'

'Really? What for?'

'To adapt to the footfall that comes here, these people have money to spend and they are used to the variety of high-standard London restaurants; international food – not just a sandwich.'

'Ah, well, that's very brave of you.' Her smile is fixed on her face. 'So, can I rely on you to support my business venture?'

'Probably not.'

She nods seriously. 'I've heard that you're not doing that well and that you've had a few viewings but no one is interested in buying this place.'

'You shouldn't listen to gossip.'

Her voice hardens. 'I've heard that you're difficult to work for and that your staff are looking for work elsewhere.'

'What would you know?'

'You'd be surprised. I know everything that goes on here.'

'Then how come you didn't know I wouldn't support you?'

'I tell you what I do know, Amber. There are so many rumours about you, and some of them aren't kind.' She holds up the palm of her hand. 'It's none of my business. You can sleep with who you like but—'

'I don't need your permission for anything.'

She stares at me and smiles. 'The thing is, Amber. There's

nothing you can do about it. I've adhered to all the planning permission conditions and there's no one who can stop me.'

'There are a number of people who are against your business venture.'

She laughs. 'You mean Frances? That nosey old goat. I won't see her in my way – or perhaps you mean Ben?' She leans over and places her hand on my shoulder. 'Do yourself a favour, Amber. If you want to stay in business in this town, then you don't want to go against me.'

She pats my arm patronisingly as if I'm a pet dog and we are the best of friends, and as she turns to walk away, Eva is leaving the flower shop. In the art gallery, Ben had also seen our exchange but he pretends he's not looking.

* * *

The next morning brings a cool northerly wind. Outside the café, at one of our tables, Mrs Mullan wears a trilby with a red rose, a purple woollen jacket and a long pink skirt with Doc Martens. Her brown Labrador is tucked under the table beside her feet and they both look frozen. She's sipping Earl Grey tea and eating a slice of lime cheesecake but her hands are shaking. 'She must be nearly eighty,' Jean says.

'Karl tells me she's almost ninety.' Lucas joins us at the counter.

I open the door and go outside.

'Come and sit inside, Mrs Mullan. You can't sit here in this cold wind. Come in and bring Dolly with you. Sit in the warm by the window near the radiator.' I pick up her coffee and cheesecake.

'Are you sure? I didn't think dogs are allowed inside.' Her

eyes are watering and her nose is red. 'But it's perishing out here and Dolly *is* getting old now.'

'No one will notice the dog,' I whisper. 'She's so well behaved and she always sits under the table.'

'That's kind of you, Amber. Thank you.' She settles herself comfortably in the window but Dolly takes longer enjoying the new smells and I'm almost dizzy watching her walk around and around until eventually she curls up on Mrs Mullan's boots and promptly falls asleep.

By four o'clock, my cold is beginning to feel a little better but my body is still shivering inside and I can't get warm.

My confrontation with JJ yesterday has again woken an anger in me. Her narcissistic personality reminds me of an old client and a court case I won a few years ago. I remember how it was covered on the TV news channels and Ralph had been very impressed. That's when talk began about me becoming a partner.

'Lucas, do you think I should put a television on one of the walls?' I ask.

His deep frown creases in mock concentration. 'That's good of you to think of me, Amber. You know how much I like the rugby.' He laughs.

'Not for you, it's for the customers.' I smile.

He looks thoughtfully around the café. 'I love it the way it is now and the music is lovely.'

Mrs Mullan sways her old body to the classic CD and the guitar strings of 'Aranjuez Mon Amour'. She hums along and her weak voice wavers and Lucas and I share a proud smile as if she's our grandmother.

'I've some new suggestions for the menu,' Lucas says.

'Great. Let's look at them together.'

There's a gust of wind and the door blows open and Eva stands there looking windswept and radiant.

'Goodness, I was almost knocked out of my shoes because of that wind.'

'Aye.' Lucas casts his eyes down her black-stockinged legs and in his best Scottish accent he says, 'Sure, tis a fierce wind out there an' them's big heels, missus.'

We all laugh.

I make coffee for us and when Lucas disappears into the kitchen, Eva whispers, 'I have to speak to you, privately.'

She pulls my arm and drags me to a table against the wall, away from the door, Mrs Mullan and Dolly.

We sit down and I sip my coffee, then rest my head on the palm of my hand. I could sit and watch Eva all day. Her face never seems to betray what she is thinking. Sometimes, I think she is sad and then when she laughs her face is transformed. Other times she appears pensive and melancholy. She is the most unusual and interesting woman that I have met for a long time.

'I saw JJ in here yesterday, what did she want?' she asks.

'She wanted me to support her.'

'And you said…?'

'I said, I'd love to JJ. I want to go into business with you. Please be my best friend.'

Eva laughs. She doesn't take me seriously and I want her to be my friend.

'You look exhausted, Amber. Are you okay?'

I nod resolutely.

'Is it because of what JJ said?'

I shrug. I haven't told her about the leak upstairs or the fact that Des wants a couple of grand to fix it or that it will take him two to four weeks, as he's fitting it in between other jobs.

'Not really.'

'There's always so much gossip and it's best not to listen to any of it,' Eva says earnestly. 'So, I thought I would come straight to you, so you can hear it from the donkey's mouth.'

'Horse's mouth,' I correct her.

'Jean told me—'

'Jean?'

'Yes, Jean,' she says firmly.

'Jean told you what?'

'Yes, and I'm delighted that she did. I thought we were friends, Amber. I thought you would have told me first. God, I've told you my fair share of problems considering we haven't known each other very long. You've listened to me whinging on about Nick and Emma. But, besides all that, I felt from the beginning that we had a lot in common and that we could be good friends – don't you?'

'I never thought that Jean was one for tittle-tattle.'

'But I can help you,' Eva says.

'You can?' I laugh aloud. 'What with?'

'Why are you laughing?' Her eyes are dark and serious. She leans across the small table, her voice a whisper, and I can smell her tangy perfume.

'Come and stay with me.'

I don't move.

'I have a spare room,' Eva says. 'Amber? Did you hear me?'

No words form on my lips.

'Jean said that you can't stay upstairs in your flat and that you need a place to stay. I have a spare bedroom. I have two! The kids aren't here, are they? Come on, what do you say?'

I don't know what to say. I can't speak.

I notice the small lines around Eva's mouth. The way the streaks in her hair are growing out and how her makeup is flawless, her carefully applied mascara, round red lips and the firmness of her soft cheeks.

'You look like you have a fever,' Eva says. 'Come on, grab a bag and let's go. You need some TLC.'

'Are you sure?' I whisper.

She smiles encouragingly. 'Let's not get too excited. Come and see it first, you might end up like my kids; you may hate the place and can't wait to leave.'

'Have you got a bath?'

'Yes.'

'Then it'll be perfect.'

Chapter 14

Eva points at the long oak table. 'It's the one thing I insisted on keeping from my marriage. James may have left me but the dining table brings us together as a family. That was the one thing I wouldn't let him take away from me.'

She continues my tour of her home as if I'm about to buy her property.

'And leading off the kitchen, at the back of the house, we have the conservatory that overlooks the tropical garden. Tropical because it is overgrown and hasn't been touched since we moved in,' she jokes.

'Wow, you're right about that. That's a job and a half.'

We stand at the back door.

'My heart isn't in it – even with a flower shop. Nick mowed the grass a few times but …I have no inclination to venture outside to look after it or to cut back the overhanging trees.'

'If I get time, I'll clear it for you. The patio at the café looks so much better.'

In the conservatory there are two comfortable sofas and several racks of magazines. She waves her arm like a tour guide, in the appropriate direction. 'And off to the right side of the kitchen is access to the garage, commonly the dumping ground for all the crates that we haven't yet unpacked from our move.'

She opens the door to the garage to prove her point and a gust of cold wind blows up my skirt. I hold it down and she pulls the door closed.

'Oh, I nearly forgot, the washing machine and dryer are here.'

'How long have you been living here?'

'Almost two years. It's been difficult, as you know, realising that I'm alone and I would have to make my own decisions, pay my own bills and look after my kids. I like the skylights in the kitchen, they add more light.'

We stand and gaze up at the sloping roof that had been an extension added by the previous owners. 'It makes the grey worktops seem lighter. It could have looked very dark in here.'

She runs her hand across the shining six-ringed hob and looks approvingly at the double oven, and in the lounge she pauses to look at the two overlarge leather sofas.

'They had been lost in my last house but now they're hard to navigate around. It was a matter of principle to keep them but there isn't much space in here.'

There's a flat screen television in the far corner and an artificial but pretty fireplace.

'The carpet was left behind by the last occupants,' she says as we walk upstairs. 'I'd like to change it. Now, this is Emma's room and I've sorted it out the best I can, leaving you space for clothes in the wardrobe and chest of drawers.'

There's a double bed with an animal print duvet pushed against the wall. It looks so cosy and comfortable, and I bite my bottom lip so my tears don't overflow.

Eva will never know how grateful I am.

'This is your bathroom. It's not ensuite. Emma normally

shares with Nick who has the converted loft. He comes downstairs to use this bathroom but as they are both away – you will have it to yourself. And, this is my room. Ta da,' she sings, pushing open the room of the master suite. 'I have my own shower room.'

'It's lovely,' I say, as I stand gazing out of the bedroom window. 'It's a perfect location. You can walk to work.'

'I'm thinking of buying a bicycle.'

'You should.'

Downstairs in the kitchen, she asks, 'Wine or tea?'

'Tea, please. I'm exhausted.'

She fusses around with the kettle as I pace around and pause periodically to look outside. It's the first proper home I've been in since I moved here.

'Was it very hard for you to move from your last house?' I ask.

'This is much smaller but at least it's home and I suppose I should add that – it's mine.'

'Are you interested in renting a room to me?' I ask. 'Just for a few weeks, while the kids are away?'

'I want to help you, Amber. Stay as long as you like.'

I wipe my eyes. 'Sometimes after a run of bad luck, you can't believe it when something good happens. It's like your brain doesn't accept it,' I say.

'After James left, I didn't know who would employ me, Amber. I worked for Tina and Mark in the flower shop and they gave me a chance, after not having worked for over twenty years. Being a housewife and mother doesn't count, of course, nor does entertaining your husband's business clients. But to work with the public and to finally earn my own money is quite…' she pauses before deciding on the right

160

word, 'liberating. I feel a sense of satisfaction and achievement, as if I am worth something.'

'You're not that old.' I laugh.

'I'm forty-five,' she says.

'Seven more than me,'

She smiles. 'Well, I never knew that they would retire and I'd be able to cobble together the money together to buy the shop.'

'You work hard, Eva.'

'Yes, but everyone needs a little luck and a few friends, Amber. Look, I'll give you a key to the house then you can come and go as you please. I sometimes go away for the weekends, I haven't seen much of my parents what with getting Emma and Nick sorted for uni, so I want to spend some more time with them.' Eva blows on her tea. 'Hopefully I'll persuade them to come here for dinner one evening and you can meet them. They're only a thirty-minute drive away.'

'I'd like that.'

As Eva passes me a packet of chocolate digestives, I'm overcome with a feeling of not just gratitude but something far more important that I can't describe. We spend the next thirty minutes chatting about the town and the local shops before I retreat upstairs for a long hot bath, and it's only when I'm climbing into bed that I understand the feeling from earlier.

Eva has made me feel valued.

* * *

A few nights later Eva insists that we order a takeaway from Sanjay's and that we share a bottle of wine.

'I can drown my sorrows,' I say. 'There was another viewing

today and well, let's just say they liked the café but they couldn't afford to do up the flat.'

I study the menu wondering what to have as I've tried just about every dish.

Eva explains. 'We both need company, Sanjay. I want to chat and have a glass of wine with a friend and not be judged by my children.' She laughs. 'Besides, Amber is good company although she's upset no one wants to buy the café.'

He shakes his head. 'Harbour Street is lovely. There's nowhere in the world like it.'

Eva continues, 'You see, it's working out perfectly. Amber's not moody like Emma, and she communicates – unlike Nick. It's such a relief to have another adult in the house, I can't tell you.'

Sanjay smiles. 'I know the feeling. My house is full of cousins. All adults and all noisy, but Little Umbar, the smallest, is often the quietest. He can't compete with them all.'

'Are you married?' I ask, thinking he must have no privacy with all those people, but he shakes his head.

'Never. I've been too busy with my business. My mother wanted an arranged marriage for me, she found a lovely girl from Mumbai but I told her I'm a modern man and I make my own choices.'

'Is she happy about that?'

He laughs. 'She tells me off every time we speak on the phone for not bringing home a lovely Indian girl to meet her.'

'I can't believe you're not married. A good-looking guy like you.'

Eva nudges me into silence but Sanjay just laughs louder.

'I believe in karma, Amber. The right woman will come along for me at the right time.'

'I hope so,' I say. 'You deserve someone special.'

He nods, pleased with my assessment of his situation.

'Don't you agree with me, Eva?' I ask.

She's engrossed in studying the menu but she looks up briefly. 'Yes, of course.'

'I'm not as handsome as Ozan and I'm not as funny as Yusef, but I like to think I have my own charm, and also, still waters run deep. I'm attracted to the quieter type of women but it's very hard working here every night.'

'Well, you're young enough to meet someone. Have you tried dating apps?' I ask.

He shakes his head. 'No way.'

'Ah, so you're going to rely on Mrs Right walking into the takeaway, are you?'

'Maybe.'

'You can't stay on your own forever, it's not good for you.'

'Well, to be honest, I do have my eyes on someone very special.'

'Really?' I ask.

Eva digs me in the ribs. 'I'm sure Sanjay doesn't need you investigating his personal relationships.'

I feel my cheeks redden and I say, 'Sorry, Sanjay.'

'It's no worry, Amber. I just hope the lady in question will think of me in that context one day.'

'Can't you ask her?' I suggest.

'Maybe.' He nods. 'Maybe I should but rejection is a hard pill to swallow.'

'Not with these delicious curries, Sanjay. Come on, Amber, let's order. I'm starving and you look like you haven't eaten in weeks.'

* * *

The next few weeks pass quickly and I'm conscious that I haven't seen much of Ben. I don't even know if he's used the voucher and I don't want to ask Ozan and Yusef if he has been to the barbers.

Jean catches me looking out of the window.

'He's away,' she says.

I must look surprised and she continues, 'Isn't that who you're looking out for?'

I shrug, turn away and wipe a table clean, conscious that the café is empty and we're about to close up.

'He sometimes takes off for a few days here and there.'

'Where does he go?'

Jean shrugs. 'He's a strange one. But it's not surprising after what happened.'

'Do you know him well?'

'Ben and Angie were childhood friends. They were best friends for a while.'

'Angie?'

'My sister's daughter. They lost touch when Angie went to art college. Ben was mad for carpentry – he was talented even back then. He always wanted to work with his hands. He would often find driftwood on the beach and make lovely decorations or sculpt it into an animal or something. He was always very creative.'

'Sensitive?'

'He was a quiet, shy boy but there was a calm determined resolve about him. An inbuilt sense of duty. He wanted to travel abroad but then his mum was diagnosed and he never left. He didn't want to leave his parents. He was a good son.'

164

'Then he went to work for JJ?' I prompt.

'It was a smaller town then. He was working in the pub to earn a bit of money. JJ was from out of town and she came in with all these fancy ideas, I don't know. To this day I'll never know what anyone sees in JJ.'

'Ben had a relationship with her?'

Jean looks horrified. 'Goodness, no.'

I'm relieved. I was convinced Ben had told me the truth and I'm pleased that other people in the town didn't think they'd had an affair.

'Was she ever married?'

'I think before she was, she came from Devon or somewhere. She's divorced now.'

'It was a sad business what happened, Ben told me about it.'

'Ben? Goodness, Amber, he must think a lot of you. He's never discussed it with anyone. Not even Angie.'

'You know he didn't do it, don't you? He never stole any money from the pub and neither did he set it on fire.'

'I never thought for one minute he did. And, it's not a coincidence that the investigating officer became JJ's boyfriend, is it?'

'That's awful. It's so wrong, Jean. And, I think Ben feels very guilty about the garage and his uncle,' I add.

'Well, William had a breakdown. It was like JJ took him under her wing and nurtured him. He was often in the pub drinking and laughing with her. I think Ben thought she was leading William on, and she persuaded him to sell her the garage. JJ took advantage of his mental state to rip him off. He sold his business for a pittance and Ben couldn't stop him.'

'JJ told me once that Ben was involved and helped broker the deal?'

Jean shakes her head. 'The opposite, Amber. JJ had already taken advantage of William's anxiety and depression and Ben was furious – he went to JJ and they had a terrible argument. Then Ben was accused of stealing and part of the pub went up in flames and the rest is history, as they say. Ben went to prison for eighteen months, and while he was away, both his parents died.'

'That's tragic.'

'He stayed away for years and then he came back last summer and opened the art gallery, I think it's deliberately to be in JJ's face as a reminder.'

'Do you think it's doing him any good?'

Jean shakes her head. 'I wouldn't think so. None at all.'

'Then it's no wonder he keeps disappearing.'

Chapter 15

The following week passes without incident. One evening Eva and I decide to go to a film together. A new romantic comedy has been released. We both enjoy the cinema and watching films, and on the way home we stop to pick up an Indian takeaway. As we tuck into the spicy sauces we discuss the merits of the film.

I hadn't liked the hero. 'He always plays the same part.'

'But he's gorgeous,' she replies, smiling.

Then her phone goes and it's her son Nick.

'Mum? We're coming home at the weekend. Can you collect us from the train station?'

Eva's so excited, she fumbles for a pen. 'How are you? How's everything? Are you enjoying it?' she gushes.

'Yeah, it's cool. I might bring the car back to London.'

'But…what's the point? We've discussed this option several times, Nick. There's no point in having a car in London––' She looks at me imploringly and I remain quiet.

'Mum. Just chill! Don't sweat it! We're just thinking about it that's all.'

'Who's we?'

'Me.'

'Why does he need the car?' Eva says to me later that evening.

'I hate the thought of him with a car in London. It will be so expensive. I'm sure James wouldn't agree.'

'But James isn't here now,' I reply. 'You have to be firm with him.'

'You're right, Amber. I will.'

* * *

I offer to move back into my own flat.

'Nonsense. It's still a mess.'

'It's so hard to get hold of Des. He's barely done a thing. He's working so slowly. Even Tracey says she hardly sees him. BUT he has promised he'll pop in one morning this week.'

'Well, it seems like the children are only coming home for one night. They want to go and see James as well. Emma has agreed to share my room. Besides, I'd like you to get to know them. You can cook, if you like.' She grins.

'I'll think of something special.' I'm already excited about the prospect of cooking a proper meal again.

They arrive home on Friday night having travelled together from London. They arrive full of enthusiasm and goodwill and I wonder if they've already shared a few drinks before coming home. I busy myself in the kitchen. It's luxury having space and although I'm enjoying their company I leave them to catch up with Eva in the lounge.

I stand for a few minutes sipping my wine, looking out of the conservatory and into the garden where I have already cleared many of the brambles and weeded the rose patch. I even managed to get out the lawnmower but the edges are still frayed and the rubbish needs clearing.

I'm conscious of their excited voices and then suddenly their tones become whispered but I can still hear their conversation.

'Do you need the money, is that why?' Nick asks.

'Amber is company for me.'

'You could have bought a puppy,' Emma chips in.

'It's only temporary while her flat is being fixed. She's lovely and she's offered to cook dinner for us all.'

'It's weird,' Nick says. 'It doesn't feel right.'

'She's a friend,' Eva insists.

'Is that all?'

'What do you mean?'

'Well, didn't she move down here with her girlfriend?'

'That was months ago and Cassie's gone now.'

'Do we need to be worried?' Nick laughs.

'Don't be ridiculous.'

'What's she cooking?' asks Emma.

* * *

I'm trying to impress them. Aside from cooking for Cassie, I haven't had the opportunity or made any friends here at all. I've had no one to cook for and I'm excited. Spending the past few weeks with Eva and for the first time having a comfortable home and proper sleep, I'm feeling much better. Much stronger.

I'm experimenting with a new menu and it reminds me of all the times I spent with my mother cooking in Italy and her mother – my maternal grandma. She lives in the countryside, in the mountains near Milan, and some of the recipes and the exotic smells, spices and flavours come flooding back to me making me homesick for them all.

I make a marinade, liquidising yogurt with fennel, cardamom seeds, oil, grated cheese then I add an egg. I stir it over the lamb chops and in a separate dish cover chicken breasts while I chop salad and add garnish.

I sip my wine as I add the chicken to the frying pan and suddenly the kitchen is filled with sizzling warm spices and my stomach rumbles appreciatively.

Emma's waist-length hair is loose and it falls across her face as she leans on the counter watching me.

'That smells amazing. I'm starving.'

'Me too,' Nick beams at me from the doorway. His beard makes him look older and his hair is longer. But his smile is open and refreshing. He grabs a cola from the fridge and Eva hands Emma a glass of wine.

'The train was heaving – so many tourists,' Emma complains.

'Nightmare,' Nick agrees.

'I bought a dress for Sasha's birthday dinner next week,' Emma says, undoing a box while Nick stands by the wall checking his mobile.

Over dinner they talk about university and the new lives they are forming for themselves. A part of me feels excluded. I see the look on Eva's face, that she's happy and excited for them but she knows that they have moved on. They will probably never come home to live with her again. And, although she hides it, I see her sadness and disappointment.

Emma is indignant at having to pay for plastic bags in shops. Nick complains about the congestion charges in London.

'So why take the car back?' Eva asks.

He avoids answering her and then we move on, discussing Harbour Street and the Halloween festival in the morning until dinner is over.

It's been a complete success.

They love the food.

'It's better than any takeaway in London,' says Nick.

'I wish I could cook like this,' adds Emma. 'Can you give me the recipe? I could impress Dad and make dinner one night.'

Eva's smile fades.

'Of course, look.' I produce the cookery book and show Emma the page. 'Take a photo of the recipes you like and if you get stuck give me a ring. This one here is easy.'

I point at a colourful photograph and we are absorbed in cooking and food and Eva turns her attention to Nick.

'About the car...'

'I know, Mum, it will just mean I can get around more easily.'

'But London Transport is so good. And you can't drink if you have the car.'

'I know but it means I can get out of London at the weekend.'

'And go where?'

'I don't know, Brighton, Suffolk, Cambridge?'

'But you've never done that before. You've always had your nose stuck to a computer.'

'I know but it's time I got out—'

'He's met someone.' Emma doesn't look up.

'Have you?' Eva asks.

He blushes and looks away.

Eva and I share a quick smile.

'If I have time in the morning I'll make you a marinade for you to take back to Liverpool,' I say to Emma, trying to deflect the attention from Nick.

'That would be great, thank you.'

'Could you make double and give me some too?' Nick smiles.

'Of course.'

Emma flicks through the pages. 'I could make loads of things,' she declares.

Nick laughs.

'Oh, what's this?' Emma is reading the inside cover of the book. 'There's a dedication. To my darling chef and my best lover…here's to more meals with you at the helm, love Cassie…'

Emma's voice trails off.

The room falls silent.

My mouth feels suddenly dry.

'Emma you shouldn't have read—' Eva says.

'That's okay.' I close the book.

Emma asks me, 'Are you gay?'

'I don't think of it like that. I fall in love with the person. Is that a problem?' I reply, feeling suddenly very defensive.

'Gender fluid?' Emma suggests.

I shrug. 'I don't have a name for it, I just call it love.'

* * *

The cost for the repairs keeps going up and I say to Des early the next day, 'I can't afford for you to keep changing your mind about what needs to be done. I haven't got a massive budget.'

'Do you want me to leave it then?'

'No, of course not but it's taking so long.'

'I thought you were happy at Eva's.'

'That's not the point. I want my own home back.'

He scratches his head. 'Well, I'm doing this as a favour, Amber. I'm doing it in my spare time. I haven't had a day off

172

for weeks.'

'You're charging me a fortune. Not even doctors make that much.'

'Then find someone else.'

'You know there isn't anyone. Since Brexit and Covid everyone's renovating their homes and costs have rocketed.'

'That's not my fault.' His mouth pouts sulkily but then it's replaced with a quick and insincere smile.

Jean listens to our exchange and after Des has gone she whispers, 'I'm so sorry, Amber. He was never this bad before. I think he's under a lot of pressure. Tracey wants a baby.'

I rub my forehead and turn at the sound of my name.

'What's wrong, Amber?'

Ben is suddenly in the café. I haven't seen him for a couple of weeks and he looks different. His stare is penetrating and he looks more handsome, stronger somehow, and younger. He even seems more friendly and I wonder if he's forgotten our last conversation.

'You look like you have the weight of the world on your shoulders.'

'Hello, stranger, where have you been?' I ask, pleased at his affable tone.

After greeting Ben, Jean goes back into the kitchen leaving us alone.

'Do you want your usual, Ben?'

'Please. I heard you moved in with Eva.'

'I had to. My flat's been flooded and I'm trying to get Des to sort it out but he's a nightmare to work with and he's also very expensive,' I blurt out.

'Can I take a look?'

'There's no point.'

'Why? Come on, show me.' Ben indicates with his head that I should go before him upstairs to my flat and I'm suddenly embarrassed. 'It's awful up there,' I warn him.

'No bother.'

I sigh heavily as I take him from the lounge to the bedroom to the bathroom, and I watch his reaction and the way he looks at Des's craftsmanship, and he tuts loudly.

'I'll do this for you,' Ben announces.

'How? I mean, you have the art gallery and everything. You've been closed for two weeks.'

'It will only take me a day or two at the most. I can do it at the weekend or in the evenings.'

'How much?' I ask.

Ben shakes his head. 'We're neighbours. It's what they do.'

I walk away, fold my arms and stand at the window looking down at the busy street. A lady leaves Eva's shop with a beautiful bouquet and Taylor's Art Gallery has a new window display. Ben must have changed it last night.

'I can't accept that, Ben. I have to pay you something.'

He doesn't reply so I turn and face him.

'I insist or I won't be comfortable. It's a lot of work.'

He smiles. 'Alright then, how about another voucher from the Turkish barbers.'

That's when I realise why he looks so different. His beard, eyebrows, and hair are all neatly sculptured.

'Wow! You actually went.' I laugh.

'Yes, and you didn't actually notice,' he replies.

Chapter 16

The custom in Harbour Street at Halloween appears to be the same each year but with the effect of Covid last year there seems to be a massive misunderstanding and no one is sure what's happening.

Jane from the jewellers comes in for her regular coffee and asks, 'What's happening later with the Halloween event?'

I shrug and I don't answer. I'm too busy checking my email from the estate agents. They're sending another potential buyer around tomorrow. The fourth person interested so far. The other three practically ran out of the place, so presumably these new people can afford the amount of work and money that's needed to make this a viable business and improve the living accommodation above.

It's Jean who answers her.

'I suppose it will be the same as every year. There will be actors who dress up as vampires and scary people covered in red paint to look like blood, it's normally like a mini parade.'

'What time will that start?' asks Karl.

Jean shrugs. 'I don't really remember, we didn't have it last year as it was cancelled.'

Sanjay pops in around lunchtime. 'What's happening this year? Does anyone know?'

'Didn't JJ say at a meeting that she was organising it?' I reply. 'You'd better ask her.'

'I'll pop and ask Eva if she knows anything,' he says.

Thirty minutes later Sanjay pops back.

'I've spoken to Kit and Jenna and they've been told nothing. Eva and Jane don't know anything either, Mario and Luke are busy so I couldn't speak to them and Ozan and Yusef have been told there's a parade at three o'clock.'

I check my watch. Fifteen minutes.

Outside in the street there isn't anything different from a normal Saturday; families, children running around, dogs on leads, couples strolling arm in arm, people window shopping – nothing special at all. Across the road Pamela is looking out of the window from the Très Chic Boutique and, as we do sometimes, we raise our hands in a wave and smile.

A large family with two baby buggies struggle to come inside the café and by the time we've settled them, a queue is forming and it's all go, we're busy serving food and cleaning tables and when I look up almost two hours have passed.

Lucas has a day off as it's the baby's christening and the café has been packed. There have been regulars who I recognise and as they greet Karl, he responds with his usual charm. He's really good at this job. He dances around like a professional boxer behind the counter. He fills cups with thick rich coffee, pours perfumed teas and mixes a blend of juices. He's happy chatting to customers and he clears tables efficiently.

Jean, in Lucas's absence, has mastered the art of cooking eggs in twenty different ways. I can also multi-task, producing smoked salmon and cream cheese bagels, guacamole and bacon wraps and a variety of sandwiches filled with chicken, tuna or thick ham.

'We don't offer a wide enough selection of dishes or vegetarian options ,' Karl complains. 'We should be doing casseroles and soups and be a proper restaurant with a licence.'

'Good idea.'

I make a mental note to speak to the estate agent, to see if it's possible to advertise the café more prolifically – have it as a featured business with a licence.

I move out of the way as a burly man pushes his way into the café and his loud voice booms across the room.

'They're thick they are, bloody foreigners! Can't understand a word. C-O-F-F-E-E,' he shouts.

A sixty-something-year-old man dressed in a charcoal grey suit is standing at the table near the window, his face screwed up in frustrated anger.

Had I seen him walking along the street on a Sunday, I would have assumed he was on his way to or from church, but now he stands facing Karl with a frown across his craggy face. Several heads have turned to look at the commotion.

'Is there a problem?' I ask quietly, moving to stand at his side.

'Is there what? Course there's a bloody problem. These foreigners can't understand a bloody thing – I only want a coffee. Bloody idiot!'

I say quietly. 'I do not tolerate bad language and abuse of my staff.' I move the chair away so he is unable to sit down.

'Bloody communists, coming over here, why don't they all go home,' he shouts. 'Hey can I get a coffee, mate?'

'Yes, but I'm busy serving this lady. I'll be with you shortly,' Karl replies.

'Hurry up, you black—' the man mumbles something but I catch the gist of it '… a monkey would be faster.'

'What did you say?' I ask the man.

He stares at me. 'What?'

'I asked you what you said to Karl.'

He tries to stare me down and clenches his fists.

I step forward. 'I'm the owner of this café and I don't like what you said.'

'I didn't say anything.'

'You're a racist and a liar. Get out.' I point at the door.

'You can't throw me out.'

'I can call the police.'

'I didn't want a coffee anyway, silly cow. This is a piss hole.' He pulls open the door and I'm still shaking with anger when he looks through the window and sticks up his middle finger.

Poor Jean's face is ashen and Karl looks uncertain. Several people in the café nod and smile in support.

'Disgraceful,' says one.

'Shameful,' adds another and a ripple of support makes me realise how a small incident can bring people together.

'I saw him in the pub,' says another.

A little later, in the afternoon when it is quieter Karl says to me, 'You threw him out. You turned away business.'

'I certainly did.'

'That was kind of you – to protect us, me,' he says.

'He'd been drinking in The Ship,' Jean says. 'Pamela saw him.'

'You didn't have to do that, Amber,' Karl says.

'Yes I did.' I pat him on the shoulder. 'You're my friend, Karl. We've got to stick together. Come on, let's see what's happening with this parade?'

Karl grins. 'It must have been so ghostly that none of us saw it.'

Jean wanders to the window and checks the street. 'He's gone now and so has the parade. I saw a couple of kids dressed up but they moved on pretty quickly... if that's the Halloween parade this year then I blinked and missed it.'

Frances, in a turquoise trouser suit and vicar's collar, walks by and I call out to her.

'Did you see the Halloween parade?'

Frances frowns. 'I haven't seen a thing. It would probably mean more if we celebrated All Saint's Day tomorrow.'

'Sorry!' I feel as though I've offended her.

'No, don't be, I'm just so fed up with JJ, she's being very uncooperative and she's put in another planning application – this time with all the necessary modifications. I'm dreading it. She really will get her own way and open the amusement arcade and there's nothing any of us can do to stop her.'

* * *

Later in the afternoon, I see JJ duck into the Très Chic Boutique. Frances's words are still ringing in my ear and I'm inflamed with a sense of injustice, JJ had said she would organise the Halloween parade but she's done nothing.

I wait a few minutes and then I cross the road and follow her into the boutique. The small bell tinkles as I enter.

JJ and Marion are at the counter. Marion's face clouds over and JJ's fake smile is as welcoming as a rattlesnake.

'Hi, I just wanted to check what time the Halloween parade begins,' I say.

Marion flicks a quick look at JJ, who smiles disarmingly.

'It's all over. All done.'

'Really? It's just that the shopkeepers were all asking what time it was on, no one was notified, and then now you say it's over. Who was in the parade?'

Marion folds her arms decisively. 'JJ has worked really hard coordinating everything. She doesn't stop working and she's always got the responsibility of the community at heart. She's the most hard-working woman I know.'

I smile.

JJ waves her arm in the air confidently. 'I hired a load of actors who dressed as zombies, vampires, ghosts—'

'And there were lots of Goths,' adds Marion.

'Did anyone get any photos?' I ask innocently.

'We've been very busy in the pub, I barely had time to look up let alone take pictures.'

'I know, one of your punters came in the café and was racially abusive to Karl.'

JJ shrugs. 'I wouldn't know. I was busy.'

'And the boutique was busy, wasn't it, Pamela?' Marion says.

I hadn't noticed Pamela standing in the shadows near a rack of expensive clothes.

'Pamela? Wasn't the shop busy?' insists Marion.

Pamela nods but she doesn't smile or speak and I can tell she feels uncomfortable.

'I'm trying to work out if it was financially worth all the effort.' I stand tall and straighten my shoulders.

'Of course it was, why are you so negative?' Marion flares.

The shop bell tinkles and Eva walks inside and I'm pleased to have an ally.

'What happened to the parade this year?' asks Eva.

'Don't tell me you missed it too?' JJ smiles. 'That's a good sign that we were all so busy.'

'I was standing outside. Sanjay had been told it was at three o'clock and so I waited.'

'It was a bit later this year,' JJ says.

'I waited.' Eva frowns. 'There were six students dressed up but it was a pathetic excuse for a parade.'

JJ shrugs. 'That's your opinion.'

'That's the truth.' Eva shakes her head angrily. 'This will change for the Christmas event. You are having nothing to do with it.'

'Don't be ridiculous, you haven't been here long enough to start trying to take over.'

'I've worked in the shop for five years and owned it for nearly two.'

'Yes.' JJ walks slowly forward. 'But you're an outsider. You're not really from around here, are you?'

'That's also racist,' I say.

'No, it's not. It's a fact.' JJ pushes between me and Eva and opens the door. 'Because, Amber, you're not from here either. You're both interlopers. Useless women. Unwanted, inept people playing at being in business.'

* * *

When I get back to the café, Ben is upstairs in the flat. I can hear him banging and hammering so I carry his coffee carefully upstairs without spilling it.

'Karl made this for you.'

'Thanks. Is he coming up?'

I shake my head. 'Karl?'

'Yes, he's offered to help me.'

I stand and look at Ben and he laughs.

'You can close your mouth, Amber. I didn't ask. Karl

181

offered.'

'Why?'

'Why not?' Ben pauses his work to drink his coffee. His eyes are smiling.

'I thought Karl was angry with me.'

Ben smiles. 'No. He's not angry with you. Why would he be?'

'JJ was rude to him in the last meeting at the church and I didn't stick up for him.'

Ben regards me carefully. 'But you went to the pub and you told her what you thought afterwards, didn't you?'

'You know about that?'

Ben puts down his coffee and climbs back up the ladder. 'Everyone does, and so does Karl.'

'You have to stop going in that pub and giving her your money.'

'I have, Amber. I'm not going back. I have more important things to do now.' He picks up the hammer and begins banging again.

* * *

Eva and I eat the leftovers from last night.

'I saw you go into the boutique and I knew JJ and Marion were both there,' she says. 'I was hoping you were complaining about the parade.'

'Well, we've said our piece and I feel better for it.'

'It won't stop her plans for the travel agents,' Eva says. 'But we must do something about Christmas.'

'I know we are both tired and annoyed with JJ but we can't keep going over the same ground.'

'So long as you'll help me stop her taking charge of anything at Christmas.'

After dinner, I take a long hot bath and retire early to bed with a book and I read about half a page before I'm asleep. In the morning I wake early, refreshed and ready to get on with the day. I'm thinking about the future and what Eva had said about the Christmas event and when I leave for work it's still dark.

I've a few ideas I'm toying with and I'm lost in thought as I cut through the alleyway and into Harbour Street. It's seven-thirty and a liquid dawn is breaking the clouds. Harbour Street is caught in an afterglow of pale yellow light making it look hauntingly beautiful. I marvel at the distinct shopfronts, some with bay windows and cluttered souvenirs or jewellery, and others with neat colourful signs in a multitude of fancy fonts; all uniquely original. Nearly all of us have canopies and in the summer these provide shade and ambience. Today the awnings are firmly tucked away, rolled up, making the street appear wider.

I'm proud of my café and, as I walk closer, I'm surprised to see streaks of red light painted across the window. I pause, wondering if it's the beginning of a beautiful sunrise reflected in the windows but I know that's not possible. I step cautiously forward until I'm in front of the building and I can see the abusive graffiti in all its revolting glory.

It's a shock.

The racist and homophobic slurs and my name and with Eva's name and then Karl's name makes me tremble with anger. I've never been a victim of such a personal assault and I'm rooted to the spot, reading and re-reading the nasty words and accusations.

183

'What the hell happened?' I turn around and Ben is at my shoulder. 'Who did this?'

I shake my head. 'I don't know.'

'They're certainly making their opinions known.'

'If Karl sees this he'll be very hurt. It's like what they do to the English footballers. How can people be so racist?'

'It's not just racism. What they're saying about you and Eva isn't very kind either.'

'Do you think I should call the police?' I ask.

He shrugs. 'I'm probably the wrong person to ask.'

'Of course, I'm sorry. I'll get some hot soapy water.'

A few minutes later he follows me into the café. 'I'll help.'

My mind is reeling. 'I want to get rid of it before Eva, Karl or anyone else sees it.'

'Of course.'

I pass him the bucket while I find a mop, cloths and detergent from the kitchen.

'Do people really think Eva and I are together?'

Ben doesn't look at me.

'Do they?' I insist.

'Well, it doesn't matter if you are, it's none of anyone's business.'

I shake my head angrily. 'Why would you think that? Can a woman not have a friend?'

'Do you want me to be honest?'

'Of course.' I look into his eyes and I'm suddenly conscious that the grooming session he had at the barbers was a great success. He's maintained the chic, younger look and it suits him. Had he been wearing a suit and tie instead of jeans and a navy shirt, he'd look like a successful businessman – a very good-looking one.

184

'I saw you holding hands with Eva. You were eating dinner here in the window of the café – and you weren't very discreet.'

I think back to the Indian takeaway we'd ordered the night Emma and Nick left for university and how sad and lonely Eva had felt. I had been comforting her as a friend but my reaction had been interpreted as a romantic gesture.

'Come on,' I say angrily, pushing past him. 'Let's get this crap off the walls before the whole street wakes up and Karl and Eva get here.'

Chapter 17

I'm scrubbing the windows; my hands are hurting and my fingers are sore.

'What's happened?'

I turn quickly, dreading the moment that someone else reads these awful words but it's Ben who replies.

'Morning, Ozan. Amber arrived this morning to find someone has written unkind comments on her windows.'

'Graffiti? You should call the police.' Ozan tilts his head, trying to read the words that I haven't yet reached. 'That's an insult to most of the people in the street. Who would have done this?'

'I don't know. But I don't want Karl or Eva to see this filth.'

Ozan stands for a while watching us silently and then he says. 'Yusef and I were born here, Sanjay and his cousins will also be very hurt, they feel they belong here in Westbay and just because this has been written on your window, if affects us all, Amber. We are with you.'

'There's also Kit and Jenna's two adopted children – what will they think?' Ben works hard, slopping water angrily against the window.

'What will you do?' Ozan asks.

'There's nothing I can do,' I reply. 'It's almost gone now.

We've nearly finished.'

'Just because you've washed away the words, the hurt will remain.' Ozan pushes his hands deeper into his pockets. He wears a black bomber jacket over his white shirt and I wonder if he's cold.

'I want to find out who did this.' Ben scrubs frantically.

'Well, it's over now. No one will know,' I reply.

'We will know.' Ozan stabs his chest with his thumb. 'I know. I have seen it.'

'Right, that's it. Now there's no proof. It's all eradicated.' I stand back and look with satisfaction at the clean windows.

'You should have called the police,' insists Ozan. 'Before you cleaned it.'

'I have photos,' says Ben.

'You took photographs?' I look at him.

'We need evidence. In case they do it again.' He looks at his phone. 'We couldn't leave it here until the police arrive because that could be ages. Then they would have to take statements, ask questions, upset all the kind and decent people and whoever did it would still get away with it. It must have been done in the night. No witnesses.'

I toss the cloth into the bucket. 'If I find out who did it, I'll confront them.' I'm already forming an idea of who could possibly want to bully me and I think back to my recent encounter with JJ and Marion.

'And, if I find out who did it—' Ben fumes.

'I can help,' Ozan interrupts him.

We both turn to look at him.

He smiles and his face lights up.

'We have CCTV outside the shop and a camera on Harbour Street pointing this way.'

187

'What? Is that allowed?' Ben asks. 'We've talked about it at the shop owners meetings…' Ben's voice trails off.

Ozan looks sheepish.

Ben laughs. 'So, it's not legal?'

Ozan smiles. 'Well, it's only been up a few days. We want to protect our business. It was Yusef's idea. Our cousin had a spare one and it's really an experiment. We've never looked at it and I'm not sure it will even extend as far as the café. Perhaps you might be able to see who came down the street and identify who did it and when.'

'You mean you have a street camera?' I ask.

'It's not general knowledge and it was only an experiment.'

Ben laughs. 'You're brilliant!'

Ozan beams proudly. 'As Yusef would say, I'm not just a pretty face.'

* * *

I insist on making them coffee and warm ham and cheese rolls.

'Why are you up so early?' I ask Ben.

'I wanted to get a few hours' head start on your flat before I open the gallery.'

'Oh, don't worry, Ben.' I rub my hand through my hair. 'It's been a rotten start to the day and I'm sure you have a lot to do without having to worry about my flat.'

'There isn't much more to do, another couple of hours maybe. Des had sorted the roof so it was just a case of making sure that it was all sealed properly.'

'Thank you. I know I owe you for the work and I won't forget it – even when I sell.'

'Look, the only thing I can say to you, is that it takes time to build up a business – probably three years to get a good reputation and of course, the right staff, let alone the right brand and products. You've only been open since April, so that's just six months. You're doing very well, and the café is very popular – not just with the tourists but also the locals, which is good in the winter when things get a little quieter.'

'Does it ever get quieter?' I grin. 'I actually like the town when it's busy and everyone is wandering along the streets on their way to the harbour.'

He smiles. 'Me too. This is home for me and always will be.'

'So you're pleased with the gallery?'

'It was a long shot when I came back. Call it fate or whatever you like but the couple who owned it before me were desperate to move to be nearer their daughter in Wales. They were grandparents for the first time.' He raises his eyes to the ceiling. 'Fortunately for me, they wanted a quick deal.'

'Did you take on all the local artists too?'

'Some of them. A few of them made it very clear that they wanted nothing to do with me. Obviously, JJ added oil to the fire and was saying awful things and reminding people I had been in prison. Lots of people didn't want an ex-con in Harbour Street but...' He sighs. 'I persevered and now, thanks to you, I'm even beginning to make friends.'

'Thanks to me?' I laugh.

'Yes, it seems like Ozan and Yusef have taken me under their wing, and more recently with Karl helping in the flat we've been chatting. He's a good guy.'

'He is,' I agree.

'Then there's Eva who has always accepted me. Since day one, she smiled and waved but I was very bad-tempered and grumpy back then when I first arrived.'

'People change,' I say.

'Life in prison was more than a sentence. I can't tell you how awful it was but the one thing it taught me was patience. I learnt to craft the chess sets for a reason.'

'Patience?'

'Revenge.'

'What? On JJ? Are you turning into a bunny boiler?'

'No, but I do want justice. It annoys me that she can get away with it – did get away with it, and I can't see how the locals haven't worked out what she's really like yet.'

'Some of us have.'

'You, maybe Eva.' He looks at me and frowns. 'Tell me that's a coincidence with the graffiti? It couldn't have been JJ, could it?'

I shrug. 'I'm guessing it could be a couple of young kids. One man got very angsty with Karl on Saturday, and he mentioned something racist under his breath.'

'What did Karl do?'

'Nothing, but I did. I told him to get out.'

'You think it could be him?'

I shrug.

'Talking of staff, I'm looking for someone to work with me in the gallery,' he says. 'I don't really know how to get anyone and my reputation still lingers.'

'The job centre?'

'They send young kids with no idea. I'd like someone mature who will be responsible and who will work weekends, not slope off early, and someone who won't turn up on a Monday with a hangover. You're very lucky with your staff, Amber. When you sell the business will you put in some clause to protect their jobs?'

I slide Ben's roll across the counter where he's leaning, sipping his coffee and watching me.

'Of course.' I hadn't actually got that far in my thinking but I remind myself, mentally making a note.

'That would be a kind thing to do,' he adds.

'Yes,' I agree.

Ozan returns and hands me the USB.

'Here's the film. You can watch it on your computer. It repeats weekly, and automatically erases the film from the week before. So I'm sorry, Amber, you will have to sit and watch the whole thing through each night.'

'No problem.' I pocket the USB. 'Thank, Ozan.' I pass his roll and coffee across the counter.

'Do you want me to look at it with you?' Ben asks.

'Nah. It's boring. I'll do it tonight but let's keep this between us, yes? It will be our secret.'

Ozan nods. 'Yes, it's best that no one knows what we've done.'

He smiles in delight as he bites into the warm roll. 'You are very kind, Amber. And, if I tell you the truth, I hate the thought of you leaving here. We are all just getting to know each other.'

* * *

It doesn't take me long to realise that Karl is not himself and I begin to wonder if he saw the graffiti, or if he's seen the stranger that came into the café again.

It's quiet between brunch and lunch, so I corner Karl near the coffee machine.

191

'Are you alright?'

He smiles but it doesn't reach his eyes. 'Fine.'

'And the truth is?' I smile at him, refusing to move, looking him in the eye.

He rubs his head and he looks tired. He's all arms and legs and gangly. 'Molly was fired from her job yesterday, and then last night they said we have to get out of the caravan.'

'Why?'

'They close the caravan park for a month every year and we have to leave. They do up the site or something but the guy that runs it was awful. He was really nasty to Molly, and I was going to put a brick through his window but Molly told me not to. She was frightened that I might hit him.'

'You don't want to do that,' I say. 'That would only cause more trouble. But don't worry, let me give it some thought and I'll come up with a plan. When do you have to be out by?'

'Friday.'

I think of my damp flat upstairs and how long it will take to dry out, and then to paint it. I couldn't offer it to them, it's uninhabitable.

'I'll think of something,' I say, and then I'm distracted. 'Frances, how lovely to see you.'

'I hope I'm not interrupting? Have you got a minute, Amber?'

'Of course.' I'm actually worried she's seen the graffiti so I lead her to a table but she refuses a coffee or anything to drink.

'It's just a quick question,' she says.

I sit opposite her and notice the lines creasing around her eyes and the light of hope she radiates. 'Amber, could I please put your name forward to organise the Christmas festivities in Harbour Street?'

I stare at her and then I laugh. 'Me?'

'Well, let's be honest, you'll hardly have sold the café before then and even if you have then you'll want to sell it with a profit, and good staff and a healthy income. You're building up your business. There are often queues outside here and it's very popular.'

'That's down to Lucas. They love his food.'

'Well, that may well be, but we need someone with a bit of business savvy to take over. Halloween was an unmitigated disaster, she wanted no help with anything and quite frankly JJ has become quite, how shall I say, rude.'

'Rude?' I hide a smile.

'She's determined to get that place across the road and turn it into an amusement arcade. She even wants to call another meeting and she's touting for everyone's votes, didn't you know that?'

I shake my head.

'She thinks that if she gets everyone on her side, then there will be no objections.'

'She came to court my vote but I told her no, and I think Ben and Eva feel the same.'

'That's as maybe but...' Frances counts on her fingers. 'She does have Marion, Derek, Ian, Luke and Mario, Jane, Tracey and now she's persuaded Kit and Jenna.'

'Really?'

'Yes. Everyone has agreed that they are sick of looking at that awful eyesore and anything will be better than an empty building. JJ's going to get her own way, Amber, and this is the only way I can think of stopping her.'

'What, me taking over the Christmas committee?'

193

'Yes, it's a strategy. I think the other shopkeepers will get to know you better. They will trust you and you will be able to tell them it's not a good idea.'

'We have Sanjay on our side,' I say, thinking frantically.

'That's not enough.'

'There must be another option?'

'No,' Frances says firmly. 'I believe you're the one to take on Christmas and make it a success.'

* * *

I'm walking back to Eva's after work, lost in thought. I've been studying the shop windows as they begin preparing for Christmas and I'm thinking of ideas for Harbour Street for the festive period. There are still three weeks until the beginning of December and it's late to be organising a big event. According to Frances, Harbour Street has never done much leading up to Christmas and we had both agreed it would be ideal if we had more time.

I pause to stare up at the golden halo of street lights, thinking of how it could be transformed into something wonderful, when I'm conscious of footsteps behind me. I turn around.

'Hi, Pamela.'

'Hello, Amber.' She pulls her coat closer to her body and she shivers. She looks frazzled and worried.

'Are you alright?'

'I'm on my way home.'

'Okay, see you tomorrow.'

'No, you won't, Amber. You won't see me again. I've quit.'

'You're not working for Marion anymore?'

'No.'

'Why?'

Pamela regards me thoughtfully, then her eyes crease and she frowns. 'Let's just say I disagree with her on certain things.'

'You shouldn't have to agree with your boss on everything. Everyone's entitled to their own opinion.'

'Your employees are lucky, with Marion it's not so easy.'

I nod in understanding. There's no point in flogging a dead horse and I know how close JJ and Marion are, but I wouldn't be a lawyer if I didn't have a curious mind.

'Do you want to talk about it?'

Pamela shakes her head and pulls the collar of her coat to her throat.

'Not now.' She turns to walk away.

'I'm sorry to see you go, Pamela. You've always been very kind to me.'

'I'd love to stay. I love working in Harbour Street. I've lived here all my life and with Ronnie so busy at work all the time, this job was a lifeline for me.' Her voice is emotional and she struggles to keep her composure. Whatever happened between her and Marion, the spark of happiness has been snuffed out. 'It gets me out of the house and meeting people. I'm normally quite shy.' She forces a grin. 'I know you probably don't believe that but when I started working in the gallery after my son David went to school it was the best thing for me—'

'The gallery?'

'Yes, before Ben bought it. In the early days before the owners' daughters started working on Saturdays.' She tuts and raises her eyes skywards and I notice then that it's beginning to rain.

'I think Ben is looking for someone in the gallery to help

him,' I say.

She stares at me.

'It's just an idea if you still want to work in Harbour Street,' I add.

'I wouldn't work for a criminal like him, Amber. He's an ex-con, a liar and a thief. I think it's disgusting he's even here and trying to ingratiate himself with everyone after what he did to JJ and her business. He's a disgrace to this town and to his family. His poor mother never got over the shock and, he killed his father and uncle too.'

Chapter 18

I'm still thinking about my conversation with Pamela when I plug the USB into my laptop. Eva has an early start in the morning, she's visiting a new garden nursery, so she's having a bath and an early night.

I pour a glass of Rioja and sit under the lamp in the living room, relishing the quiet and the comfort of a warm home, and I think about Karl and Molly in their caravan.

If my flat was finished, I'd offer them a room but as it is, I'm already homeless. I've picked through my possessions and tried to store and clear most things and Ben's installed a machine he reckons will dry out the flat quicker than normal but I don't hold my breath.

My shoulders ache and I'm tired.

I spend a few minutes online checking the estate agents, and although I've had a couple of recent viewings all of the prospective buyers have run from the property after they've seen the state of the flat.

I've tidied up the patio and there are lovely pots of flowers I bought from Eva at cost. It's a sociable outdoor space for people to sit safely with their children and dogs but it's rarely used. They prefer to be outside on the street or inside in the warm.

I check the estate agent listings, and then I check the job opportunities online for lawyers in London. The salary alone makes me well up with frustration – my salary was six figures, now I barely have one at all. My costs are higher; the mortgage for the café and the flat is extortionate, then there's insurance, rates, taxes, staff, overheads of the business and running expenses like my van and then me. But I haven't even had a regular haircut since I cropped my hair when I first moved here, as an experiment for a new look. It's since grown out and now it's like rats' tails. A regular massage is a thing of the past, and as for meals out in popular gastro restaurants with expensive wines and a business account, I now rely on Sanjay's Indian takeaways. Fortunately, they are as good as any London restaurant, but having been through the whole menu, I begin looking for something economical and tasty to cook at home. I've always loved cooking and Eva certainly enjoys my concoctions; tonight it was chicken with crème fraîche, brandy, mushrooms and Dijon mustard served with wild rice. It reminds me of a recipe I'd been trying to think of all day. Karl had mentioned winter stews again and I remember my grandmother used to make a wonderful lamb dish with vegetables but the secret was in the seasoning.

I scan through various websites, thinking of different herbs, remembering as a child how I used to cook with my family, during the long Italian summer holidays on the hillside with the sound of the braying donkeys, goats and sheep for company.

I close my eyes remembering happier and certainly easier days and the warmth and love I'd felt while growing up, never realising how lucky I was, and before I know it, I fall into a deep and happy sleep.

* * *

The following morning Eva runs over to the café.

'Nick and Emma are coming down tonight. I can't believe it. It's Wednesday, for heaven's sake! They've never come home midweek. Mum and Dad are coming for dinner and they've decided to come home too but now I've got flowers and plants being delivered to the shop between six and seven, and I won't be home in time. I can hardly cancel and tell them not to come and I can't afford to invite everyone out for dinner. I'm saving really hard for Christmas and James is being particularly difficult. He told me last night he wants to take them away skiing this year. On Boxing Day. I can't believe it, Amber. What can I do? I can't manage Christmas without them. Not my children. I want to see them and spend time with them. If only they'd given me some notice. I could have changed the delivery day or, oh, I don't know what to do, Amber—'

'Go and sort out your business. We're pretty quiet here and Jean and Karl won't mind if I leave early. I'll pop to the butchers and I'll think of something. I'll make a lovely dinner and it will all be ready for when you get home.'

Eva smiles. Tears well up in her eyes. 'You're such a good friend.'

I glance over her shoulder at the flower shop.

'Stop worrying! Look, you'd better go, you have a customer in the shop. Just come home when you can and it will all be okay.'

* * *

In the end I opt for the easiest dinner. A rib of beef with Yorkshire pudding, a head of fresh carrots, fluffy parsnips and crispy roast potatoes, and for good measure, I make a leek soufflé. Eva arrives home in time to run into the bathroom and repair her makeup, then by coincidence they all arrive together.

Eva's father, Mikołaj, still has a strong Polish accent. 'You look beautiful, Eva,' he says proudly.

She beams at him. 'Thanks, Papa.' She stands with her arms around him and she turns to me.

'Do we look alike?'

'You have the same straight nose and blue eyes.'

'Papa fell in love with Mum when he came here forty years ago.'

'1989, after the fall of socialism,' he adds proudly.

'But they always took me home for the summer, or I went to stay with cousins.'

'Our culture is important too.'

'I know, Papa, and our language.'

He nods. 'I think Nick and Emma's Polish is a little rusty.'

'Then you can practise with them later.' Eva kisses his cheek. Neither of them looks up. Both Nick and Emma are subdued and they barely acknowledge me. For some reason, I've an inkling that they've already stopped somewhere and had a drink. Emma's face is flushed and Nick's frown is deeper than usual.

Eva's Mum Gloria is petite and I can see how pretty she would have been in her youth.

After the introductions, Eva pours wine and they all settle in the conservatory. I can hear them, and I can see them as I move around preparing the gravy and setting places at Eva's lovely family dining table, wandering between the rooms.

'I know we've surprised you, but the change of scene will do us good. Your Papa needed a change of scene, you know what he gets like,' Gloria says, 'We haven't been here since the summer – remember? It was that very warm week.'

'In June, Mama.'

'Yes, well, it's been a few months and Papa got it in his head he had to see you. Then he called Nick and Emma.' She lowers her voice. 'He even paid for their train tickets. You know what he's like when he gets these notions in his head.'

Mikołaj opens the patio doors and heads outside into the garden to inspect the tubs and pots.

'You've worked hard, Eva darling. You've done all the gardening. That was some job – it was all overgrown.'

'Amber helped me. I couldn't have done it without her.' Eva smiles.

Nick and Emma swap a glance.

'Is she staying long?' Gloria whispers.

I move away, further into the kitchen. I don't want to be caught listening.

'Until her apartment is fixed. Nick, get off the phone and be sociable,' Eva moans, then says to her mother. 'Emma wants clothes for her holiday. They want to go skiing with their father.'

'Can't James give her money?'

'He seems to think he's absolved of duties as he's paying for their airfare.'

Mikołaj comes inside.

'It's a bit too cold for me this evening.' He rubs his hands together and he wanders into the kitchen to refill his sherry. 'Family,' he whispers to me. 'I've been very worried about

Eva. Since James left her, she's been very sad and I don't understand him. Silly man. Do you know in all the years they were married he never even learnt one Polish word.' He shakes his head and moves away. 'Silly, silly man.'

Over dinner the conversation flows easily. We talk about food, recipes, gardening, and I feel that they are keeping the conversation neutral so that I can join in, and although I'm pleased to be a part of their conversation I'm conscious that Nick and Emma mostly listen. They don't look at me.

Eva talks about the Darling Buds and Blooms. 'I developed a love of flowers from Papa,' she explains to me.

'You had a lovely garden in your last home,' Gloria says.

Nick stretches his legs. 'We don't need to be reminded of what we had.'

Everyone ignores his rudeness.

Gloria asks about the café but I don't mention Cassie or the fact I was a lawyer in London and I'm vague about the details.

'Are you married?' she asks me.

They all seem to wait. It's as if the table takes a silent but uniform gasp.

'No. I'm not.' I smile.

Nick coughs.

Emma stares at her plate, then raises her eyes to stare at me.

'Of course, with Eva's addiction to coffee it's understandable you are friends, Eva adores coffee.' Gloria reaches for her daughter's hand.

'That's true,' I smile. 'We have to send her regular cups across the road to keep her fortified.'

'I'm surprised you're not married – a good looking girl like you – and no boyfriend either?' Gloria asks.

I hold my breath and in the ensuing silence Mikołaj says,

'Stop your nonsense, all these questions. This is the nicest piece of beef I've had in years, Amber. Thank you.'

I smile and Eva meets my gaze across the table.

'It's delicious,' she agrees.

'Dessert is bread and butter pudding.' I stand and clear the plates.

It is perfectly browned and served with thick cream.

'You should open a restaurant,' Mikołaj says, accepting a second helping.

'That's what I keep telling her,' Eva says.

'I'm only just getting the café sorted out,' I reply.

'Dad was a farmer,' Eva explains.

'He had his own farm all his life,' Gloria adds.

'It seems a long time ago now...' he says and he seems absorbed in his dessert. 'I can't remember when I ate such a good pudding.'

'Nonsense, I made you one a few weeks ago.' Gloria bristles.

'This is much better.' Mikołaj winks at me and grins.

Nick looks at his phone.

Emma stares out of the window.

After the meal, I insist they go to the lounge and leave me to tidy the kitchen. But Emma and Nick are ordered to help me and they work silently, moving around the kitchen in perfect harmony trying not to touch each other, stacking the dishwasher, and cleaning pots and pans.

'Did you try cooking any recipes we looked at yet, Emma?' I ask.

'No.'

'You liked the last—'

'I've been busy.'

When I ask them about uni they close up and it's obvious

they don't want to speak to me. I don't push them. I'm tired and besides, I reason, they're not my kids.

'I'm going to make coffee before they leave.' Eva says, coming into the kitchen. Her hair is askew and she looks sleepy.

'Of course.' I fill the kettle. 'I'll say goodnight. I've an early start tomorrow.'

'Thanks for a wonderful meal.' Eva grins at me and rubs my shoulder as I pass by walking toward the lounge to say goodnight. 'It's just what we all needed.'

'It's been a pleasure. You're very lucky to have wonderful parents.'

'Thank you.'

'There's never anything on television.' Mikołaj wanders in with the TV magazine in his hands. 'I used to look forward to a good drama but it's all rubbish – even on a Sunday night.'

'I prefer the radio – the plays are far more interesting and there's much more variety,' Gloria calls out.

I take my leave of them quickly and, Nick and Emma, who are now on the couch, barely look up.

'Promise you'll come and see us,' Gloria says, and to my surprise she wraps me in a hug.

'That would be lovely,' I reply.

'I'll show you the sunflowers I grew from seeds and the seedlings growing in the green house.' Mikołaj kisses me on both cheeks.

'That's a promise,' I reply.

As I walk upstairs to sleep in Emma's room I feel her hostility on my back. She's sleeping on the couch tonight and, as Eva told her, you knew that before you came home – so why have they both been so rude?

* * *

In the morning the house has a sleepy feel to it. When I go downstairs the door to the lounge is closed and although someone has lifted the blind in the kitchen, there's no one around. Outside trees are waving manically as if they are trying to capture my attention and I pause to stare at the changing colours in the leaves. They look beautiful and I think about the robin that often perches on the fence while I'm working outside.

If I wasn't in such a hurry to get out of the house and to avoid the family, I would have stood at the window and enjoyed the beauty, but instead I search frantically for my car keys.

The kitchen is cluttered with Emma's bags, discarded shoes and Nick's jacket hanging on the back of the chair. The worktop I cleaned last night is strewn with a crumb-laden chopping board, a knife coated with peanut butter and empty juice glasses.

I search the kitchen. It is past seven o'clock but I feel like a thief in the night. I finally find my bag hidden in the conservatory and I pull out my car keys just as the kitchen door opens.

Startled, I pause.

Nick stands in the doorway staring at me. His fists are balled into the pockets of his baggy combat trousers and he leans against the door frame.

'Morning. Found them.' I rattle my keys triumphantly in the air. 'Have a good day, Nick.'

His low voice cuts across the room and halts me in my stride.

'Don't even think about going near my mother,' he says.

He stands between me and the hallway, the pathway to my

escape.

Pulling his hands from his pockets, he folds his arms. His lips are in a tight straight line.

'Don't be ridiculous! I'm off to work.'

'You've been staying here too long.'

'It is none of your business.'

'I mean it. My mother doesn't need your shit in her life.'

'My shit – as you call it – won't affect your mother.'

'It had better not… she's not a lesbian.'

'That doesn't even dignify a reply.'

'Then what are you doing with her all the time?'

'I'm sure she's already told you. She kindly offered me a room because my flat was flooded.'

'Are you sleeping with her?'

'Do you fancy every girl you meet?' I say, hoping he won't hear the tremor of anger in my voice. 'Do you?' I insist quietly. 'Fat – thin – tall – dark – funny, seriously?'

'No.'

'Exactly – and neither do I.'

I push past him and the lounge door opens and Emma stands dressed in pyjamas. Have they been lying in wait for me?

'Morning, Emma,' I say politely.

She doesn't reply. She simply blocks my path to the front door.

'Excuse me.' I move to open the latch.

'Don't touch me. You're not my type.'

She squeezed herself dramatically against the wall as if touching me would give her a disease. 'Ooohhh, careful. There are girls like you at uni. They want to touch me.'

I shake my head. 'Grow up, children.'

I throw open the front door. My blood pressure levels are

rising. I step outside into the fresh November air into a cold wind but it's what I need to bring me to my senses.

How can they make me feel like this?

How dare they?

I wait with my hand on the gate then I turn quickly and go back inside. They are in the hallway whispering quietly, their heads bent close together and they are surprised to see me.

My voice is quiet and controlled.

'It's just as well that you've both gone to university. While you're there I hope you learn that life is about tolerance and understanding. Hopefully, you'll mature and realise that there are too many bigoted, narrow-minded and immature people in this world. If you want to be one of them – then the choice is yours. Your attitude is shameful. You are an insult to the education and opportunity that your parents have provided for you. We live in a better world than we did years ago. Now, everyone has the right to be whoever they like – without labels and without shame.'

At the top of the stairs Eva stands with her hand on the banister looking at me. Her face is aghast. I turn on my heel.

I don't stop. I keep walking.

Chapter 19

The beach is damp and dark. A sea mist has curled in across the beach causing droplets to form on the pebbles. I dig my hands into my coat pockets and stride determinedly along the promenade with only a few dog walkers to keep me company. I watch a couple of cross-breeds chase each other and wonder if perhaps one day I may get a dog. A cat would be better. One like Scruff-bucket; independent, loving, reliable and friendly.

It would be far more preferable than having another relationship.

I will never get involved with anyone again.

It's all too much effort and too sad. I couldn't cope with another emotional fallout. Although Cassie left over six months ago, sometimes I still find it hard. Being alone doesn't bother me. It's having no one to confide in, no one to mull things over with.

I miss Martin. He had been my colleague and friend since we were at university together and now he's living on the far side of the world. Although we've chatted a few times on Skype it's mostly been about his new life and family. I haven't the heart to dump my problems on him now he is so far away.

I rest my arms on the edge of the sea wall and wonder what life is all about.

I think of Karl and the worry he has in the caravan with Molly, and compare it to the spoilt life of Emma and Nick.

James left Eva.

Cassie left me.

JJ lied about Ben.

Ben went to prison for something he didn't do.

And Pamela, like a lot of people, believes JJ's lies.

I walk back to Harbour Street via the small working harbour, inhaling the warm diesel from the fishing boats and the tangy salty water. I pause to admire the boats and seagulls squawking overhead. The rows of old fishermen's houses are pretty, and I look in their gardens, revelling in the smell of shrubs and plants and listening to the sounds of the rustling trees. Nearby, a robin rests on a branch and it reminds me of Eva's garden. A garden she didn't want to go into, a house she didn't want to like – was it for fear of being disloyal to her previous home, her family and old life?

Who do we lead our lives for – our partners, our children or ourselves?

How selfish are we allowed to be?

How protective of our families are we?

Eva's face this morning was murderous. I think she would have killed me for confronting her smart, wonderful bright and educated children. She's sensitive and protective towards them both after her divorce, especially after the cutbacks in her financial arrangements. They had to uproot their home and live somewhere much smaller.

But now, I'm a guest in Eva's house – or I was – perhaps I should have behaved more appropriately.

The path emerges into the glow of the street lamps. There are two ladies power-walking and a jogger, who with his breath like fog, pants past me.

I can't continue living like this. I'll be better off back in my flat. And, I'll see if I can take out a bigger loan and sort out a new financial business strategy that will see me through the winter until I sell the café.

I calculate quickly, I probably have six to eight weeks left to generate more income before Christmas. I head to the café, determined to make an appointment with the bank manger today.

* * *

'No sooner has Halloween ended and the pumpkins are gone, fireworks take over and then they're displaced by Santa's cheery face and reindeers in all shapes and sizes.' Jean bustles around behind the counter, moaning. 'The first few days of November have passed so quickly I've barely had time to think about Christmas presents. Now all the shops in Harbour Street remind me that the festive season is upon us, jingling their delights for the season of goodwill and reminding me that we must prepare for the perfect Christmas.'

Lucas agrees. 'Everyone dreams of the perfect Christmas, Jean.'

'And it never happens,' she announces. 'People argue or fight or drink too much.'

'Or they have a screaming baby.' Lucas smiles.

'I'd like a white Christmas,' announces Karl.

'Today is freezing and snow is forecast.' Lucas checks his weather app.

'You can't believe the weather people,' Jean says.

Each time the door opens a gust of cold wind sweeps around

my long woollen skirt. Business is steady and customers are even asking if we cater for special dinners, parties or Christmas celebrations.

Karl says, 'We should branch out. Diversify.'

Jean agrees, 'It's busy enough.'

Lucas tells them about a new recipe for a Hungarian stew he's been practising.

'Morning,' I say as a pink-haired lady wrapped in a woollen coat stomps in wearing heavy boots.

'Isn't it cold?' she replies. 'I think we're forecast snow.'

The old lady rubs her leather-gloved hands. Her unprotected eyes are bloodshot from the wind and she reaches inside her coat pocket for a tissue. She wipes her nose before answering. 'We might have a white Christmas,' she concludes.

Karl bounces over smiling. 'Here's your usual, Kathy.' He places a hot croissant and a latte on the table.

'You're a good boy, Karl. Thank you.' She unbuttons her coat. 'I went into the church to light a candle for a friend and Frances said there's a meeting tonight for the shop owners about what you're doing for Christmas. Are you going, Amber?'

'Yes.'

'Good. It's about time everyone made an effort. This street was always the worst in the town when I grew up. All the business events were around the square and the church and it was always very festive with Christmas carols. No one ventured into Harbour Street in those days. These used to be the old houses that the fishermen lived in and sometimes they sold their fresh catch from their front rooms. No one wanted to live here or have a business because of the smell of the fish. It's like the smell seeped into the floorboards, the whole place was considered to be common and smelly.' She grins. 'But now look at it. In the last twenty years it's changed so much and I really thought it was all going so well…'

'It is, isn't it?'

'Not if you think of that empty place across the street being turned into an amusement arcade.'

'Is that definitely happening?' I ask.

'Well, there's no stopping that JJ. She's walking around the town like she owns the place and rumour has it that she's going to be the mayor next year.'

'Oh, no!' Karl says. 'That's awful. She's already making a move on the caravan park.'

'What do you mean?' I ask.

'Well, the caretaker told us last night, it's one of the reasons we have to get out tomorrow. JJ is wanting to buy the caravan park but she wants it all done up first.'

Kathy shakes her head. 'Will no one stop that awful woman?'

'That would take a Christmas miracle,' mumbles Karl.

* * *

The meeting is in the church at six o'clock and Frances flutters around flapping her arms and guiding shop owners into the front pews.

'Are we all here?'

'JJ's not here,' Jane says.

Ian replies, 'She's not coming.'

'Why?' asks Frances.

'It's probably because the Halloween parade was a disaster,' whispers Sanjay loudly.

Karl laughs.

212

Marion stands up. 'JJ has a prior business meeting but she has allowed me to cast her vote.'

Frances nods. 'Right. This meeting is about Christmas and what we will do in Harbour Street this year. I nominate Amber to be the Chair.'

'Seconded,' Sanjay shouts.

'Any objections?' Frances looks around.

I catch Marion's eye but she looks quickly away.

'That's decided. Right, over to you, Amber.'

I clear my throat, conscious that everyone is looking at me.

'I believe that years ago Harbour Street was an undesirable location because of its close proximity to the harbour. Since then, there have been a lot of changes and things have improved but more recently, because of Covid and the lockdown, businesses have struggled. What I'd like to do is to make this a Christmas no one will forget. I'd like to have your suggestions, no matter how outrageous or costly, to make this the best Christmas EVER in Harbour Street.'

Karl puts his fingers in his mouth and whistles.

Frances shushes him but laughs and claps delightedly.

Sanjay gives a whoop of delight and Eva beams happily.

The rest of the shop owners look either bored or at me with unconcealed contempt and resentment.

* * *

It's late when I arrive back at Eva's and she's already eaten.

'I ate in Sanjay's,' she says. 'He insisted. You know, at one of the three tables where people usually wait for their takeaways. It was warmer in there.'

'I don't blame you.' I flop onto the chair opposite where she's stretched on the sofa. She mutes the TV and yawns. 'How did you get on in the flat?'

'Ben has put in a dehumidifier and I've had the heating on full blast and it's pretty much dry. Karl's added a second coat of paint to the bedrooms, and I've cleaned up and it's actually looking quite normal, in fact better than I could have imagined. I'd stored all my books, they're still stacked in boxes, and I've packed away most of my clothes and hidden them in the small attic space and although it's smelling strongly of paint the flat looks very respectable.'

'Are you sure it's alright?' Eva asks.

'Yes, you've been really kind to put up with me for these past few weeks, I really appreciate it.'

'Is this about Nick and Emma?'

'No.'

'I heard what you said to them this morning, and after you left, I also spoke to them…'

I let the silence fill the room. She doesn't know about the graffiti that was daubed on the windows of the café and I don't think it will make her feel better if I tell her now, but it reminds me that I haven't yet checked the CCTV camera. I fell asleep the first night and since then I've cooked for Eva's family and I've been sorting out my own flat. Besides, Ozan said the camera might not have reached the café and there might be nothing to see anyway.

'It turns out,' she continues, 'that Nick and Emma had a couple of drinks in The Ship before they came home last night, and they heard rumours in the pub that you've moved in with me… because, rumour has it, we're romantically linked.'

'Umm.' I think of my encounter with JJ and Marion and I'm not surprised. 'That must have been upsetting for them.'

'I can imagine JJ spreading these lies,' Eva says. 'I want to tackle her about it but I have no proof it was her.'

'Perhaps they were shocked,' I say.

'They were upset, but rather than coming home and discussing it with me, they decided to have a go at you and I told them that was unacceptable. It was very rude of them and I'm sorry, Amber.'

'It's fine. They put two and two together and came up with a random number, thanks to the rumour machine in The Ship.'

'It's not fine. I brought them up to be better people and so did their father. They will apologise to you.'

'So long as you've spoken to them and they know the truth, that's enough for me.'

'Is this why you're moving out so quickly?' she asks.

'No. I need to sort out my life. I came to Westbay because of Cassie but I can't seem to sell the café and I have to make money to get through the winter. If there's another lockdown, then many businesses won't survive, including the café. I've spent the small amount of savings I had and I've arranged to speak to the bank manager again next week.' I sigh. 'But I feel that I must look after Karl, Jean and Lucas – they've been so loyal to me during the summer. Especially Karl. He could have left at any time to work in one of the bigger retailers but he's stood by me for the meagre amount of profit share I give him each month, and he's even pitched in to help paint my flat.'

'Karl is very special.'

'I know and I'm sometimes quite humbled by him.'

'You don't need to leave here, Amber. You're making some good friends and this could be the start to something wonderful.'

215

I stare at the moving silent mouths of the characters on the television and I think of all the people I've met here and I'm suddenly overwhelmed.

'I can't stay, Eva. It's all too… complicated. Everyone has a story and there's too much emotion here all bubbling away under the surface; anger, bitterness, jealousy—'

'And love and kindness and, most importantly, friendship.'

'At least when I was practising law I didn't have to get involved with emotions. It was just the facts and they're far easier to deal with. This is just all too much for me.'

'Then, if you must, apply that same principle to your life here. Don't get involved but stay, Amber. Harbour Street needs you.'

* * *

'Have dinner with us tonight?' I say.

Ben looks around the flat, his hands on his hips nodding at Karl's paintwork, and then his eyes rest on mine.

'I'm getting fish and chips for us all to celebrate Karl and Molly moving in. I've given them my credit card and they've gone to get them, please say yes and I'll text Karl.' I wave my mobile and smile.

Ben nods. 'Okay. Thank you.'

I text Karl: *4 x fish and chips. Ben is staying. x*

Karl replies immediately: *Great. X*

Then suddenly another message pops up.

Hello baby, hope you're OK? It's been a long time but I can't stop thinking of you, love Cassie xx

My mouth turns dry but I ignore the message and toss my

mobile on the table. While we wait for Karl and Molly, Ben walks around the flat with a carpenter's eye. 'We could put some shelves up, if you like.'

I find plates, knives and forks, salt and vinegar, ketchup and mayonnaise. 'That's a good idea.'

Karl comes running up the stairs closely followed by Molly. She's breathless and her cheeks are red and her eyes bright with excitement. She's only young and she has a number of tattoos around her hands and wrists and deep, dark eyes that look older than her nineteen years.

Ben looks at the fish and chips approvingly.

'You've worked hard.' He smiles at Karl. 'Good paint job.'

'I didn't expect Amber would offer us a place to stay.'

'And she's given us the bigger bedroom,' Molly adds. 'The master bedroom. That's so kind of you.'

'I don't need much space.' I open a bottle of wine and pour us all a glass and leave the bottle on the table.

'It won't be for long, I promise.' Karl sticks a chip in his mouth. 'It just gives us some time until we can find something else.'

'It's such a cosy flat.' Molly looks adoringly at Karl and he grins at her and squeezes her knee under the table.

I raise my glass in a toast.

'It's all down to you, Ben. Thank you for all your hard work.'

'You're very kind offering Karl and Molly a place to stay.' He looks down into Harbour Street. 'If you ignore the travel agents, it's a pretty view from here.'

'I actually like the view. It's very interesting and it's always changing with different people and the seasons.'

I think back to the summer and how lonely I'd felt in the beginning but now, tonight, I feel different. It's like the flat has been cleansed of Cassie and the past, so why has she texted me – tonight of all nights?

The new sage candle that Molly bought as a flat-warming present gives out a calming and relaxing aroma, and for the first time in a long while I feel content and relaxed in my own flat.

'It's a shame the travel agents closed. That building is terrible.' Ben looks sad. 'So much has changed here.'

Karl speaks with his mouth full. 'But we can make it better again. We can stop JJ and, we can have the best Christmas ever.'

I sit companionably beside Ben and share the view outside. 'An amusement arcade would be awful, wouldn't it?'

Ben nods. 'I blocked her last planning permission but I have a feeling she'll get the next one through.'

'She's taking over the town, the caravan park is next and then she'll be mayor. She will be unbearable and she'll make our lives a misery.' Karl dabs his mouth with the kitchen paper I put out as napkins. 'Unless we stop her.'

'But how?' asks Molly.

'That's the problem,' Ben replies. 'We can't now. It's all too late.'

Chapter 20

I call it open house and, after business is finished for the day, I open the café from seven until nine o'clock. I've printed out a note to all the shop owners and invited them to pop into the café to discuss their ideas for the Christmas festival in Harbour Street. And, for anyone not able to come (or not willing) I've enclosed a blank sheet of paper and envelope. I emphasise that there are no reasons why everyone can't have their say and their voices will be heard. I also promise that once the ideas have been put forward and the budget (controlled by Frances) is agreed, then there will be a short list of ideas with costs, and a democratic vote will take place.

Karl wants to be downstairs with me but I don't want anyone to feel inhibited with their ideas if they think my staff are present, so he's upstairs watching TV with Molly while Frances and I sit companionably waiting to see who will turn up.

Sanjay is first. He's only next door and he says it's pretty quiet but the only thing he'd like is a proper Santa Claus and a procession if possible.

'I know I'm not a Christian, sorry, Frances, but Christmas is one of my favourite times. I have wonderful memories of my first years in England when I was a boy. Each year my parents took me and my sisters to John Lewis, and Santa looked so real with his white beard and big jolly costume. One year he gave me a yellow bath duck and I still have it. But it wasn't about the gift, it was all so exciting, and it helped make me settle into this country and feel part of life here.'

Frances smiles and writes down *Santa*.

'So how could the procession work?'

Sanjay shrugs. 'Sorry, Amber, I'm hopeless at working out things like this. That's why I'm suited to my business. I take the orders, and work out the price and then one of my cousins delivers the food.'

Next to arrive are Ian, the grocer, and Jane. They have come together, so I wonder if they feel there is safety in numbers.

Ian says, 'We don't want anything too noisy or rowdy. I think JJ's right, after the lockdown people are being cautious and we must take that same level of responsibility. I can put together some fruit and veg parcels like I do every year, a raffle of some sort.'

Frances makes a note.

Jane adds, 'I don't know how I can be of any use. Jewellery is jewellery. I've never done anything special, I just put some lights and a few small decorations in the window and make sure there are romantic choices; rings are particularly popular for obvious reasons.'

Tracey turns up just as they are leaving and her eyes are bloodshot and swollen as if she's been crying.

'I'm so sorry,' she gushes, 'Des is such a pain. He's so unreliable. I really wanted him to help you do up your flat but he's always so busy.' Tears begin to roll down her cheeks and I find a napkin for her. 'We've been planning a baby for months but it's not happening and I don't think he cares anymore. He won't commit. He's out working all the time and I rarely see him and I don't know if he's having an affair… I don't know what to do.'

Frances meets my eyes and turns quickly away.

'It's a difficult time for you,' I murmur.

'It is, Amber. You're so right. I'm short-staffed. The Polish girls I had working with me have left because of Brexit. Over 90,000 Poles have left the country *so we're all* short-staffed. And, no one likes the unsociable hours and the zero hour contracts. I can't get any help. I don't even have a receptionist. It's coming up to a really busy time of year as everyone wants their nails done, or a fake tan and a massage before Christmas and I'm losing customers because there's no one to even answer the phone.' She dries her eyes and then checks her watch. 'I'd better dash, Des said he'd be home by now.' She stands up. 'Oh, and with the Christmas thingy, I'm happy to go along with anything just so long as it doesn't cost me any money.'

Derek the butcher saunters in just after eight with his hands in his pockets, looking red-nosed and cold. 'It's Baltic out there,' he complains. 'Look, I've been told to tell you I'm not getting involved but to be honest, Frances, I respect you. I'm a God-fearing man and I'll help at Christmas if I can.'

Frances smiles brightly. 'Thanks, Derek, we appreciate that.'

'Well, I was thinking we could have a few lights about the place. We've never done that before. I think there must be some in the church hall. Can't we borrow those?'

'They will be up in the church garden.'

'Ah,' he nods thoughtfully. 'Well, unless we all delve deep and buy our own lights, I can't see another option.'

Eva comes in. 'Another option for what?'

'Christmas lights along Harbour Street,' explains Frances.

'Well, I thought it would be nice if everyone had red buckets outside their shops with mini Christmas trees. One each side of the entrance. I could get a trade price from the nursery. I'll check next week.'

'That's a good idea.' Frances makes a note.

Freddy from the mobile shop puts his head around the door. 'Hi, guys, look I haven't got a lot of time. I'm in a hurry but if you're doing a Christmas raffle I'm happy to put up an old phone. It would be second-hand but let me know?'

'Thank you,' Frances calls to his retreating back.

'We could sort out a hamper for a raffle,' Derek says. 'You know, a bit of meat and cheese and I could get Ian to put in a few fruit and veg and maybe a few nuts.'

Frances writes this all down and she puts down her pen as Mario and Luke arrive. They have with them a grey wrinkled pug, and a lean lurcher.

'*Porgy and Bess*,' Luke jokes. 'Some of my favourite songs.' He begins to sing Gershwin's 'Summertime' and he's actually quite good. We all maintain a respectful silence until Mario suddenly claps enthusiastically and we all join in. Luke bows theatrically.

'You should be in the church choir,' Eva says, patting Bess.

'I am.' Luke beams proudly.

'That's another idea,' I say, nodding at Frances to write it down. 'The choir might sing.'

'I used to belong to a rock choir, we could jazz up some Christmas songs so it's not just carols,' Luke suggests.

'Good idea.' Eva beams.

'We could have some carols though?' Frances smiles and we all agree with her. That's when Kit and Jenna walk through the door.

'Are we late?' Kit asks.

'Not at all, come in…' I offer them a seat and although Jenna sits down, Kit stands, leaning his lanky skinny frame against the glass window.

'What can we do to help?' He pats his stomach. 'Shall I volunteer to be Santa?' he jokes.

Frances reads out the list, 'Santa, procession, Christmas lights, mini Christmas trees, church choir, and a raffle – a hamper and a second-hand mobile.'

Jenna shakes her head. 'It's hard asking people to contribute anything, we've all taken a big hit in the past eighteen months and we've hardly made any money to cover our costs let alone the extras needed for something like this.'

'Covid and lockdown almost finished us,' agrees Kit. 'If it wasn't for furlough I don't know what we would have done but now all the subsidies for rates and taxes are over, we'll have to pay the price for the support we've all had for the past eighteen months.'

'Perhaps we should give Christmas a miss this year?' Derek suggests, and for some reason they all turn to stare at me.

'Well, let's see what we can do,' I say with more optimism than I feel. 'It's early days yet and we still have a few weeks until December.'

Frances checks her watch and it's gone nine o'clock. 'What about Marion, Ben and, Ozan and Yusef?' she asks.

'I don't think they're coming,' replies Jenna.

Feeling deflated and demotivated, by nine-thirty we decide that no one else is turning up and head home.

* * *

When I go upstairs, I find Karl and Molly snuggled up on the sofa watching a film. They move apart, and are about to stand up and turn it off but I wave my hand.

'Please, guys, relax, this is your home.'

'But if you want to watch TV we can…' Karl's voice drifts off. 'How was the meeting?'

'Pretty awful. No one has any money and they have even fewer ideas but hey ho. I'm going to have a shower and an early night.'

They settle back down on the sofa and I'm on my way to the bathroom and I suddenly remember.

'Molly, didn't you lose your job at the caravan site?'

Molly nods. She has dark circles under her eyes.

'Well, perhaps in the morning you could call into Tracey, at the salon next door. She's looking for some help.'

'Me? I've never done anything like that before; treatments and stuff…'

'You can answer a phone politely and take a message, can't you?'

'Oh yes, no problem. I used to do the bookings at the park.'

'Well, she's desperate for a receptionist.' As I turn and walk away I see Molly looking adoringly into Karl's eyes smiling happily.

After my shower, I pull on my pyjamas. The bedroom is much neater and I can even see out of the glass doors and step onto the small terrace. Earlier, I'd admired the rooftops and the distant sea view, now I close the blinds. I like the white walls and I feel I have head space to think. I lie on the bed and open my laptop then rummage in my bag for the CCTV recording that Ozan gave me last week. I can't believe it's taken me this long to dig it out but this time I'm determined to stay awake. It's been a long week, cooking for Eva's family and the scene that followed and then sorting out my own flat, but it's been worth it and strangely, hugely rewarding.

I'm happy that Karl and Molly are cuddled up on my sofa, looking relaxed and comfortable. It's been worth the effort and as I begin watching the picture on my laptop of the grainy image of Harbour Street, I wonder where on earth Ben has gone to and why he keeps disappearing.

It's almost two o'clock in the morning, Karl and Molly have long since gone to bed, and after the sound of them murmuring for a while there are loud snores coming from their bedroom.

My back aches, and I'm tired. I've watched the shop owners closing up for the night, and then I'm amazed at how busy Harbour Street becomes, after dark, as people walk dogs, go jogging and others walk through the street to the fish and chip shop in the harbour. Eventually it all falls quiet. The Ship closes. A few couples walk home and a man stands to urinate outside Freddy's mobile phone shop, only two doors down from the boarded travel agents. I'm thinking how Harbour Street will change if JJ gets her own way, and then two people appear on the screen. They walk toward the café, wearing hoodies and very quickly they each produce a spray can from their pockets and begin to deface my property. The time on the CCTV is 3.05am.

I swing my legs off the bed and sit up.

They work quickly and when one spray can is finished they produce another, making sure they take their empty cans with them.

I hold my bedside lamp closer to the screen, watching their movements, taking in the details of their clothes. One is

225

slightly taller and wears trainers. The other wears a puffy jacket and high heels. They are enjoying themselves and seem to be making comments and laughing. Then one of them turns to look down the street and in that moment I capture her image on the screen and I pause the tape.

'Hello, JJ,' I whisper.

* * *

The following morning once the breakfast rush is over and there's a break in the customers, I dash over to Taylor's Art Gallery. It's quiet compared to the café but a few people are browsing and classical music plays in the background. At the workbench, Ben's head is lowered in concentration as he studies the small figurine in his hand. He looks up and his face breaks into a grin.

'Ah, the Christmas fairy.'

'Karl insisted I bring you coffee,' I say.

'He's a keeper, that one.' He takes the coffee gratefully, removes the lid and blows before sipping slowly. 'So, how did it go last night?'

'You didn't turn up or give us any Christmas ideas.'

'I'm not an ideas type of guy.'

'These are beautiful,' I say, picking up a hand-carved chess piece. 'It's a T-Rex.'

'True, and this is a Triceratops and this is an Allosaurus. I'm still working on the rest.'

'How cool is that. It would make a fantastic Christmas gift.' He smiles tolerantly at me.

'Ah, you're getting ready for the Christmas trade.' I grin.

'I'm doing my best. So, what happened last night?'

226

'It's classified. If you didn't show up, then you don't get to know what's going on.'

'Ah… so the power of being the Christmas Chair has gone to your head?'

'Absolutely, and the only way, you can redeem yourself—'

'Redeem?'

'Yes for not coming and supporting me, is to find me three barrows.'

'What sort of barrows?'

'To put displays on; fruit, veg, that sort of thing.'

He sighs dramatically. 'What makes you think I can do that?'

'You can do anything, Ben. You're the 'go-to' man for this project.'

When he laughs the tension leaves his face and he looks so much younger and happier. His eyes twinkle and he holds my gaze.

I walk over to the door and on way out, I call over my shoulder.

'Oh, and by the way, I'll need them for the first weekend of December for the parade.'

'Okay, I'll do my best, but only if you tell me one thing.'

I pause at the door.

'Did you ever look at Ozan's CCTV?'

I nod and then shake my head. 'Yes, but there was nothing.'

'Nothing?' He looks disappointed.

'Couldn't see a thing, the camera didn't stretch as far as the café, so it's best we forget about it.'

Chapter 21

My next visit is to Sanjay. I wait until he opens for the evening trade at five o'clock and he's standing behind the counter reading a book. He looks up, surprised.

'You're early tonight, Amber. Hungry?'

My phone buzzes and I pull it out of my pocket.

Hey baby, we have to talk. I miss you and I need to speak to you. When are you free? CX

I delete Cassie's message without answering and pocket my phone before turning my attention to Sanjay.

'You remind me of a newsreader on television,' I say.

He grins. 'Because you only see my top half.'

'Exactly.'

'How can I help you?' He hands me a menu but I shake my head.

'I'm cooking for Eva, Karl and Molly tonight. I'm trying out a new recipe.'

'Are you going into competition with me?'

'Nothing compares to your delicious cuisine, Sanjay.'

He grins. 'You are a very charming lady.'

'And you are a very kind young man.'

'I'm not so young, Amber, as you well know. I'm older than

you and perhaps even older than Eva. Can't you tell?' He points to the hair greying at his temple. 'But you didn't come here to pay me compliments, did you?'

'How well you know me.' I lean on the counter. 'I need a favour.'

'No problem, Amber, but on one condition.'

'What's that?'

'I also need a favour.' He tugs on his bottom lip. 'And, I think you are the only person who can help me.'

* * *

Dinner is simple to prepare; rack of lamb with pea jus and mashed potatoes with chives. The mood is happy and we're exchanging silly comments.

'I'm eating like a king,' Karl declares.

'I wasn't sure if I should cook salmon for a main course,' I reply.

'Do you like braised pheasant?' asks Eva.

'I'm not politically inclined,' I joke.

'Murder most fowl...' Eva grins.

'Swordfish?' Karl says.

'That's a great murder weapon,' Molly giggles, and we all laugh.

'Maybe I'll try experimenting with a vegetarian recipe next time.'

Eva wipes her mouth at the corners. 'I'm not sure if the shrimps in Pernod are my favourite or the main course.'

'Definitely the lamb,' Molly says.

'Well, it's a celebration dinner for you, Molly. Congratulations on your new job.'

229

Molly's eyes sparkle as we raise our glasses in a toast. 'I'm so lucky, Amber. Thank you.'

'You deserve it.'

Eva says, 'Tracey came and bought flowers today and she says you worked really hard catching up with all the appointment confirmations. She's really pleased.'

'No, I mean all of this. You're all so kind.' Tears well up in Molly's normally troubled eyes and she looks at Karl who beams back at her. 'You've given us your bedroom, you won't charge us rent, you found me a job and now this delicious meal. My mum never did anything like this for me.'

'Your mum was like my dad.' Karl takes her fingers and holds her hand tightly. 'He was a gambler and your mum was an alcoholic. They only thought about themselves. They were addicts. They couldn't help themselves.'

'You're right. Besides,' Eva says with firmness, 'none of us know what's ahead of us. The past is to learn from, the present is to enjoy and the future is to savour.'

'I'll drink to that – cheers!' I say, raising my glass. 'And thank you for the wine, Molly. It's delicious.'

Molly talks about her job as the receptionist in Tracey's salon and we talk mostly about Harbour Street and the other shop owners.

Karl finishes his dinner and places his knife and fork neatly together. 'Ben's incredible. What he knows about wood and carpentry is amazing. I learnt a lot from him doing up the flat, I really enjoyed it.'

'Have you met Ozan and Yusef?' I ask Molly. 'They're lovely.'

'Yes, Karl took me over there. I wanted to see how they groom him.' She laughs playfully and runs her hand down his cheek. 'I also met Sanjay and he's so gorgeous, really friendly,'

Molly says.

'Sanjay is one of the nicest people,' Eva agrees.

'And he's very attractive, don't you think?' I ask her.

'He looks like one of those Bollywood film stars.' Karl laughs. 'You know the ones, Molly. The music films with all the dancing and singing we watch when you're feeling low.'

'Bhangra, I love the music,' Molly cries. 'The films are uplifting and romantic. Maybe he should start dance classes. I'd love to learn how to move like that. ' She gazes adoringly at Karl.

Eva's mobile rings and as she goes to find her handbag I stand up to clear the plates. Karl stands up to help me but I hold up my hand.

'Relax. This is your night off.'

Karl grins and sits back down at the table.

In the corner of the room, Eva suddenly gasps. She covers her mouth and her face pales as she slips onto the dining chair.

'Oh my God…when…how…?' She listens carefully. 'Okay, yes…of course. 'She ends the call and when she turns to us her eyes are filled with disbelief and tears.

'It's Dad,' she says. 'Dad's – a heart-attack. Just now, an hour ago at home. He's… he's gone…'

I sit beside her and hold her in my arms. Her body is shaking and I wait knowing she's processing this sad news. Karl brings her a glass of water and Molly gives her a tissue.

'I only saw him last week.'

Molly sits on the arm of the sofa gently rubbing Eva's arm, and Karl hovers behind us as we talk quietly about her father and make plans for the coming days.

'I have to go,' she says, standing up.

'Will you be okay? Shall I come with you?' I ask.

'No, thanks. I'll be fine. I said to Mum I'd go straight away. I'll have to contact Emma and Nick.'

'Are you alright? We've all had a drink so—'

'I won't drive. I'll call a taxi and I'll phone Emma and Nick from the car.'

Karl has his phone out and he's already asking for a cab.

'I'm so sorry,' I say while we wait in the street for the taxi. 'I know how much he meant to you. He was a very special man and a wonderful father.'

'Thank you, Amber. I'm pleased you had the opportunity to know him. He was the best.'

As the taxi draws up I pull Eva into a hug and she holds me tightly. 'Thank you,' she whispers, as we pull apart. 'I needed that hug.'

* * *

'Poor Eva,' Ozan says. 'I wish we could help her.'

'I don't like that her shop is closed. The street looks very sad without her display of plants and flowers.' Yusef looks pensively out of the window.

'Well, it's still important that we forge ahead with our Christmas Harbour Street opening on the first Saturday in December,' I say. 'I know you guys missed the meeting and Christmas probably isn't your thing but—'

'You're joking! I love Christmas,' Yusef says brightly. 'I love the kids' faces and the excitement of it all.'

'I was wondering if you had any ideas, we've had a few suggestions from the shop owners.'

'Like what?'

'Well, Kit has volunteered to be Santa...'

232

'How will he get around?' Ozan asks.

'Walk, I suppose. I haven't really got to that bit yet.'

'Well, maybe we could borrow Jack's Harley?' Ozan looks at Yusef.

'Harley Davidson?' I brighten at the thought. 'That would help the procession.'

Yusef leaps up. 'Yes, our cuz has a red one, we could get him to bring Santa on the back of it, that would be cool. The kids would love it.'

'Great idea, if you think he'd do it.'

Yusef punches the air. 'He owes us, man. I'll call him now.'

'We could be outriders,' Ozan suggests, 'We've both got smaller bikes – Yamaha's. We could decorate them and ride in front of Santa and wave at all the kids and throw them sweets and things.'

I smile at their enthusiasm. 'Okay. If you're sure.'

'Man, this is going to be the best Christmas ever, you mean we get to ride in convoy with Santa, man, that's wicked!' Yusef punches the air again and in seconds he's already on his phone talking in Turkish and he puts up his thumb and winks. After he finishes his call he says, 'Can we wear whatever we like?'

'I suppose so. What do you have in mind?'

Yusef grins and taps the side of his nose. 'We've got some great costumes that we wore to a party last week in London that the kids will love.'

'Do you want to tell me—'

'No, definitely not. It will be a surprise.'

'What sort of party?' I ask.

Ozan laughs. 'It was movie-themed.'

That's when I begin to worry what costumes they will wear and what I've let myself in for.

* * *

The night before the Harbour Street Christmas parade and the arrival of Santa on a Harley Davidson, I pop over to the flower shop. Eva has been away all week staying with her mother and organising her father's funeral that's taking place today.

During the week she phoned Pamela to ask for her help with the shop. I hadn't realised they were friends but then I'm not surprised as the Très Chic Boutique is right beside Darling Buds and Blooms.

'I can't afford to stay closed,' Eva had said to me on the phone. 'I'm only sorry I won't be there to help you set everything up but I'll do my best to make it to the parade.'

'Don't worry, Eva. Sanjay, Ben and Karl are amazing. They're all helping and everything is sorted.' It wasn't but I didn't want to stress her unnecessarily.

Eva's shop looks magnificent. There's an assortment of festive gifts; fresh flowers, red and cream poinsettias, decorative watering cans, wellington boots and gardening gloves, as well as colourful pots and a vast array of small cacti.

I'm still uncomfortable after what Pamela had said to me about Ben but I have to put my prejudices to one side so I walk in with a bright smile.

'Hello, Pamela, Eva said the Christmas trees will be here today. Can I help distribute them?'

'Thanks, Amber, but they actually came late last night.' Pamela looks relaxed and confident. 'I've put them out the back, there are so many of them and they are quite heavy so it would be great to have some help.'

'Sanjay, Ben and Karl have offered to help after work. It's

going to be a bit crazy trying to organise everything tonight.'

'I see the lights are up.' Pamela looks happier and younger than when I last spoke to her and she seems a natural in the flower shop, dealing with phone calls and making notes as we speak.

'Sanjay managed to borrow them for us. They normally use them in his cousin's community for Diwali – the festival of light. They hung them up last night and turned them on briefly to test and make sure they work and to be honest, they are spectacular.'

'There's certainly a lot of them.'

She's right. The lanterns hang outside all the shops on both sides of the street. I was a little doubtful at first, there seemed so many, but Sanjay was insistent and he was right. They took my breath away and I stood there speechless at how pretty Harbour Street looked.

'We'll turn them on tomorrow – when it is almost dark and everyone is here for the parade.' I rub my hands, feeling excited.

'Everyone seems very exhilarated, Amber. There's a great buzz in the street and it's already quite busy. I hear some reporter from the radio is coming.'

'Well, that would be fantastic. That would be great publicity. And Harbour Street will look even better tonight when we have all the Christmas trees outside the front of the shops.'

'I've got the decorations for them and I'll sort them when I get a moment, just a bit of tinsel, nothing expensive or valuable but they will be pretty.'

'You're doing a great job, Pamela,' I say. 'Eva will be thrilled.'

'She gave me a one-day crash course when she came to collect her car, before she went back to her mum's, and we labelled everything and she's managed to do all the ordering. All I have to do is wrap everything in red and gold paper, it's simple really.'

'Fab. I'll see you later.'

'Amber, before you go…'

I pause.

'I just want to say, I'm sorry for what I said about Ben.'

I nod but I can't bring myself to reply.

'He was so good to me last night. He saw the delivery truck arrive and he insisted on helping. He carried all the trees and buckets into the shop and he was so lovely, nothing was too much trouble.'

'He's a kind man,' I reply.

'I know that now.'

* * *

When I close the café it's already dark. Kit and Jenna, along with Mario and Luke, are placing two Christmas trees either side of the entrance of each shop in Harbour Street. It's a hive of activity and they are bantering, calling out across the street, teasing each other as to whose decorations look the best. There's a festive mood and when Frances appears she's positively bursting with excitement.

'Have you tested the lights?' she asks, standing beside me, hopping from one foot to the other.

'Yes, we did last night. I think everyone will be amazed – they are incredible.'

'Do you want to run through the timetable of events for tomorrow?'

'Let's do a quick check, if you like.'

'I know you've planned everything to perfection, Amber, but I just want to make sure,' she says.

'I want it to be the best Christmas parade ever.'

'It will be. John Gently is the church organist and his daughter works for the local television. He's trying to get her here for it.'

'Brilliant. That should put Harbour Street on the map for Christmas.'

'Where's Ben?'

'I haven't seen him all day,' I reply.

'I've hardly seen Marion for the past week either,' Frances says, nodding at the closed boutique.

'She's scurried in and out but as JJ isn't involved in any of the Christmas preparations, I think Marion's being loyal to her. Sanjay's put the Christmas trees outside her shop though.'

Frances sighs. 'People should be entitled to have their own relationships and not be coerced into behaving toward other people the way someone else wants them to. Marion was never like this before. I don't understand it.'

'JJ needs her loyal followers.'

'We must be kinder to each other. I just wish JJ was more approachable. But it seems that her way is the only way and if you disagree with her then you're cast out. Everyone has to agree with her or she accuses them of being disloyal and she wants nothing to do with you and you're blanked.'

'Ghosted, is the modern term.'

'Ghostcd?'

'Yes, when you're ignored or someone blocks your calls. It's all part of this social media lingo.'

'Perhaps I should speak to her.'

I smile. Frances isn't wearing her vicar's collar for nothing.

Christmas is an important time in the Christian calendar and she appears very aware of her flock in the town.

'Do you know Marion well?' I ask, then we both turn at the sight of a large white van cruising slowly from the square and into Harbour Street.

'Well, she's stopped coming to church and that concerns me. Oh, who's this driving the big van?'

On cue, Ben leans out of the window. 'I had to hire a van,' he calls.

'Whatever for?' Frances asks.

'To keep madam happy.' He nods at me.

'Me?'

'Yes.' He parks outside the boarded-up travel agents and leaps down. Karl stops helping Sanjay with the trees, and he fist-bumps Ben in greeting and they both disappear to the back of the van.

Frances and I wait, and a few minutes later they emerge pushing a big dray cart; one that used to be pulled by horses, this one is covered in distressed blue paint and has two large rustic wheels.

'Does madam like?'

'Madam does like, thank you,' I reply, matching his sarcastic tone.

'You wanted three of these?'

I grin. 'I expected oversized wheelbarrows. These are proper carts. I'm impressed.'

'Amber, I don't do anything by halves, surely you know that by now.'

He and Karl push the first cart to its position outside the butcher's window then Ben stands chatting with Derek for a few minutes.

'I'm not getting involved as I can see Derek's shock at having to fill such a large display,' I say to Frances.

'Derek will sort it.'

'I don't know how you managed to persuade him to cook hotdogs and burgers tomorrow.'

Frances grins at me. 'Well, let's be honest, Amber, it's about time he stepped up to the plate. He's been supporting JJ's plans and I think this is his way to keep the balance in the community.'

'The power of the church?'

'No, I think he's more frightened of me than of Him.'

We both laugh.

'Wow, the carts are going to look magnificent.' Pamela comes to stand beside us.

'There's two more,' Ben cries cheerfully, as he and Karl head back to the van and reappear with a distressed cart painted red.

'These are beautiful,' I say.

Ben smiles and nods proudly.

'Where's Molly?' calls Karl, as they leave the red cart outside my café.

'She's inside.' I point at the door. 'Helping Jean to prepare the mulled wine and hot chocolate. We're serving drinks from the cart with homemade warm donuts that Lucas will make in the morning.'

Karl grins before going off to help Ben with the third cart painted olive green. Ian carries baskets of fruit and vegetables from his shop, sizing up the space, deciding on the display, and Jane from the jewellers helps him.

'I want to be on duty outside tomorrow,' Karl says, rubbing his hands.

'Mulled wine? I thought you need a licence to sell alcohol,' Jane says, coming up beside us.

'I applied for one a while ago, JJ tried to block it but I have it now,' I reply.

'It was my idea,' calls Karl over his shoulder, as he disappears inside. 'One of my many brilliant ones.'

'You're a very organised businesswoman,' Frances says with approval. 'I knew you'd be good at this.'

'No, the alcohol licence was actually Karl's idea,' I say.

'Harbour Street is looking very festive, aren't we so lucky to have such a fantastic community spirit.' Jane tucks her scarf closer to her neck.

Tracey comes out of the salon and looks around with surprise. 'My goodness, this is going to be incredible tomorrow. What time does it all kick off?'

'We'll open in the morning at the usual time and Kit, AKA Santa, will arrive at four o'clock, the choir will be singing a mixture of Christmas carols and rock songs, then Sanjay will switch on the lights.'

'And, we'll hold the raffle just after that.' Frances checks her notes. 'The donations have been amazing, Amber. We have hampers and everything.'

'What's Ben done with the art gallery?' asks Jane, peering over at the window. 'It looks incredible in there.'

Frances beams. 'He spent last night with Ozan and Yusef turning it into Santa's grotto. So when Kit arrives tomorrow, he will go inside with presents donated by shopkeepers and local people, mostly from the church, and the children can visit him in there.'

'They must be quite jealous in the square.' Jane rubs her hands and grins. 'The smells coming from inside the café are incredible, Amber. I can't wait for you to open tomorrow.'

Chapter 22

On Saturday morning there is heavy cloud and it's bitterly cold.

'It won't rain,' Karl announces, checking his phone. 'But it will be dark early and overcast.'

'Perfect, we will see the lanterns much better in the dark.'

It seems that people have heard about our Christmas parade because by eleven o'clock Harbour Street is rammed. The smell of sizzling onions is carried on the wind, and queues have formed at the dray cart outside the butchers where Derek and his staff are cooking hot dogs and beef burgers. In the middle of the street, a small area is blocked off for the large amplifiers and speakers, and the choir led by Luke is singing Christmas carols. People are stopping to watch and listen and they join in, clapping appreciatively afterwards.

Eva arrives at lunchtime. 'It's so crowded everywhere. It's taken us almost twenty minutes to walk from the clock tower.'

'I didn't think you were going to make it,' I reply.

'Ian is selling raffle tickets like they're lottery tickets.' She's flushed with excitement and nerves and she strides forward and wraps me in a bear hug. 'I feel so guilty,' she says. 'Papa's funeral was only yesterday but Mama insisted we come.'

'Is she alright?'

'My aunt, her sister, is staying with her for the weekend. They will have some special sister-time together.'

Over her shoulder Emma and Nick stroll towards me, jostling between shoppers, and I remember our last unfortunate encounter in Eva's house.

Eva links her arm through mine. 'Everything looks amazing, Amber. You've done a wonderful job. I can't believe these dray carts. Derek and Ian have put out such a wonderful display, and Ian even looks as though he's enjoying himself.'

'It's been the whole community, Eva. I couldn't have done it on my own.'

'Don't the Christmas trees outside the shops look amazing?' Emma says, coming up to us.

'Yes, Pamela has done a great job,' I reply.

'What time are the lights coming on?' Nick asks with a tone of friendliness.

'Four o'clock.'

He checks his watch and when he looks up at me, he says, 'We both want to say we're sorry, Amber.'

'Yes, very sorry,' Emma adds.

Eva smiles proudly at them both.

'That's fine. Let's forget it, shall we?'

'It's taught us not to listen to rumours,' Emma adds, smiling.

'Is there anything Emma and I can do to help?' Nick asks me.

'Now, that's an opportunity I can't turn down, thank you, Nick. One of you can help Jean in the kitchen and the other can help Molly on the cart serving hot drinks until Santa arrives then Molly will go across the road and help in the grotto. She's turning into an elf.'

I nod at Taylor's Art Gallery.

Eva squeezes my arm. 'I'm going to say hello to Ben and take a proper look and see what he's done in there. Oh look, there's Pamela. What a fab display she's done with those cream and red poinsettias. I'll see you guys later.' She unhooks her arm and heads across the street.

Nick and Emma look at me expectantly.

'Come on then, you two. I'll introduce you to your new bosses.'

* * *

The two outriders on Yamahas, Ozan and Yusef, are making their way slowly through the crowd. They are dressed in Batman and Robin costumes, and masks cover their faces.

'You like the outfit?' Yusef shouts to me above the crowd.

'Very handsome,' I call back.

Behind them a massive red Harley-Davidson appears and Kit, dressed as Santa and riding on the back, is waving frantically. His red gloves, white beard and thick padded suit make him unrecognisable.

Outside From The Heart Gift Shop, Jenna stands with their two teenage children Sia and Kanan who are laughing and waving proudly at their adopted father.

'Who would have thought?' Jenna calls over to me, laughing and pointing at her husband.

'It suits him,' I call back.

Ozan blows kisses and the crowd think this is very funny, and a loud cheer goes up as they ride past. They all come to a stop outside the art gallery and excited families gather closer and the younger children push to the front.

Kit manages to swing his leg off the bike, carrying the weight of the Santa suit with expertise. His beard is slightly lopsided and he keeps tugging it back into place which make the crowd laugh more. He pulls up his big black buckle, reaches into his sack and then throws wrapped sweets into the air. They fall like confetti and the younger children scrabble on the ground.

Outside the Kingdom Pets shop the choir has finished their repertoire of Christmas carols and they begin to sing more upbeat Christmas rock songs; 'Santa Claus is Coming to Town', 'Rockin' Around the Christmas Tree', 'Jingle Bell Rock' and 'Feliz Navidad'.

Luke and the other ten singers are swaying and moving with rhythm. They hold microphones and the sound system, on loan from another cousin of the Turkish barbers, carries their joyful voices along the street like a wave of rhythmic euphoria and the crowd joins in, singing along with them.

Outside the closed travel agent, Eva's two Christmas trees in red pots have brought life to the empty façade. There's a sudden gust and a flurry of fake snow is blasted out from a big machine, courtesy of another Turkish cousin. Smaller children giggle and they run to catch it, bending down to gather it in their mittens, wondering at its sudden disappearance.

'I always thought that Diwali was my favourite time of year, Uncle Sanjay, but this is lovely.'

Beside me, Little Umar is holding his Uncle Sanjay's hand.

'Ah, Little Umar, how right you are. It is proper for people to celebrate their own traditions. We perform our ceremonies for Lakshmi, the goddess of prosperity and wealth and we light the world and enjoy family feasts. We share gifts, and we say our puja. We are not so different, my little nephew, kindness and tolerance is in all our teachings.'

245

Ben stands to one side of the art gallery watching the scene unfold before him. He's dressed in a thick, warm jacket and he's maintained his neat beard and tousled short hair. Even from this distance he looks ruggedly handsome, someone who is capable, independent and kind. When he smiles indulgently at the children I can't help but smile too. He sees me and raises his hand and, feeling suddenly self-conscious but happy, I wave back.

Molly, dressed as an elf, is one of Santa's helpers and Jenna and Tracey have also volunteered to guide the children inside to visit Santa. They ask the parents and children to form an orderly queue once the lights have been switched on.

'Uncle Sanjay, did you know that inside Santa's grotto, there's a film of *The Snowman?*'

'We're very lucky, Little Umar, that our Turkish friends have been so generous in lending us their technology.'

'It's on the wall, not even a screen, and it's massive.'

'Yes, Little Umar, it's a special projector that you can set up anywhere to watch a film or a video or any sort of recording.'

'Do you think we can we get one for Christmas?' he asks.

Come on, let's go and ask Santa.' Sanjay pats the boy lovingly on the shoulder and smiles at me before setting off though the crowd toward the grotto.

Outside the café Emma is serving hot drinks. She's wearing fingerless gloves and she's smiling and interacting with the customers. Beside her, couples and families stand holding warm mugs of mulled wine and hot chocolate.

Lucas has been making batches of donuts since dawn, sizzling them in the deep fat fryer until crispy brown and covering them in sugar. They've been a great hit. Now he is standing in the doorway of the café with his wife Aaliyah, and

246

although their baby daughter Sunita is too young to know what's going on, she is alert and gurgling happily in his arms.

When Sanjay switches on the Christmas lanterns there's a gasp of disbelief and then spontaneous applause and laughter ring out. Harbour Street is bathed in the light from lanterns hanging across the shops' awnings and as Batman and Robin fool around everyone cheers and claps harder, I feel an immense sense of pride and pleasure.

'They look incredible.' Ben is suddenly beside me and his presence is reassuring and comfortable.

'Don't they,' I agree.

'You've done a wonderful job, Amber.'

'I couldn't have done it without you or Sanjay.'

'No, that's true.' Ben nudges me with his shoulder and I giggle.

'Well, I probably could have,' I tease.

Santa goes inside the grotto and the crowd breaks up, children queue to visit Santa and the rock choir sings a medley of Christmas tunes, so I take a few minutes to nip inside the café where Jean and Nick are talking, as they work companionably behind the counter.

'Hi, is everything alright?' I ask them.

Jean beams happily. 'It's great to have this young man's help.'

'It's probably the only thing I'm good at; stacking a dishwasher and drying plates.' He casts his eyes up to the ceiling.

I grin. 'Keep up the good work and maybe I'll give you a job in the holidays.'

He puts up a wet thumb.

I head out to the street and behind them I hear their exchange.

'I prefer it in the back here, Jean. Do you?'

247

'Yes, I do.'

'It's like, you don't have to speak to anyone and you can just get on with things…'

* * *

The excitement continues for a few hours then as the temperature drops and visitors begin to leave town we are left clearing up the debris; collecting the discarded trash in the street, taking in the goods from the dray carts and storing away the sound system.

Yusef and Ozan work diligently carrying the expensive equipment back to their barbers.

I glance into the art gallery and see the grotto is empty but I'm drawn to the large film playing on the wall. *The Snowman* is projected along one side of the gallery and it's mesmerising. I stand listening to the well-known tune and I'm lost, transfixed by its beauty and powerful imagery.

'Isn't it a great idea?' Ben says. He stands close to me, our shoulders touching. 'You know, those boys Ozan and Yusef are incredible. They loved dressing up today and being part of it all. I think they've had the best day ever.'

I laugh. 'They're kids at heart.'

'Perhaps we all are.' Ben smiles. 'I mean, there isn't one person here who hasn't enjoyed today.'

'I haven't seen JJ, have you?'

'No, but Marion did come out of the boutique for a few minutes to see Santa.'

'So, even she couldn't resist seeing Kit dressed up, how wonderful.'

Eva calls from the doorway. 'Hey, you guys, Sanjay wants

to invite us all to a takeaway, can we use the café?'

'Of course, how kind of him.'

Eva is looking flushed and happy, and I smile, knowing that Sanjay is pleased she's back home.

'Who has he invited?' asks Ben.

Eva walks in to stand beside us. 'My goodness, that's very powerful to see a film like that so large on the wall.' She rubs Ben affectionately on the arm. 'Everyone is invited. All of us, including you, Ben Taylor. You guys have all worked so hard and I feel so guilty for doing nothing.'

Ben reaches down and gives her a hug. 'I'm really sorry about your father, Eva.'

'Thanks, Ben.' Eva's voice is thick with emotion.

When he straightens up I can see the tears in his eyes and I know he's thinking of his own grief, pain and hurt.

You're never too old to lose a parent. You're never too old to be an orphan.

'Come on then, you two, I'm starving. I could murder a chicken curry,' I say brightly.

* * *

Emma and Molly move the furniture in the café to make one long table down the middle of the room. I find some red paper tablecloths and napkins and Nick produces beer and wine glasses from the kitchen.

'Jean had to leave,' he says. 'She wanted to get home. She was tired.'

'I'm sure she was pleased with your help today, thank you.'

We're distracted as Ozan arrives still dressed as Batman. Yusef is also in his skin-tight Robin costume enjoying the limelight and they make a flying entrance, holding their capes wide and singing the TV theme tune. Yusef runs around the table and it makes us laugh.

'My bro is the main man, 'cos he's the eldest. He's Batman,' Yusef explains. 'I'm the better guy though, the good-looking one.'

'Yeah, yeah.' Ozan punches his brother's arm.

Yusef turns his attention to Kit and slaps him. 'Hey Santa, man. You're looking hot in that gear. You're seriously cool, dude.'

Kit seems relieved when he pulls off his beard and dumps his hat on the table. He rubs his blond hair. 'It itches.'

Jenna steps forward and kisses him on the cheek. 'I like you with a bit of weight on.'

Sia takes his hand. 'I prefer my daddy like this.'

Kanan puts on the white beard. 'Ho, ho, ho.'

Kit laughs.

Frances, Derek and Ian stand to one side of the café talking animatedly and I know they are pleased with the success of the raffle and also the dray carts that Ben provided.

'Harbour Street looks incredible,' Frances gushes.

'Freddy couldn't come this evening, he's gone to see his daughter in Devon,' explains Derek. 'That man barely looks up from his phone but he has a heart of gold. If it wasn't for him the raffle wouldn't have been nearly as successful. We sold so many tickets this year. They all wanted a phone.'

Pamela says, 'Freddy's been here for years and although I hardly see him, he's always very supportive.'

Tracey appears with Des at her side and she whispers,' I hope you don't mind Des coming. I know he hasn't helped much but he's been working so hard and I haven't seen him for ages.'

Des stands with his hands in his pockets and nods at me from a distance. He looks surly and uncomfortable.

'That's not a problem, Tracey, everyone is welcome,' I reply, although I'm not happy to see Des after he ripped me off with the building work in the flat and never finished it.

'Oh, and by the way, thanks for sending Molly to work with me. She's a real treat.'

'She's very happy, Tracey. I'm pleased it's worked out.'

Ben carries in a couple of boxes of wine followed by Jane who announces loudly, 'I haven't done much to help with this lovely day, so the least I can do is to provide the wine.'

For which she receives resounding applause.

Karl twists the caps off the bottles with a flourish, and serves drinks. He places the extra bottles on the table along with water and soft drinks from the café. I fuss around getting people seated and Nick fiddles with the music system and finds a Michael Bublé Christmas CD.

'More Christmas music.' Emma raises her eyes to the ceiling.

Nick grins. 'Suck it up, sister.'

As I busy myself, I overhear snatches of random conversations and Jane is humming to the song about Santa kissing Mommy under the Christmas tree. Luke joins in and so Jane sings louder, encouraged by his earlier performance in the street and they sing along to a few songs until Sanjay and Eva arrive together carrying bags of Indian food.

'It smells delicious,' I cry.

'How lovely.' Frances claps her hands.

'I've worked up an appetite.' Luke pulls out a chair beside Mario, and as we all find a place to sit, the food is soon distributed between us.

The atmosphere and excitement are contagious and we talk about the fun parts of the day, swapping stories and experiences. The banter is funny and fast then Yusef asks, 'Did the TV reporter come?'

'Yes, she did,' replies Frances.

Jane says, 'I saw her too. She was outside my shop at one stage.'

'I served her some hot chocolate,' adds Emma.

'Will I be on TV?' Yusef asks, and pulls out his mobile. 'I'll have to check it out, man. I could be famous.'

'Didn't she interview you, Ben?' Pamela asks.

Ben nods. 'She wanted to know about the grotto.'

'Kit got filmed, didn't you, honey?' adds Jenna, proudly. 'And you said a few words, didn't you?'

'Hot Santa, man,' cries Yusef. 'See the vid here, man.' He raises his phone. 'We made the news, man. Look at us, baby! Wow, those lanterns are awesome – and, this curry is hot, Sanjay-man.'

'Cheers, Sanjay, thank you for this.' Frances raises her glass.

Toasts are made and a cheer goes up for Sanjay. He sits beside Eva smiling happily, nodding in appreciation of our praise and thanks.

Nick and Emma chat happily with Karl and Molly, and as I look around the table I'm overcome with the most incredible sense of belonging. The chatter and banter goes on around me and it's like I drift behind an invisible cloud and the sounds in the room become muted. I see everyone for who they really are and the kindness in this room. It dawns on me then that this is what a community is really like; this is how people of different backgrounds, cultures, experiences and ages all thrive. They help each other. They care. I see how my relationship with them all has matured and grown and developed over these past months. Each of us has a story, each of us has our problems and our dreams and we all face our own daily challenges. We are separate but united together. This is a family like the one I have in Italy. And I'm reminded of my Italian roots and of sunny days, warm Italian piazzas, sitting under awnings at long tables full of food, laugher and fun. And, more importantly, perhaps even love.

Sanjay and Eva's heads are bent together in quiet discussion, and Mario and Luke discussing the merits of owning a mixed-breed as opposed to pure bred dog with Frances. The shopkeepers who have been in Harbour Street the longest, Derek, Ian, Pamela and Jane, have now accepted us. We are all Harbour Street traders and although we may not always agree, I am secretly happy that I have helped with the success of the Christmas parade. I'm proud to be a part of this wonderful community.

Ben is sitting across the table from me and he's smiling at something Yusef has said and he throws back his head and laughs. Then he catches me looking at him and he winks so I wrinkle my nose at him.

'Who's that at the window?' Emma points. 'Do they want to come in?'

The conversation dwindles, and we all look up to see a bewildered face pressed against the glass.

Then, very slowly the door opens.

'Hello?'

'Cassie,' I gasp.

Chapter 23

'I can't believe what you've done to the place,' she says.

We are upstairs in the apartment and Cassie is twirling around like a well-rehearsed film star with a faux fur coat tucked under her chin. Her red, fox-like hair hangs down her back and her eyes are heavily made up. She looks sultry, sexy and very provocative.

'I wish you'd done this when I was here, darling. I wish you'd gone to this trouble then.'

'What do you want, Cassie?'

'Well, to begin with, I think you were very rude to drag me away from the party downstairs. I'd like to have met everyone. Was Marion there? I didn't even get a chance to look.'

When Cassie had opened the door to the café and stepped inside, everyone had fallen silent. I'd grabbed her hand and mumbled something about taking Cassie upstairs for a chat, leaving them to carry on, but Cassie had resisted the pull of her arm.

'The café looks amazing, Amber. This is how I imagined it would look and you've used all my ideas. Look, you even have the orange lights.'

I'd pulled her hand then she'd shrieked, 'Karl is that you? OMG.' She had leaned over his seat and wrapped her arms around his neck as if he was a dying friend. 'Karl!' she cried dramatically.

Poor Karl's eyes were wide with fright and once he'd removed Cassie's arms, he'd looked embarrassed and shy, as Molly looked on with an open mouth.

Cassie went sullen. 'Don't you remember me, Karl?'

'Come on, Cassie,' I'd said sternly. 'Upstairs! Now!'

In the flat she wanders around and pushing open the bathroom door she whistles. 'You've made a real go of this, haven't you, Amber?'

She pulls off her coat revealing a tight black skirt and cream blouse. 'I came straight after the matinee. I had to see you. Why haven't you answered my messages?'

'I've been busy. Why aren't you on stage tonight?'

'I didn't feel well. The understudy is taking over.' Cassie flops on the sofa, crosses her legs and looks around. 'You've changed everything, baby. It all looks much cleaner and neater.'

I pour water from the tap and stand at the sink drinking. I need a clear head.

What is she doing here?

Outside, the shop owners from downstairs are spilling out into Harbour Street, saying muted goodbyes, and there are hugs and air kisses as they go their separate ways.

Yusef calls out and suddenly he's racing down the middle of Harbour Street with his arms wide and his cape taut behind him, singing the theme tune of Batman.

'Why are you hiding in the kitchen?' Cassie's voice comes from the door way.

'I'm not hiding but I'm tired, Cassie, so cut the crap. Why are you here?'

'I thought I'd get a better welcome than this.' She sulks.

'Why—' I can't finish, I'm confused seeing her again.

Cassie whispers softly, 'Look, I'm really sorry, but I miss you, Amber.'

I look at her pouting in the doorway and I wonder if it's a scene she's rehearsed in her mind, as if she's playing a part in a blockbuster film.

'You didn't miss me eight months ago when you went off to London.'

'I know, but I was lonely here. If it wasn't for Marion and JJ, my life would have been hell.'

I bristle at the mention of their names.

'Anyway,' she says brightly. 'I couldn't believe the coincidence, I was on the train down here and then I saw the local news. Westbay was on television, and the reporter was interviewing Santa and some other residents in Harbour Street. It looked amazing. Really cool with all the lights and lanterns and the little Christmas trees at the shop doors. It's cute like a film set, and there was even snow.' She laughs. 'You had a snow machine?'

I smile. 'It was spectacular.'

'Have you any wine?' she asks.

I find half a bottle on the kitchen counter and pour her a small glass of Rioja.

'Are you not drinking?'

'No, I've a busy day tomorrow.' I fold my arms.

'Come and sit with me on the sofa and let's catch up. I'm dying to hear everything.'

I walk with her into the lounge but I pause to look down into Harbour Street where Ben is letting himself into the art gallery. I think of all the work he's done, turning his shop into Santa's grotto, then making the three dray carts, helping Pamela and putting up all the lights with Sanjay.

'Are you even listening to me?' she moans.

'I'm not sure why you're here, Cassie. So just tell me the truth.'

'Are you moving back to London?' she asks.

'Why?'

'I miss you and I want you back. And Scruff-bucket needs you.'

* * *

Cassie is surprised when, an hour later, Karl knocks apologetically on the door. 'I'm really sorry, Amber.'

'Nonsense, this is your home, come in, Karl, and you too, Molly. Cassie and I will go downstairs.'

'Really, we can—'

'No, Karl, please. You must both be exhausted.'

There's an awkward moment when we all pass each other in the narrow hallway. We murmur goodnight as we brush past each other and I push Cassie downstairs into the café. She's clearly bewildered.

'What's going on? Is Karl and that other girl staying here?'

'Yes.'

'Why?'

'They were evicted from the caravan park.'

'But—'

'But what?' I ask angrily, flicking on the kettle in the café's kitchen.

'But, how long are they here for?'

'I don't know and it's not important.' I sigh. 'They needed a place to stay and I have a spare room.'

'But that's our room.'

'No,' I say firmly. 'It isn't *our* room. You left, remember.'

'I made a mistake.'

'You've made a lot of mistakes, Cassie. You don't know what you want.'

'I do now.'

I place our coffee on the table in the back of the café, away from the window and the street lamps, and I light a candle.

'Very romantic,' she says, reaching for my hand. Her voice lowers and in the half-light she whispers, 'Do you remember last summer when we came here? We were so in love and I chased you into the sea and I've never seen you so happy…'

We spend the night talking and the following morning, when it's still dark, I walk her to the station and she leaves on the early London train.

* * *

'Since the Christmas parade was on the television, interest in the town has surged and in particular the quaint little road called Harbour Street.' The estate agent, Charlie, is positively jumping up and down with delight.

I guide him to the back of the café so we can have some privacy from the curious customers and staff who are still happily remembering the events of the Christmas parade.

'They love Harbour Street and look at it, Amber. It's packed with Christmas shoppers all buying presents for the festive season. It's incredible. It's prime real estate.'

As I take Charlie upstairs, I feel Jean, Lucas and Karl's eyes on us but I take no notice. I'm still buoyed-up from the success of the Christmas parade last weekend and now the excitement of possibly selling the café.

'I think everyone is very happy with how it all worked out,' I reply.

'And so they should be. We'll have this off your hands by Christmas,' Charlie says, rubbing his hands. 'We've a viewing today and clients are coming back for a second viewing tomorrow. It's all very positive.'

'That's great. You have a key but please check with Karl first.'

'Karl?'

'He's staying here and I'm going up to London later. I may not be back in time.'

He nods seriously. He looks like a boy in a grown-up man's three-piece grey suit, and I wonder if we can sell my property before we close for the holidays.

'Did you hear about JJ?' Charlie asks, standing at the window and nodding at the travel agents. 'She's finally got the planning permission for that building. She's going to open the amusement arcade. You'll be pleased to have that eyesore opposite gone, won't you?'

'Is that definite?' I stand beside him and gaze out of the window at the boarded-up building.

Beside it, Ben is opening up his art gallery and Eva's flowers are already prominently displayed in the street.

'Amber?'

'Yes.' I turn from the window.

'Will you take an offer on this property? I've a good feeling about today.'

'Let's see what happens,' I say, checking my watch.

I don't want to miss the train.

* * *

My old office looks austere yet polished; glass, chrome, shiny and sleek and very much like its owner Ralph Stewart, my ex-boss. He's dressed in a light brown suit and matching check waistcoat. There are expensive cufflinks on his wrists as well as a heavy gold ring on his pinkie.

He greets me like an old friend, taking my shoulders firmly and kissing me on both cheeks.

'Come in, come in, Amber. It's lovely to see you. You've cut your hair, it suits you.'

He ushers me into his office and I'm still impressed with the view from the tenth floor and the double-fronted aspect of the Thames and the whole of London stretched out before me. My office was a few doors along the corridor and I remember the view of the skyline, the Embankment and the London Eye, with a mixture of excitement and nostalgia.

Ralph presses an intercom, which seems old-fashioned, and orders coffee. While we wait we make small talk until his PA, who I've never met before, brings coffee and biscuits. Although she gives me a sidelong curious glance, he doesn't introduce us.

'So, Westbay seems to agree with you now. You look much better, Amber. How's it all going?'

I spend a few minutes bringing him up to date with the café and Harbour Street and finish with the successful parade and Santa arriving on the back of a Harley, and the Christmas lights switch-on.

'You seem to have made a go of it.' He nods approvingly, smiling broadly. 'You've tapped into your business skills.'

'I think you're right but I never knew it could be so

problematic, the politics of a small street are—'

His phone rings and he's distracted.

'Sorry, Amber. I should have put that on silent but I am waiting for an important call. As you were saying…'

But I've lost my thread. My train of thought has been diverted and I remember all those important calls from clients, from sources to support the case, private investigators, people in offices and working in jobs who provide the right information that could crack a problem wide open and suddenly my heart is ringing with excitement. The thrill of a new case, the weight of the yellow files and the painstaking problem-solving into the night.

'Do they have a mayor?' Ralph asks suddenly.

'A mayor?' I repeat.

'In Westbay?'

'Yes, there is one, but there's a pub landlady who's a narcissist and she's bullied most of the town for years.'

'Really? And you're letting her get away with that?' He laughs. 'I'm surprised. That was always one thing that you hated, bullying. You used to be like a Rottweiler going after some of our clients. You can be very feisty, Amber, so I can imagine you're giving her a run for her money.'

I'm surprised and disappointed at his appraisal of me. 'She's actually really nasty. She sprayed racist and homophobic graffiti over my shop window.'

He taps his fingernail on the desk.

'That's an offence,' he says. 'A prison sentence. What did you do?'

'Nothing.'

'Have you gone soft? I always remember you having a strong sense of justice, of right and wrong. You would fight to the end and it would take a lot to beat you. You were good at your job but it was your integrity and sense of right and wrong that was your strength.'

'I'm still like that,' I say, and I tell him about the time I confronted Marion and JJ in the boutique.

He laughs at my account and my descriptions, and I remember how amenable he is and how charming he can be. He's also a good listener which is essential in our line of business. When he takes another quick call and leaves the office, it gives me time to reflect on some of the cases I've worked on; all commerce related, merchandising, trade and sales. My initial role as a junior in the company was to deal with merchant shipping, accident and insurance, and after a ship had caught fire in Canary Wharf, I had successfully won the case. It had involved a lot of research in the legal battle to prove a fault in the ship's wiring. People had lied and I'd been determined to fight and find out the truth. Afterwards there had been a substantial payout and my reputation had been secured and my path to the top was inevitable. A partnership.

Until Cassie.

I stretch my back and neck, and yawn with satisfaction, feeling comfortable in my environment. I love the challenge of a new case, reading, researching, rooting through the finest detail to find deliberate errors, lies, cover-ups, simple mistakes or to find the legal support in the appropriate laws. It was in my blood, as much as cooking Italian food was in my soul.

I smile. This is my family. This is my tribe.

That's when Ralph comes bounding into the room with renewed energy and I can smell the scent of a new case and my senses are stirred.

I want to be involved.

'So, Amber. Tell me. How's the sabbatical going?'

'This is what I want to speak to you about.'

He smiles. 'Good. We can't wait to have you back.'

Chapter 24

The next few days are quite bizarre. During the day, the café is busy and it seems everyone is too preoccupied and engrossed in their work to make small talk. Karl and Molly are out most nights, either at the cinema or they go out for a meal. One night they even drive up to London to visit Karl's mum and I begin to wonder if they're avoiding me.

When I pop over to Darling Buds and Blooms, Eva is always busy showing Pamela more details of shop life, and they huddle together in the back room too busy to talk.

'Is it urgent, Amber? I'm showing Pamela how we do orders.'

'No, I can pop back.'

I put my hand against the glass window of the art gallery to shade my eyes and peer inside. Although Ben has dismantled the grotto, the shop is closed and when I get back to the café, I ask, 'Has anyone seen Ben?'

Jean is the only one who looks up. 'No.'

'I wonder where he's gone.'

'You know he often disappears.'

'He's been closed for a few days now.'

Jean shrugs.

Karl and Lucas ignore me.

Feeling disconcerted, I wander over to the pet shop. Luke

264

is serving a customer and Mario dives into the storeroom. In From The Heart Gift Shop, Kit and Jenna are busy unpacking boxes, stocking shelves and serving customers.

'We've been so busy.' Kit turns away and I have a feeling he's avoiding any further conversation.

It's the same with Jane the jeweller, Ian the grocer and Derek the butcher. It's only Freddy who hasn't changed, he just looks up, smiles, and returns to his work – as usual.

I stand in Harbour Street looking at the new sign hanging up across the window of the boarded-up travel agency.

UNDER NEW MANAGEMENT
COMING SOON – AMUSEMENT ARCADE

They were right, JJ got her own way, and I decide this is what is upsetting everyone.

* * *

After the second week in December the local mood hasn't improved. Everyone seems sullen and quiet, and while I chivvy them along, trying to be festive, they are unresponsive and often ignore me.

I'm in the café kitchen when my mobile rings.

'Amber?' says Charlie. 'Good news. I've got the price you want.'

I've forgotten that my mobile phone is on loudspeaker so while Lucas is serving Hungarian stew, and Jean is buttering bread for sandwiches and Karl is making coffee, they all hear the news at the same time.

'Will I say yes to them?'

I barely pause. 'Yes.'

After I hang up Jean stares at me. Her eyes are dull and her mouth is set in a firm line.

'Charlie's sold the café,' I say.

'So I heard,' she replies, turning away and carrying the sandwiches to the table in the café.

I grab my jacket and head outside. My plan is to tell Eva but in the flower shop Pamela tells me she's gone to the garden centre as they've run out of decorative vases.

'But I hear you're leaving,' Pamela says.

'That news travelled fast, I've only just heard myself. Charlie's literally only just called me to say he's sold it,' I reply.

She stares at me, not smiling.

'Oh? I didn't know you'd sold the café,' Pamela replies.

'Then how did you know I was leaving?'

'Well, everyone knows. Cassie came back and you've been up to London a couple of times. Eva thinks your sabbatical has come to an end.'

'They all know I've been up in London?'

'It's a small town and even Ben said he saw you on the train yesterday.'

'Is he back?'

'Yes.'

* * *

Ben is carrying wood from the stockroom to his workbench in the far corner of the gallery. He doesn't look surprised to see me or particularly happy.

'Hi, Ben. How are you?'

'I'm fine.'

266

'I didn't know you were back.'

'So?'

'Oh for heaven's sake, don't you turn monosyllabic on me as well.'

He frowns.

I continue, 'It's like the whole atmosphere of Harbour Street has changed. Everyone seems annoyed with me or they're ignoring me. What's happened since our successful Christmas parade when everyone was so happy?'

He looks at a piece of wood carefully, turning it in his fingers, concentrating.

'Would you please tell me, Ben? What's going on?'

He looks up and I see his beard has grown; he hasn't shaved for a while and there are dark circles around his eyes.

He sighs. 'They think that you arranged the Christmas parade to suit yourself, that you did it to get on TV so that you could sell the café. They all feel used and betrayed.'

'But that's not true.'

'Isn't it?'

'Is that what you believe too?'

'The evidence points that way.'

'Since when were you a bloody criminal lawyer?' I say angrily and his face darkens. 'I'm sorry, Ben, but that's not fair of them,' I moan.

'Life isn't fair, Amber. Get used to it.'

'What's happened to you? I thought we were – we are friends, and Eva, she's been avoiding me too.'

'She's upset. Can't you see that?' He throws his hands in the air and the wood crashes on the bench. 'Everyone's upset, Amber.'

'Why, because they think I was promoting my own business?

267

Well, for your information, and you can tell 'all' the people from me, I only wanted to help Harbour Street. I didn't even want the job. It was Frances who insisted. No one wanted JJ to be involved after her last disaster at Halloween. For heaven's sake,' I shout. 'It was a success for everyone. We all benefited and just because I've had an offer on the café, it doesn't mean that I'm the only one to make money from it. Everyone's doing great business-wise and it's still very busy. And besides all of that – it was *fun*. It brought together the whole community.' I'm running out of steam and I lower my voice. 'It was so magical, with us all working together to make it a success and with Santa and Batman and Robin.' I laugh, and unwelcome tears burn my eyes. 'And then the meal that Sanjay provided in the café for us and the fun we were all having...'

'Exactly,' he says quietly. He stares intensely at me.

'What do you mean?'

'And then Cassie turned up.'

'What's this got to do with Cassie?' I explode.

Ben picks up the wood and tosses it in his hands. 'You're obviously going back to London, Amber, so just cut the crap and leave everyone to get on with their lives.'

* * *

I wait until I see Darling Buds and Blooms closing up for the night and then I head across the street.

'Eva,' I say. 'I must speak to you.'

'You'd better hurry up, I'm going out.'

'Sorry, I don't want to hold you up.'

'What is it?' Her face is serious and she's obviously in a

hurry; either she has a date or she doesn't want to speak to me.

'Everyone is being very unfriendly with me and Ben says it's because the shop owners think I arranged the parade so that I could sell the café. You know, the fact that the parade was so successful and it was on television. Is that true? Is that what they think?'

'You tell me, Amber. Have you sold the café?'

'Yes.'

'And did the buyers see Harbour Street on television?'

'Charlie said they did. Yes.'

'Then it's not rocket science, is it?'

I feel my anger stirring inside. 'But the café has always been for sale. It's a coincidence.'

Eva puts her hand on my shoulder.

'Look, don't worry about it, Amber. You've sold the café, it's what you want. You can go back to London and by this time next year everyone will have forgotten and you won't even remember you lived here.'

'But they're all upset with me. They probably think I'm like JJ.'

Eva closes the drawer from behind the counter and looks up.

'Well, there's that too. Lots of us are upset about JJ getting the planning permission through. We don't want an amusement arcade. Then she hangs that dirty great sign across the window to ram it all down our throats. To be honest, Amber, I think that because the parade was so successful they all thought, or assumed, you'd have the courage and you'd challenge JJ.'

'Challenge her?'

269

'Yes, you're a lawyer. A commercial lawyer, and they thought you'd do it for them, for Harbour Street and for the town.'

I stare at Eva, confused.

She continues, 'I think they thought you were their saviour but you're not. And now it's all too late to stop her. As we both know, nothing ever works out how you plan it.'

I rub my hand through my hair. 'You can't keep rejecting a business proposal unless there's a legitimate reason not to open it. It's up to the City Council – not me.'

'They don't see it that way.'

'But everyone is so angry with me, even Ben—'

'Ben is a different matter.'

'Different, why?'

'Because Ben cares about you – a lot. You've helped him get back into the community and to be accepted and to belong here again.'

'I didn't do that. He's a good person. He's lovely and he's kind.'

'So are you, Amber. You don't realise how many people you've helped; Karl, Molly, Ben, Lucas and of course, me.'

I sigh. 'So why the hell is everyone so pissed off with me?'

'For one very simple reason. You're our friend. We don't want you to go.'

* * *

The beach is cold and windy. The pebbles are hard to sit on and they dig into my skin but I don't care. I snuggle behind the breakwater with my coat zipped to my neck and my arms wrapped around my waist. The wind whips around my head and then I hear a voice calling and I look out to sea where, on the horizon, red lights from ships are passing in the night. 'Like friendships,' I mutter miserably. 'Like bloody friendships.'

'Amber?'

My body stiffens.

'Amber?'

I hear the crunching of boots on pebbles and a huge figure comes out of the darkness and hunkers down beside me.

'I thought I saw you coming this way. Are you alright?'

'Ben.' I sigh.

'What are you doing out here? It's cold.'

'What do you want?'

He sits beside me and stretches out his legs. 'I need some fresh air too.'

'Why?'

He doesn't reply and his eyes concentrate on the horizon. 'It's been a tough few days.'

'You disappeared again?'

'Yes.'

'Where do you go?'

'I go back to prison.'

'What? Why?' I glance at his ankle and he smiles.

'I don't wear a tag if that's what you're thinking. I go back to help the others.'

'What others?'

'The ones I left behind.'

'I don't understand.'

He folds his hands together and rests them on his legs as if he's not cold and I lean closer to him, taking refuge and comfort in his solid presence.

In the half-light he speaks quietly.

'I believe that out of everything bad comes something good. When I was in prison, I was lucky to be able to use my crafts and skills to teach others. Carpentry is one of the oldest skills and traditions and, to be honest, it's the one thing I'm good at. I ended up teaching lots of men, boys... some of them just kids really. And, I know that when some of them come out they are not as lucky as me. I had a home to come to. I had a town where I grew up and spent most of my life, but some of them have nothing; no one waiting for them and nowhere to go. So, I created a workshop, it's a social venue as much as it's a carpentry workshop. It's somewhere where they can belong and they can practise their carpentry skills so they don't feel it was all a waste of time.'

'Like a charity?'

'Yes.'

'And they make things?'

'It's early days yet. I only began this project in the summer.'

'But that's where you go?'

I can feel his smile in the darkness.

'I've self-funded a lot of the project but I've been trying to raise money. I want to apply for charity status and get some grants and financial help – although it's tough at the moment.'

'What a kind thing to do.'

'Those three dray carts in Harbour Street were made by the guys in the workshop.'

'Really?'

He nods and smiles proudly. 'It gave them a purpose to build those. I showed them the news programme and photographs afterwards and they loved it. They were really proud of themselves.'

272

'It's no wonder you look tired, working here and going back to London.'

He yawns, rubs his cheek and scratches at the stubble.

'I haven't slept. One of the boys, Larry, went missing. He's a troubled soul and he didn't turn up as he usually did, so I went out with the homeless charity on the streets looking for him.'

'Did you find him?'

'Yes, he'd passed out – drugs again – but we got him to hospital.'

'Will he be okay?'

Ben shrugs. 'I hope so, we can only support him. He's twenty-five, and he's had a tough time. He's in and out of rehab. He steals to feed his addiction. It's an ongoing story and there are lots of them like it, men, women – some of them just children. And most of the time it's quite overwhelming.'

He wipes his eyes with the back of his hand.

'You're a kind man,' I whisper.

'For a lot of them, it's just a case of muddling through life; surviving each day.'

'It shouldn't have to be like that.' I reach out for Ben's hand and I'm comforted by his strength and warmth as I squeeze his fingers. 'You've had a tough time too. Who cares for you?'

He doesn't answer.

In the darkness I ask quietly, 'Did you read your mother's letter yet?'

He shakes his head.

'Then maybe it's time you did, Ben. I think it might help you.'

Chapter 25

It's one week until Christmas Eve and I can't sleep. I lie awake most of the night thinking about Ben and the homeless on the streets in the cities in England and abroad. I think about Karl and Molly in the other bedroom, Nick and Emma and the next generation. I think about Eva's divorce from James and how Sanjay looks at her, Ben's kindness and Lucas's new baby daughter Sunita. I think about the years Derek, Ian, Jane and Frances have lived here and the changes they've seen. And I smile in the darkness when I remember Ozan and Yusef in their fancy dress costumes.

I close my eyes, and printed in my memory is Harbour Street Café, my café, the clock tower leading to the harbour and The Ship; half in Harbour Street and the other half in the square. I think of JJ and the development across the road and I see Marion's drunken smile when she was with Cassie in the pub. Before Cassie left me and took Scruff-bucket.

Then I remember what Ralph had said to me, that I was driven by the need to fight for those that couldn't defend themselves. I was someone who would help those who aren't always in a position to help themselves. The strong must care for the weak. Fight for what you love, believe in, and for justice.

I shower and dress, and when I leave the flat Karl and Molly are sleeping.

Downstairs, it's still dark and I spend half an hour in the café and measure the Italian prints hanging on the wall and check a few apps on my mobile.

As light dawns and the town stirs, I make my way to the north end of town, away from Harbour Street and further from the square and I'm first in the queue waiting for the shop to open.

I have a plan and I need to get things right. My legal brain kicks in and I focus on the details. This is important. Everything must be exact. They must be the right size.

It's mid-morning when I call into the Turkish barbers and the boys are busy.

Yusef doesn't smile or joke, and he barely looks at me.

I ignore his rudeness. I know he's hurt.

'I need a big favour,' I whisper to Ozan. 'Will you trust me?'

He listens carefully and although he says nothing, he disappears into the back room to get me what I need. When he returns with the box he doesn't smile. There is no warmth from them either of them but I'm grateful they are still generous and kind to me.

While the café is busy downstairs, I wait upstairs in the flat. After making the first phone call, I make notes and then I phone Ralph Stewart at mid-day.

At one o'clock I venture down into the café and give Karl a voucher.

'What's this?'

'This is my thank you, to you and Molly. I've booked a table for you tonight, be ready for seven o'clock.'

He opens the envelope. 'But, Amber. This is crazy. It's for

one of the best restaurants. It's so expensive.'

His smile is unsure. It's also one of complete disbelief.

'I've ordered a taxi for you, there and back. Enjoy it and order whatever you like. And, make sure you both get dressed up. Think of it as a special date together.'

It's mid-afternoon when I call into The Ship with a hand-written note for JJ.

I go back to the café and wait patiently for the café to close and for Karl and Molly to go out for dinner.

Then I do what I should have done a long time ago.

* * *

The café is subtly illuminated and I've made some changes to the layout of the room. I go over my plan then I sit at the table in the middle of the café. When she taps on the glass door, I stand up, straighten my shirt, and open the door.

'JJ, thank you for coming.' I smile professionally and wave her inside as if she's my client.

Outside it's blowing a gale and raindrops are falling heavily. I'm pleased. It makes Harbour Street quieter. No one wants to go out on a night like this which means no one will notice the lights on in the café.

I lock the door softly behind her.

'What's this all about?' she demands.

JJ wears a short bomber jacket over blue jeans and an open-necked shirt. There's a silver cross pendant hanging around her neck. Her nails are painted red and her fingers are adorned with chunky costume rings.

'Would you like coffee or a drink?' I ask.

'No, I'm fine.'

'Please sit here.' I indicate to the chair opposite me. She's facing inwards, toward the kitchen with her back to the door.

She hesitates and so I sit down.

'So, what do you want, Amber?'

JJ's face is heavily made up and her dark eyeliner makes her look like an imitation Egyptian goddess. 'It's busy in the pub and I haven't got long.'

'Look, I just wanted to find out what you're going to do with the building opposite. I've heard rumours of course, but to be honest, I'd like to ask you directly. You see, it will affect me a lot.'

'Well, you've seen the sign I've put up. The building is an eyesore and everyone agrees with me. It can't lie vacant and boarded up any longer—'

'I agree with you, JJ. Have you thought about designs or colours or even a timeframe of when you'll start?'

She stares at me, pulls out the chair and sits down. 'I can't believe you're interested. I thought you were one of the shopkeepers against me.'

'We haven't always got on, that's true.'

'Well, to be honest, Amber, I thought you were jealous of me. I had a really good relationship with Cassie. She was really lovely, kind and sort of vulnerable. Not like you. You've always been rude and you're not a kind or very nice person. Over these past few months you really have been quite aggressive and antagonistic—'

I smile. 'Is that why you sprayed graffiti all over my café windows?'

She barely pauses. 'I didn't do anything of the sort.'

'You're lying, JJ.'

She stands up and pushes her hands in her pockets. 'Is this

why you've asked me here, so that you can make up lies?'

I reach out for the cord at my fingertips, lying on the table, and as I pull it toward me the material covering three giant canvases falls away and the photographs are revealed. I've even adjusted the café spotlights so they illuminate and highlight the printed images of the scornful faces.

JJ's eyes narrow and she regards them closely in silence. They take up almost one length of the entire café. In the first frozen image, a screen shot from the CCTV, JJ is dressed in a hoodie. She's pulled out a spray can from her pocket. Her accomplice in high heels has done the same.

In the second image, their words are very clear; inflammatory, accusatory, racist and homophobic.

In the final image, nearer the door, I managed to freeze the frame of the assailants' faces; JJ and Marion.

There's no doubt it's them.

'This is ridiculous.' She looks at the last one for a few seconds before turning back to me then very slowly she smiles.

'You've superimposed these images. It's photographic trickery. You can do anything these days with a camera and a computer.'

'I thought you might say that.'

I pick up the remote from the table and flick a switch. On the white wall opposite the canvas prints, I've taken down the blackboard with Today's Specials and the film comes to life.

Instead of *The Snowman*, I've plugged in the USB with the CCTV. It shows JJ and Marion running down the street, pulling spray cans from their pockets and writing their filthy words on my café window. Marion is tottering on high heels. JJ pulls her hoodie over her face. Then they turn to look down the street and, in that moment, their images are captured. I've frozen their faces for a few seconds. There is no doubt.

'How did you…?'

'CCTV,' I reply.

She shakes her head in disbelief. 'This is—'

'You see, JJ. You can't hide who you really are. If your nastiness is ingrained then the truth will always come out in the end. This is a criminal offence and you could both go to prison.'

She's like a marble statue, standing still, staring at the moving image of herself defacing my property.

'You're a liar,' she hisses.

'And you are racist and homophobic and, just for the record, your accusations are both offensive and filthy. I'm neither straight nor gay. I don't need a label. I fall in love with the person. And, Karl maybe black and proud, but Eva is not gay and we've never been lovers and, more importantly, none of these despicable bigoted things you wrote are legal. This is a heinous crime.'

'We don't want people like you here,' JJ spits. 'You're a blow-in, go back to London, Amber.'

'Why don't you tell me about Toby Johnson?'

'Toby?'

'Yes, you remember him, don't you? You were his carer twelve years ago in Devon. You looked after him and, after he died, he conveniently left you his life savings.'

'What? How did you – you can't prove anything—'

'What should I prove? I'm just saying that's where you got the money to buy The Ship.'

'He left me that money,' she says angrily.

'Yes, but ten years ago you were using the same tactic on William, weren't you? You played on his anxiety and

279

depression and you manipulated him, so he signed over the garage to you at a value far less than the market price, but Ben found out, didn't he?'

JJ stares up at the moving images. I have the film on a loop. JJ and Marion are running off into the night but they come running back out of the darkness again, pulling the spray cans from their pockets.

'You're lying,' she says, unable to take her eyes from the film and the absolute proof of her actions.

'You framed Ben. You accused him of stealing money from the pub and then, in a moment of bravado that you seem always to think you can get away with…' I point at the screen and the abusive words they are spraying on my windows. 'You caused a public argument with him and forced him to lose his temper, then you set light to your own pub and planted evidence at Ben's flat to incriminate him. Were you so angry because he wouldn't sleep with you? Or because you were so desperate to get hold of the garage so you could develop that piece of land into your pub patio?'

'How dare you?' She lunges for me but I side-step, move behind the table and hold up my hand.

'Careful, JJ. You don't want to commit any more crimes.'

She stops and glares at me, her hand on the back of the chair as if she's about to pick it up and hurl it at me. Her face is full of fury, her eyes blazing and her lips curled like an angry hyena.

'How do you think your reputation will stand up after I show all this to the town? I can upload this video to just about every platform on social media in five minutes and the whole world will see it. You will be finished here. Everyone will know what you're really like. Here's the proof. Here's the evidence that the landlady of The Ship is racist and homophobic. That won't go down very well, will it? It's hardly good for business and I'm sure the brewery wouldn't be too happy. Everyone will know the real you. You poison people, JJ. Even when Emma and Nick called into the pub you had to spread your lies about me and Eva. And poor Karl, who has done so much for this community, doesn't deserve to be treated like this. You wrote some awful things, JJ.'

'I didn't mean it.' She shakes her head and hugs her bomber jacket closer to her waist. 'I didn't. It was—'

'Which part didn't you mean? The graffiti or ruining Ben's life? Sending an innocent man to prison? Knowing his mother and father both died while he was locked away because of your lies? Or continuing to treat him badly when he came back to Harbour Street, spreading more lies to ruin his reputation and business?'

'I never expected him to come back. He wanted to go away, so I just—'

'He wanted to travel, not go to prison. Why did you send an innocent man to prison?'

'It all just got out of hand. He wouldn't support me. He wouldn't persuade William to…' She sits at the table and puts her head in her hands. When she wipes her eyes, she leaves a streak of mascara across her cheek. 'Then when he did come back here, he started sitting in the pub every night. He'd just stare at me. You've no idea what I've been though, Amber. It's been torture for me. His father even came into the pub once to plead with me, Ben's mother was dying but I had no idea. I didn't know until it was too late… I feel so awful. '

'William took his own life,' I whisper, 'because of you.'

'I didn't know what to do,' she whimpers.

281

I fold my arms. 'You could have told the truth.'

Her eyes darken and her mouth is set in a furious straight line. Suddenly she stands up and hurls the chair to one side. 'You can't prove any of this, you stupid bitch!'

'I have the private investigator's report about Toby and I think these pictures and this CCTV are perfectly adequate for the police.'

'Where is the tape?' She begins frantically looking around for the projector that I borrowed from Ozan.

I stand watching her and my tone is measured and calm. 'Even if you do find it, I have plenty of copies, JJ.'

She bites her lip before answering. 'Okay, what do you want?'

'I want you to stay away from the travel agents building. I want you to sell it. No one wants an amusement arcade in Harbour Street.'

'No.'

'I think you will.'

'And if I don't?'

'You know what I'll do, JJ. I'm a lawyer.'

We stand facing each other and I'm conscious of the scene still playing on a loop on the wall. She's spraying my windows in red letters over and over again and again and again.

'This is blackmail,' she hisses.

'No, this is reality.'

'If I agree, will you give me the CCTV and the canvas images?'

'No.'

'You'll never prove this. I'll fight you every inch of the way.' She turns away and heads to the door. 'You're dead, Amber. You're so bloody DEAD.'

'Oh, JJ, I forgot to tell you. Before you go there's one more thing.'

She turns, her face is full of hatred and also fear.

I point up to the mini camera above the counter that I put up an hour ago in the corner of the café.

'I've been recording all of this. So, I have your confession and your threat. It's all nicely filmed so I can upload this to social media or take it to the police.'

She fumbles for the lock.

I call out, 'The choice is yours, JJ. No one will trust you or even like you when they know the damage you've done to so many lives.'

'Fuck you, Amber.'

'You wish.'

The door slams in her wake.

Chapter 26

A few minutes later, in the quietness of the café, I stop the loop of the CCTV. I put the USB in my computer case and hold Ozan and Yusef's mini projector in my hands. If I was a gamer or wanted a projector for outdoor movies this would be great. It's certainly served its purpose tonight.

I put it to one side. I'll return it to them in the morning.

I take down the canvas images that I'd had printed this morning in the photographic shop. It had been worth the wait but now this morning seems a long time ago. I replace them with the café's original posters, pretty Italian village scenes, and make a mental note to call my family.

Ralph had given me all the support and guidance I needed. He's a good friend. It hadn't taken me long to piece things together once Ralph's private investigator had turned up the information about JJ and Toby Johnson.

There was nothing illegal that anyone could prove. Toby Johnson had no family to contest the will, which had been changed just three months after JJ had started caring for him. She was, at best, unscrupulous. I just hope she was kind to him.

I carry the canvas prints upstairs to my bedroom where I lean them against the wall and cover them with an old sheet so they are hidden from view while I decide how to dispose of them.

I check my watch. Karl and Molly will be back soon and none the wiser about my encounter with JJ. It had been important to keep them out of the way and it was also an important gesture for their support and friendship. Karl had helped Ben paint the flat without ever thinking I'd ask him and Molly to move in, which proves that one act of kindness creates a ripple effect.

In the kitchen I pour a celebratory glass of Rioja and, as I stand at the window looking into Harbour Street, I raise my glass to the boarded-up property opposite the café.

'Cheers,' I say. 'That's a relief to have that over. Now, let's see what the future brings.'

* * *

Karl and Molly arrive back at the flat laughing and in good spirits and they're surprised to see me sitting at the dining table in the window nursing a second glass of wine.

'Amber, we've had the most amazing time.' Molly flings herself at me and wraps me in a warm hug. 'I've never been anywhere as posh as that. EVER!'

'Good. That's the idea. How was your meal?'

I smell sweet wine on her breath.

'I've eaten too much.' Karl grins. 'I had the best monkfish.'

'And I had lamb.'

'It was gorgeous.' Karl sits opposite me and when Molly lets me go, she naturally slides onto his knee. 'It was sooo good but I'll be honest, Amber. I think you're a better cook.'

I laugh.

Molly's arms are a pattern of tattoos, an Aztec sleeve on her left arm and hearts and names and dates on the other, and then I notice the names Molly and Karl entwined with a heart on her wrist.

'Have you been sitting here on your own all evening?' Molly asks.

'No.' I smile.

'Did you eat anything?' asks Karl.

'I forgot.'

'You've just been drinking wine?' He frowns.

'It's only my second glass.'

Karl looks unsure. 'Are you alright? You look tired but sort of different.'

I smile and take a deep breath.

'I've decided to stay.'

Karl's eyes widen in shock. 'What? Stay here?'

I nod and smile at their disbelief then joy.

Molly leaps up to hug me again. 'You're staying?' she cries.

'You mean, you're not selling the café?' Karl hasn't moved.

'I'm not selling the café,' I confirm.

'I can't believe it.' He stares at me. 'But what's happened to change your mind? I thought you and Cassie... I mean, you went up to London and everything and—'

I hold up my hand.

'I went up to London to see my ex-boss about a few other things. Cassie and I were over last April. She came here because she wanted me to move back to London to be with her but I realised that wasn't what I wanted. When she left me that was one thing, but when she took Scruff-bucket, I could never forgive her for that.'

'Scruff-bucket?' asks Molly.

'Our cat.'

Karl shakes his head and grins. 'You're really staying?'

'Yes.'

He looks out of the window and appears to be absorbing this new information and then says quietly, 'I've been so worried about finding a new job and getting work. What about the buyer? You know, the people who made you an offer? You said yes.'

'Nothing is signed. I'll tell them tomorrow I'm pulling out.'

'What made you change your mind?' asks Molly, letting me go and putting her arms around Karl's neck.

'I think Harbour Street suits me.'

Karl shakes his head and there are tears in his eyes. 'You don't know how happy that makes me,' he whispers.

'I do.' I reach out and take his hand.

He pulls at his bottom lip. 'I've been so worried.'

'Well, not anymore, Karl. It will all be okay. Everything is okay. You have a place to live and you both have a job.'

'Now all we have to do is to stop JJ making a mess of that building across the road and wrecking our street.' He nods his head toward the window and, suddenly I'm overcome with a sense of relief and calm. The tension in my neck and shoulders tingles but the pain eases and I smile, feeling full of optimism and hope.

'Well, let's see what happens. As Eva says, you never know in life how things are going to turn out.'

* * *

The rumour mill works very quickly in Harbour Street. By the time I've been to see my bank manager with my new business

287

plans and I've called into the estate agents and told Charlie to reject the offer on the café and to take my property off the market, and then to Ozan and Yusef to return the projector, the atmosphere in the café is upbeat and lively.

The hissing of the coffee machine and the warm smells of fresh bread, coffee, and background Christmas music greet me. It's busy and full of laughter and excited friends and families planning for the Christmas festivities.

I pause for a moment at the door to inhale my business as if seeing it properly for the first time, before smiling and greeting them all as if they are sitting in my home and they are my best friends.

I draw Jean and Lucas to one side and I tell them that I'm not selling the café and they are relieved and happy but not surprised. I suspect that Karl has already spread the word and I have no doubt that Molly is doing the same thing in the salon. Soon the whole of Harbour Street will be aware of my decision.

'We will close for four days over Christmas. You all need a proper break and it's important you spend time with your families,' I announce.

'What about you?' Lucas asks.

'I spoke to my parents this morning. They are in Italy but they'll come over in the New Year. This year I'm happy to stay here in Harbour Street.'

Papa and Mama had asked me to return to Milan but I had refused. 'For the first time, I want to make this my home and I want to be here,' I'd told them, and although they were sad they wouldn't see me until the New Year, they understood my decision.

'We only want you to be happy,' Papa had said.

'Is there anyone special?' Mama had asked.

'There are a lot of very special people and I can't wait for you to meet them all,' I reply. 'I can't believe how lucky I am.'

'Would it be alright if we stayed in the flat over Christmas?' Karl asks, drawing me out of my reverie. 'Will we be in your way?'

'No, of course you'll be here. This is your home. I'll cook Christmas lunch with turkey and all the trimmings for us all.'

Karl smiles. 'I've never had a proper Christmas lunch before. Molly will love it.'

Mrs Richards feeds Bertie discreetly under the table in the corner, Karl carries a takeaway coffee across the road to Eva and Pamela, and Jean busies herself behind the counter telling me about the Christmas presents she's buying for her boys.

And then suddenly Luke appears beaming happily.

'Mario and I can't believe you're not selling the café. It's a dream come true. We never wanted you to leave,' he says quietly, then glancing over his shoulder says, 'Is it common knowledge yet?'

I grin. 'You can speak up, Luke. It's alright. The café is staying open. I'm not going anywhere.'

Luke beams happily. 'Good. Because, I've got a small favour to ask you, Amber. Well, it's not so small really but it is, if you know what I mean? I'm sorry it's all such short notice.' Luke leans across the counter and continues to whisper, 'I've asked Frances to give Mario and me a church blessing. It's not a wedding as such but it will mean so much to us, especially to Mario, you know what he's like…'

I didn't but I say nothing.

'It will mean so much to be accepted and, Frances has a gap on Christmas Eve around lunchtime and we want to celebrate.

So, I was thinking, perhaps we could hire the café and have a small gathering. You know, with family and all our friends here in Harbour Street.'

'How lovely. Congratulations. That's so exciting.'

'I know it's short notice but Eva has already agreed to do the flowers and she said she'll coordinate with you and decorate the café, is that alright?'

I smile; today my heart is lighter and anyone could ask me anything and I'd probably agree. 'Definitely.'

'Can I pop over later and discuss the details and...' He holds a finger in the air. 'This is our secret. I don't want Mario to know. It's all going to be the most marvellous surprise for him.'

* * *

'When is a wedding not a wedding?' Eva asks, laughing. She's at her counter rearranging a floral door wreath with professionalism, and I sit on the high stool at the counter watching her.

'When it's a blessing?' I laugh.

Luke holds his hands up, good-naturedly laughing. 'I know, I know. I can't believe it. After all these years. You may tease me but I've even got Banjo trained to bring in our rings.'

I prompt. 'Banjo the—?'

'Banjo's our new rescue, he's a Boxer. He'll wear them around his neck in a red velvet box. Frances said that's fine with her so long as he doesn't poop in the church because the children's nativity starts at four o'clock and she doesn't want the church smelling of dog poo.'

'Blame it on the donkey.' Eva laughs.

290

'It's got to be the ass's fault,' I agree.

'Now, are you sure we're all set for the big day?'

'Yes.'

'Yes.'

'Do I need to—'

'No.'

'No.'

'Nothing?'

'No,' we both say together.

'Go and relax. It's all under control.'

After Luke has gone, I'm happy to watch Eva working, weaving flowers through the wicker frame. It's intricate work but she works quickly and every so often she stops to look at it before continuing again.

'Well, at least it's something to look forward to,' she says. Her eyes are dark and sad. 'Did I tell you that Nick and Emma aren't coming home for Christmas at all now?'

'I'm sorry, Eva. Are they definitely going skiing then?'

'It's not your fault, Amber. They're flying out early on Boxing Day. James has been waiting for this moment ever since he walked out on me. Sometimes there are just no words for how you feel, are there? I mean, it's bad enough that he did what he did, you know, leaving us and then we had to sell our beautiful house and seven acres of land—'

'I didn't know you had such a large home.'

'Emma even had a horse but he didn't care. Everything is disposable and when it came to money he made sure his lifestyle wasn't affected. It was us who had to downgrade, and then I was supposed to be grateful that he even paid maintenance for the kids. Of course, that's all stopped now they've gone. He took great delight in telling me that I'd have to stand on my own two feet and be independent. I'm so lucky, Amber, that I started my own business.'

'At least you're in control now. You don't need him for anything.'

'That's the problem, Amber. I'm not. He's still controlling, but now he's controlling them with money. He buys them all the time; ski-ing at Christmas, safari in Africa at Easter, sailing around the Greek Islands next summer but they don't see it, or they don't want to. He manipulates their minds. He encourages their sense of worth through control and he says things like—' She deepens her voice. '"Have money and you can go where you want and do what you want and have no regard for anyone else. Be like me and live life to the full and enjoy the best of everything". He encourages them to be mercenary, Amber. He's always looked down on the Polish side of the family as if they're poor relations but they have good and kind hearts. When Papa died, James sent Mama expensive flowers but he couldn't even pick up the phone. His affection is fake, he just wants the kids like possessions to prop up his ego, but family and friends are more important than that.'

'You can't buy love,' I reply, looking at the Christmas bouquets set aside on the counter.

'He wants to prove a point. With them spending Christmas with him, it's like he's saying "they love me more than they love you. Now they can choose who they want to be with at Christmas. I'm the better parent".'

'But you know that's not true. He shouldn't play them like this and besides you can't really blame them, it's just how kids are.'

'Disloyal?' Eva jokes.

'They don't see it that way. He's their dad and most kids are just opportunists. They'll do what they want.'

She cuts red ribbon angrily and tosses the scissors back on the counter. 'I know. I'm sorry. I just feel abandoned and I'm disappointed. It will be my first Christmas without them ever. They'll fly out on Boxing Day to Zurich but he's insisting they spend Christmas Day with him.'

'Well, you'll have to let them go, Eva, but I hope you're coming to me for Christmas lunch.'

'In the flat?'

'In the café. I'm cooking a traditional Christmas lunch for Karl and Molly. You can help me, you know, you can do the important jobs like peel potatoes, Brussels sprouts, parsnips and—'

'Pluck the turkey?'

'Maybe.' I grin.

Eva smiles. 'Thank you and although you haven't told me officially. I'm pleased you're not selling the café and leaving here.'

'To be honest, I quite forgot. I assumed Karl would have told everyone.' I grin. 'So much has been happening recently.'

'What made you change your mind?'

'I think there are a few things, not one big one but you know, like pebbles, they mount up and then suddenly life tips you in a different direction.'

'I could never think of you leaving. You belong here,' she adds simply then she looks at me. 'What about Ben?'

I shrug. 'I haven't seen him for a few days. He's been going up to London.'

'He's brought a young lad back to work with him. Someone he met while he was travelling.'

'Really?'

Eva stands back to look at her display and then she places it to one side. 'He's only a young lad and he seems quite shy. Anyway, thank you, Amber. Christmas lunch will be fantastic and I'm really looking forward to it.' She smiles. 'Will you ask Ben too?'

* * *

There's a light on inside Taylor's Art Gallery and I guess Ben's working late. The door isn't locked so I step inside. There is new artwork on the walls; several large winter landscapes, beach scenes with snow and several of Harbour Street, one in particular grabs my attention; it's a night scene and there's a small light glowing in the café window. I smile and lean forward to check the signature. Ben Taylor.

On the display shelf in the window the dragon chess set is finished and I'm admiring the intricate details, in awe of the precision of the arduous detailed work, when Ben appears from the workroom wiping his hands.

'Hi, Amber,' he says softly.

'I thought I'd come and tell you that I'm not selling the café.'

'I heard.'

'Oh.' I pause. 'Karl told you?'

'Of course. I think he sang from the clock tower.' His smile turns to a frown. 'I'm really pleased, Amber. You're good for Harbour Street.'

'Harbour Street is good for me.'

He smiles. 'I think you're good for me and everyone else here too.'

'That's a nice thing to say.' I grin and step forward, closer to him. 'I believe – oh, hello.' Over Ben's shoulder there's a shadow and a young boy steps into the light.

Ben turns around to follow my gaze. 'This is Ricky,' Ben says. 'A friend of mine, we met travelling. Ricky, this is Amber.'

'Hello.'

'Hi, Ricky.'

He steps forward with a shy smile. He looks as if he's wearing someone else's clothes. His legs are too long for his trousers and his jumper is too big for his narrow shoulders. He's pale and he looks like he could do with a decent meal.

'Ricky will be staying with me for a while and he's looking for a job if you know of anything?' Ben says.

Ricky won't look up or meet my eye but he doesn't take his eyes off Ben.

'I'll give it some thought,' I reply.

'Thank you,' Ricky mumbles.

'Ricky, if you want to take those chess tables I showed you just now, and stack them in the van out the back, I'll be there in a few minutes.'

Ricky leaves us and when he's out of earshot, Ben moves toward me and takes my elbow and leads me away toward the shop door.

'Ricky suffers from anxiety and depression. He's had it tough and I couldn't let him stay on his own.'

'Is this the lad who went missing in London?'

'No, this is another lad. The charity said he's only just appeared on the streets and it's better to keep him away from all the junkies before he becomes totally filled with despair. He's helped me in the workshop but he's a bit lost.'

'He's just a kid himself.'

'He's barely eighteen. He's from a broken home and the

parents aren't around. He's been in and out of foster homes since he was thirteen.'

'Bless him.'

'Look, Amber, I just want to say that, well you know, it's a difficult time right now but I'm pleased you're staying here. It's good to have you around. I like being with you.' His eyes are soft and intense.

'Me too, Ben. I'm pleased I'm staying. Now tell me, what are you doing on Christmas Day – and Ricky, of course?'

Chapter 27

The day before Luke and Mario's blessing on Christmas Eve, Frances comes into the café. She orders a coffee and then asks if I have time to sit with her, which I don't, but I perch on the edge of the seat anyway trying not to check my watch.

'Are you alright?' she asks. 'You look very nervous.'

'I'm waiting for a phone call,' I reply.

I've spent most of the morning upstairs in the flat on the phone to Ralph. I asked him for a favour and I'm waiting to see if he can help me. I need someone who isn't from Westbay and he's the only person I trust to help me solve one last problem.

'Is it important?' Frances asks.

'It will make my Christmas very happy,' I reply.

'Oh, well, lots of luck. Now, is everything ready for tomorrow?'

'It's manic,' I say. 'Luke and Mario's blessing plans are worse than Madonna's wedding could possibly have been to organise.'

'The Madonna?' She raises an eyebrow.

'Oops, sorry, Frances, wrong analogy.' I grin and she laughs aloud.

'Luke's a diva, bless him.' I laugh. 'He's been over here every day checking to make sure we have everything organised. Is

297

this really all a secret from Mario? If it is, he must be walking around with a blindfold and headphones on.'

Frances smiles but she seems preoccupied. 'Everyone is sworn to secrecy.' Her voice trails off.

'Well, Eva and Pamela are coming over with the flowers in the morning and – are you alright, Frances?'

She grasps her fingers together and rests her hands on the table. Her tone is measured and serious.

'I think everything is alright, Amber. It's just that something really strange is happening in Harbour Street.'

'Really?'

'Yes. JJ has left.'

'Oh.'

'Did you know?'

I shake my head innocently. 'She didn't tell me.'

Frances stares at me. 'Do you have any idea why she would leave?' Her gaze is unwavering and I feel she would have been better suited as an interrogation officer.

I shrug and shake my head. 'Nope.'

'And, she's selling the pub.'

'Oh.'

'And you have no idea why?'

I shake my head. 'Maybe she's had an epiphany? It is that time of year.' My smile dies on my lips as Frances continues to watch me without a reaction.

She continues, 'It seems very strange that she's upped and gone without a word to anyone. She emailed Charlie to put The Ship on the market and she's gone, just like that and no one knows why.'

'Strange,' I mutter.

'Marion came to see me. She is very upset. They were good

friends and she knew nothing.'

I scratch my head and look puzzled. 'I haven't seen Marion for a while. She's like the Scarlet Pimpernel. She never even joined in with the Christmas parade arrangements.'

'Well, rumour in the pub now says that Marion will be closing the boutique too.'

'Goodness. Rumours? I didn't think you went in the pub.'

'I don't but my parishioners do and some of them are very concerned.'

'Parishioners gossip?'

'Graham went for a quick drink with an ex-colleague from university at lunchtime.'

'Ah.' I smile.

Frances continues earnestly, 'It makes me wonder what could possibly have happened for JJ to leave Harbour Street so suddenly especially after she gets planning permission and puts up that awful sign and everyone thinks the amusement arcade is going ahead.'

'Ummm. I don't know.'

'It's so sudden.' Frances leans forward. 'There's no sense to any of this.'

'Umm, it is strange,' I agree.

'And you know nothing?'

I cast my eyes around the café and wave my arms.

'Look around you, Frances, I've enough on my plate to worry about, without thinking about JJ and Marion. It's crazy in here.'

'It all seems a coincidence that with JJ selling the pub and leaving and Marion closing her shop, and now you're staying in Harbour Street and—'

'What an incredible coincidence.' I pretend to look shocked, surprised and even a little excited. 'Where is your faith, Frances? God clearly works in very mysterious ways and, to be honest, I've always believed that good will triumph over evil.'

My heart is racing excitedly but I draw a line at punching the air with my fist in triumph.

* * *

I'm invited to the church service for the blessing and I stand between Eva and Ben. My hair is cut shorter and I'm wearing makeup and even lipstick for the first time in months. I'm also wearing a colourful blue dress, navy leggings and boots.

For the first time since last April, I am me.

I know who I am and what I want.

Frances waits expectantly looking happy and radiant as Luke and Mario, wearing matching white suits, with Banjo in a white harness and a red velvet box on his collar, walk down the aisle together. A soloist from the choir sings a Judy Garland song, 'I Can't Give You Anything But Love'.

Luke's voice trembles emotionally.

'Because of our love, we give each other wings to fly, roots to come back to and reasons to stay. It's all about today and today is the day to love, laugh and definitely to live.'

Frances's voice fills the church with a simple and beautiful blessing.

'Amen,' we all whisper.

Tears fill my eyes and Eva passes me a tissue and raises her moist eyes to the vaulted ceiling to cover her own emotions.

They place rings on each other's fingers, self-consciously grinning, and Mario removes his glasses to wipe his eyes before they share a light kiss on the lips.

Ben slips his hand into mine and gently squeezes my fingers. I smile gratefully at him, surprised at the tenderness and love in his eyes.

When the blessing is over and as the couple leave the church, the choir perform a simple melody of Elton John's 'Something About The Way You Look Tonight', and then it's all over and everyone is back to the café.

Jean is bustling around the kitchen. She's wearing the red silk blouse I gave her for her birthday and she beams at me.

'You look lovely,' I say.

'It's my favourite blouse,' she replies. 'The café looks amazing, Eva and Pamela have been such a help.'

Festive red and gold stars and shimmering ribbons hang from the ceiling, and in the corner a Nordic pine tree is adorned with hand-crafted wooden figures; angels, snowmen and snowflakes made by Ben's students.

It looks idyllic.

The married couple are cheered by family and friends, champagne corks are popped and the music goes on.

Karl jumps eagerly around, rearranging chairs, lining up plates and cutlery, adjusting a glass out of place like a professional maître d'.

'Tell me I've come a long way since working in the pet shop,' he says.

'You've come a long way since working in a pet shop—'

'No, really.'

'I think you've come even further than the undertakers,' I reply.

'You're dead funny.' He laughs.

In the kitchen, Lucas looks tired; a combination of sleepless nights with a young baby and the café kitchen is taking its toll. He's worked hard but today is his last job, as he's taking extra leave until the New Year. He's also asked to leave early so he can spend time with his baby daughter. It's Sunita's first Christmas and he hugs everyone before he leaves.

I give him a massive hug and slip him an envelope with a very generous tip. 'We open on the 2nd, so get plenty of rest, we'll have lots to do in the New Year.'

Lucas looks doubtful. 'January is never busy, Amber. No one has any money after Christmas.'

'Maybe you're right.' I smile. 'But, as Eva says, you never know what the future holds. Happy Christmas.'

Jean isn't far behind him. She has her own family to celebrate with and she takes me to one side. 'I love working here, Amber. It gives me a sense of purpose. And you've done so much for everyone. Look around you. Take stock and see what you have done. You've brought together a whole community of people and you've brought one thing to Harbour Street that was lacking...' She pauses. 'You've brought true community spirit.'

'Oh, I don't think that it's me who has done that.'

She pulls me into a hug. 'Happy Christmas, Amber. You will never know how much we all appreciate what you've done for us. You're a very special lady and we are all very lucky to call you our friend.'

I take a while to control my emotions. I'd never expected such an outpouring of emotion from Jean, and her words are still echoing in my head as the local traders begin to arrive to celebrate the blessing.

Ian and Derek, Jane, Kit and Jenna, Tracey and Molly, then later Freddy make an appearance and toward the end of the afternoon, Ozan and Yusef arrive with energy and excitement.

Ozan immediately comes over to me and whispers, 'Whatever you did, congratulations.'

I frown and look puzzled.

'Well, you must have put the projector to some good use, did it involve JJ?'

'Maybe.'

He kisses my cheek. 'Well done.'

Yusef checks his appearance in the café window before turning his attention to me. 'So pleased, man, that you're not leaving, aren't we, bro? We didn't want Ambie to leave, did we? You're looking so hot too, babe. You get your hair cut? You look steamin'. And that dress, OMG, you are sizzling.'

'I had to go to town so I thought I'd treat myself.'

'Loving the style, girl. You're a cool chick. Isn't she, Ben, my man, how are you, dude? Loving your look, my man. And this black shirt and yellow tie, man, you're like a male model. You two are really glam-or-ous.'

Yusef rubs Ben's cheek teasingly and Ben grins back then says to me, 'You do look lovely, Amber. That style suits you.'

'And I've never seen you so smart.' I smile.

'It's a special day.'

I raise my eyebrow and he smiles. 'You know, the blessing.'

'The life sentence,' I grin.

'Ah, you've got your romantic hat on, have you?'

'I threw that away a long time ago.'

'Not everyone is like Cassie,' he says, looking into my eyes.

'After she left, I was angry with myself for investing in this place.' I link my arm through his and pull him away to whisper quietly. 'But you know something, I'm really pleased she wanted to buy a café and that I followed my heart and not my head or none of this would ever have happened.'

'Out of everything bad comes something good.' His lips twitch into a smile. 'No regrets about not going back to London to be with her?'

'That was never on the cards. That night she turned up here was a complete surprise. She'd been texting me but I'd never replied. No means no. I can't go back once the trust is broken.'

'I hope you can trust me?'

'I do, Ben. I really do. I don't think you'd have stolen Scruff-bucket either. Come on, let's congratulate the happy couple.'

I lead him toward Luke and Mario, standing near the buffet displaying the vast array of fish, shellfish and salads along the far wall, before our conversation turns dangerously emotional. I'm still reeling from Jean's kind words and I don't want any more kindness. It might make me melt and break down in tears.

'I want you to try Lucas's vegetarian curry.'

Sanjay is suddenly beside us. 'Are you in competition with me, Amber? It smells very good.'

'Have you tried it?' I ask.

'Umm, it's not too bad.' He smiles.

'Do you celebrate Christmas?' I ask.

He shakes his head. 'Sort of, we have a meal, you know, the family, all the cousins together.'

'Would they miss you this year if you came and had Christmas lunch with us?'

He looks surprised. 'With you and Ben?'

'And Eva.'

* * *

The last of the guests have left the café, all heading home for Christmas Eve. Karl and Molly have helped clean and tidy the café and now they are upstairs, probably watching a film. Everything is ready for me to prepare lunch tomorrow, but now I have a chance to be alone, reflect and to be calm and quiet.

I dim the lights. I'm happy to sit alone in the café window with a glass of wine.

Christmas Eve is always a special time for me and I remember many family dinners in Italy and hope that next year I might go back and join them, but this year I'm very happy to be where I am.

Very happy.

I imagine Martin in Australia and his family celebrating on the beach. Ralph, who phoned me earlier and did me one last favour before leaving with his family to holiday in the Caribbean. And Cassie texted to say she was going back to her family in Edinburgh for Christmas. She said the show had run its course and she was undecided as to what she would do in the future. She said she might even travel. She'd always wanted to visit Brazil and I'd wished her well. I hope she will be happy.

This had been her dream not mine.

A year ago, the café in Harbour Street had been only an idea – our plan for a new future. An exciting journey, she'd said. Now, when I look back I hadn't thought about the lifestyle and how everything would change. I'd only wanted Cassie to be happy and I'd taken my security, my home, my savings and I'd invested them in Cassie.

True friendship, love and dreams cannot be bought.

There's a tap at the window and a smiling face appears.

I open the door.

'Do you want to be alone or would you like company?'

'I'd like *your* company.'

Ben waves a bottle of red wine in the air. 'Good. I went to the off-licence.'

While he settles at the table I find a corkscrew and another glass, and as he opens the wine he whispers, 'It's a strange old world, isn't it, Amber? You never know how things are going to turn out.'

'Never.'

'Who would have thought this time last year that I'd be sitting here with you, and I'd be accepted back into the community in Harbour Street?'

'It's a strange world,' I agree.

He looks intently at me. 'It's also strange that JJ has left, isn't it?'

'I suppose so.'

'Do you know why?'

'I don't know her well enough.'

He pauses with his wine glass at his lips. 'And you know nothing?'

I shrug. 'Maybe she'd just had enough of it here.'

'Maybe.'

'But it is for the best, isn't it?' I ask.

'Of course. But I did speak to Frances and she thinks it's most peculiar too. JJ went very quickly and the brewery have had to put in a temporary landlord over Christmas until it's sold.'

'That's good.'

'I didn't get a chance to get even with her.'

'Well, hopefully you won't hear from her again and you can

draw a line under it all.'

He frowns. 'With her going, I feel I can breathe. I can relax again. Does that make sense?'

'Yes.'

'You'll think I'm crazy, Amber. I don't know why, but I feel braver now. Does that make me sound weak?'

'No, you've been very hurt and you probably feel a terrible sense of injustice and that's left you feeling helpless.'

'I want to take control now. I want to change.' Ben reaches into his jacket pocket and brings out an envelope, and he lays it between us on the table with his fingers just touching the outer edges.

'This is the letter from my mum.'

'Have you read it?'

'I want to, Amber. Will you stay with me while I do?'

'Of course.'

He slides the letter from the envelope and my eyes turn misty, burning at the thought of his mother, ten years ago, writing this letter to a son she would never see again. A letter that he kept hidden and was never confident enough to open – until now.

In the flickering candlelight I watch him read and I see the changing emotions register on his face until finally he looks up at me. His voice croaks with emotion. 'She knew I didn't do it.'

'I know.'

'You knew?' He frowns. 'How?'

'The same way that she knew, Ben. You're too kind. You'd never have done that.'

Ben's chest is heaving in silent sobs and he wipes his eyes with the back of his hands.

'I thought she'd… I thought she was disappointed but—' He hands me the letter. 'She loved me. She never stopped loving me. She understood.'

'I'm pleased.'

'She says she knew what her brother William was like. He went to see her after I went to prison and he told her that it was all JJ's fault. He'd been smitten with her and he'd wanted to please her. He thought she loved him.'

I nod with understanding. It was JJ's modus operandi. The same one she'd used before.

'Mum also says that I must be strong and one day the truth will come out and I won't be ashamed or frightened of what people will say. Please read it, Amber.' He hands it to me with shaking fingers.

I read slowly. It's a private, warm and loving letter written from a mother's heart to her son in prison. It's full of love, it's full of hope and it's also full of warmth and optimism for his future.

'She must have been a lovely woman. I wish I'd known her.'

I hand him back the letter and he folds it away.

'She would have loved you, Amber,' he pauses. 'Mum was always an optimist. Did you read what she wrote at the end? She said I must learn to love and to trust again. She says I must have courage.' His eyes meet mine and I look away into the deserted street outside and reply.

'Well, now that JJ has gone, you will find peace, Ben. You can live again and without fear.'

Ben sits back in his seat and stretches out his legs and gives me a slow smile.

'I'm not like Frances,' he says. 'I don't believe that God works in mysterious ways.'

'Is that what she told you?'

'She told me that's what you'd said to her when you heard JJ had gone.'

I stay silent and Ben continues to stare at me then very quietly he says, 'I saw you.'

I turn my attention again to the street and I gaze out of the window.

'I saw JJ come in here,' he adds.

I watch a couple walk quickly past and their muffled voices float into the café, their footsteps clicking on the pavement.

Ben leans across the table.

'Amber, please tell me the truth. I need to know what happened and what you said to her. She wouldn't just get up and go of her own accord. She is a vindictive and evil person and if I don't know the truth, I'll never be able to relax. I'll always be looking over my shoulder thinking she's going to come back and... I served my time, Amber. But emotionally I still have a long way to go.'

'I know. I understand, Ben.'

I stand up and walk over to the counter and when I return I sit back down opposite him and slide a small gold package wrapped elegantly with a bright red bow across the table.

'Happy Christmas, Ben. Watch it when you are on your own. Then you can decide what you want to do.'

Chapter 28

I don't allow Karl and Molly in the café. I insisted they either stay in the flat or go out for a walk and enjoy Christmas Day. 'Make it special, create happy memories,' I say.

When they arrive in the café for a drink before lunch, they gasp in surprise at the beautiful table decorations and pretty flowers. In the kitchen everything is cooking nicely; turkey, bacon-wrapped sausages, stuffing, fluffy roast potatoes, crispy parsnips, Brussels sprouts, carrots and peas.

'I hope you don't mind, Amber, but I've invited Tracey to come for Christmas lunch,' Molly says. 'She phoned early this morning and was sobbing. She's really sad, she's all on her own. Des dumped her last night. He told her he didn't want a family and he wasn't ready to commit, but I've overheard him on the phone before to someone and I think he's having an affair.'

'Poor Tracey,' Karl says. 'She doesn't deserve that.'

'No one deserves that,' Molly agrees. 'She's better off without him.'

'There's no problem, Molly. We have plenty of food. Just set another place at the table and pour her a drink when she gets here.'

'Well, who's counted the place settings?' Molly asks. 'There's too many.'

'It's fine,' I say.

The door opens and Eva comes into the café at the same time as Tracey.

'Here we go,' Eva says brightly. 'Come in, Tracey, you're with friends now.'

'Thank you.' Her swollen eyes have dark circles and she looks like she's been crying all night. 'I couldn't go home to my parents, Amber. I'd never hear the end of it. They always warned me about Des. They told me he was rotten but I never thought he'd break my heart.'

I hug her tightly. 'It's a tough time for you but you will come through it. I did.'

'You've done brilliantly and this is so kind of you.'

'It's a pleasure, Tracey. The only condition is that you relax and have fun.'

'I will.'

Eva came over earlier this morning and insisted on helping me with the lunch preparations. Then she went home to shower and change clothes. 'Where do I put the Secret Santa present?' Eva pulls off her coat; now she's wearing a pretty dress with colourful snowmen.

'Under the tree?' Sanjay is wearing a festive Christmas tie. He arrived ten minutes ago and has spent the entire time looking out of the window waiting. 'You can put it beside mine – and no peeking.' It seems that he doesn't want to leave her side and, as he takes her elbow, he leads her to where his gift is under the tree.

'It all smells delicious.' Karl sniffs the air appreciatively and defaults to his comfort zone of pouring drinks for everyone.

'We had a lovely walk on the beach and I'm starving,' declares

311

Molly. 'Do you want spoons or forks for Lucas's homemade Christmas pudding and brandy sauce?'

'Both,' I reply.

'I've never eaten at such a pretty Christmas table.'

'Have we enough peanuts and cashews on the table?' ask Karl. 'Do we need crisps?'

'Plenty. We'll eat soon.' Then I call out, 'Eva, I need to talk to you.'

She's standing by the Christmas tree giggling with Sanjay. Their heads are close together and they're whispering.

'Come on, Eva.' I beckon her over. 'I have a surprise for you.'

Molly, Karl and Tracey wait, watching us both.

'I don't need any surprises—' Eva gasps and then covers her mouth as Nick and Emma hurry from the kitchen with their arms outstretched.

'Happy Christmas, Mum,' they chorus.

'Surprise!' says Emma.

'What are you doing here?' Eva cries, hugging them close, tears sliding silently down her cheeks.

'I couldn't leave you, Mum.' Emma says, wiping away a tear. 'Christmas wouldn't be the same without you.'

'You are our Christmas,' Nick agrees. 'It wasn't right for us not to be with you.'

'But what about your dad?'

'We told him last night we weren't going ski-ing.'

'But why?'

'We want to be with you,' Emma says.

'He must have been furious.' Eva laughs.

'He'll lose the money on the holiday but he can afford it.' Nick pulls out his mobile phone. 'So, then we phoned Amber, early this morning. We wanted to surprise you and she invited us here for lunch and the thought of her delicious crispy potatoes and honey roasted parsnips—'

'And, you'll come home with me tonight?' Eva asks.

'Of course. We're staying until the New Year.'

'I can't believe it.' Eva looks at me. 'Thank you, Amber.'

I raise my glass. 'Happy Christmas.'

Everyone is smiling, even Tracey looks like she's finally stopped crying. It's only Sanjay who, although still smiling, now looks slightly crestfallen but I know that there will be plenty of time for them to be together in the New Year.

Eva confided in me this morning that she had feelings for Sanjay. I didn't tell her that Sanjay had asked for my help – a favour he'd called it – and I know I'll have to tell him one day that he's managed perfectly well on his own.

'Right, come on, Karl, let's get this party started. More cocktails, sherry or Prosecco?' I call out.

'Where's Ben?' asks Molly.

'He's still not here?' says Karl. 'We can't eat without him.'

I stand with my festive apron tied around my waist. 'I might go over to the art gallery and if he's not there I'll go to his house.' I wonder if my Christmas present of the USB file I gave him last night has upset him.

'I'll come with you,' says Karl.

That's when the door flies open and Ben comes in smiling broadly. Behind him Ricky, the young lad from London, is carrying a box.

'Sorry we're late, everyone, meet my friend Ricky,' Ben announces and he steps purposefully toward me. 'Hi, Amber.'

'Will I take the wine?' Karl reaches out for the box but Ben takes it.

'This is a special present. It's for Amber.'

Suddenly there's a small noise, a squeal, from inside the box and the conversation in the café stops.

'What's that noise?' I ask.

Ben is like a magician with a top hat and he lifts the lid with a dramatic flurry. 'Ta da.'

I glance inside and into the eyes of the most adorable silver tabby kitten.

'Oh my goodness—'

Then I see two more eyes. Four eyes.

'There's two of them,' I cry.

'Happy Christmas,' Ben whispers. 'We all know how much you miss Scruff-bucket!'

'They are so adorable.' I pick one up and hold it in my arms against my cheek and the other one is already crawling onto the edge of the box and wants to escape. Eva catches it.

'How will we manage with two kittens?' I ask.

'Are they boys or girls?' Eva lifts to look.

'One of each,' Ricky replies.

'I'll help look after them,' Molly says.

'And me.' Karl tickles the kitten in my arms under the chin and it purrs loudly.

'We'll all help,' Eva adds. 'You're not keeping them to yourself, Amber. They are so cute.'

'They look identical,' says Sanjay, stroking the kitten in Eva's arms.

'What will you call them?' asks Emma.

'Potato and Parsnip?' suggests Nick.

'Peanut and Cashew?' says Molly.

'Salt and Pepper,' adds Karl.

'You could have a Cat Café, a Kitten Café, they've got them in London,' Ricky says. 'They're very popular.'

314

'What a fabulous idea.' Tracey claps her hand and laughs. 'Animals are far better than a boyfriend.'

'Have another drink, Tracey,' says Molly, winking at Karl.

I smile at Ben. 'They are gorgeous. Thank you. I thought you weren't coming,' I whisper.

'I wouldn't let you down. We're late because we collected the kittens this morning from a friend with a rescue centre.'

He kisses my cheek and I'm surprised at the tenderness of his touch and the softness of his lips. He whispers, 'And thank you for my Christmas present, Amber. It's the best present of all.'

'I didn't want it to upset you.'

'The opposite,' he replies.

'So, what did Amber get you for Christmas, Ben?' Eva asks.

'Yes, come on, what could Amber possibly get you, that's better than these two adorable kittens?' Molly nudges Karl but he ignores her. He's staring out of the window with his mouth open.

'Karl? Karl? What are you doing? Look at these kittens, aren't they gorgeous.' Molly nudges him.

Karl is transfixed by something outside in the street and he points. 'Look at that!'

'Is it snowing?' asks Sanjay moving to the window. 'I've never seen a white Christmas.'

One by one everyone turns to look but there isn't any snow.

There are Christmas lights and a giant banner illuminating a new sign hanging from the first floor of the travel agent's windows in big red letters.

COMING SOON
NEW INTERNATIONAL BISTRO

'Why didn't we see it before?' Karl says.

'We've all been too busy,' replies Eva, passing the kitten to Molly and moving closer to the window beside Sanjay and the rest of our friends.

I stay where I am looking at Karl and Molly, Eva, Nick, Emma and Sanjay, Ricky and Tracey and Ben as they all stare out of the window. Each of us with our problems, hopes, fears and dreams for the future and I'm feeling lucky to be surrounded by these incredible people that I can now call my friends.

I hug the purring kitten to my chest, feeling its warm beating heart and the dry little lick she gives me on my finger.

'Oh my goodness,' exclaims Eva. 'Would you believe it! Someone has bought the travel agents.'

'Who put that sign up there?' asks Karl.

'It's going to be a restaurant,' exclaims Tracey.

'But who's the new owner?' asks Sanjay.

Molly slips her arm through Karl's.

'This is exciting,' says Emma. 'Isn't it?'

'I guess it depends who owns it,' replies Nick. 'Doesn't it, Mum?'

They're all too busy to notice me. Except Ben. He turns around and stares meaningfully at me before breaking into a wide smile but suddenly I'm too busy playing with the kitten in my arms to look up at him.

It hadn't taken me long to put up the sign.

Ralph negotiated the deal in secret for me, yesterday morning, purchasing it from JJ for a very low price on the condition of a very quick sale.

* * *

It's New Year's Eve and we are sitting on the sofa together beside the roaring open-fire in Ben's house, drinking champagne.

'So, tell me the truth.'

'Okay.'

'No secrets and no pretending. We must be totally honest with each other. We have to be ourselves.'

'Okay.'

'When did you decide you fancied me?'

'From the minute I first saw you.'

'And when did you decide you wanted me – you know – physically?'

'The first time you touched me.'

'And when did you decide you wanted to spend the rest of your life with me?'

'When I sat with you on the beach.'

'Wow!'

'My turn?'

'Yes.'

'When did you decide—'

'The minute I saw you. I looked at you—'

'In the café—'

'It was as if I had known you all my life.'

'Me too.'

'I love your smile.'

'I love all of you.'

'I love you more.'

'Enough to clean the litter tray?'

End.

Janet Pywell's Books

Ronda George Thrillers:
The Concealers
The Influencers
The Manipulators
The Ronda George Thriller Boxset - books 1-3

Mikky dos Santos Thrillers:
Golden Icon – *The Prequel*
Masterpiece
Book of Hours
Stolen Script
Faking Game
Truthful Lies
Broken Windows

Boxsets
Volume 1 – Masterpiece, Book of Hours & Stolen Script
Volume 2 – Faking Game, Truthful Lies & Broken Windows

Other Books by Janet Pywell:
Red Shoes and Other Short Stories
Bedtime Reads
Ellie Bravo
Someone Else's Dream

For more information visit:
  website: www. janetpywellauthor.wordpress.com

All books are available online and can be ordered through major book stores.

If you enjoy my books then please do leave a review from wherever you purchased the book. Your opinion is important to me. I read them all. It also helps other readers to find my work.

Thank you.

About the Author

Author Janet Pywell's storytelling is as mesmerizing and complex as her characters.

Janet's latest novel Someone Else's Dream is a heart-warming, uplifting, feel-good novel about courage, integrity and friendship.

In the Mikky dos Santos international crime thriller series - art forger, artist and photographer Mikky is a uniquely lovable female: a tough, tattooed, yet vulnerable protagonist who will steal your heart. Each book is a stand-alone exciting action-adventure novel, set in three uniquely different countries/locations.

In the first series of domestic crime thrillers, Ronda George is a kickboxing *Masterchef*. After ten years in the British Army assigned to some of the world's most dangerous places, Ronda is enlisted by Inspector Joachin García Abascal to infiltrate the murky underworld of greed, corruption and betrayal.

These books are a must-read for devotees of complex female sleuths - a female James Bond.

Janet has a background in travel and tourism and she writes

using her knowledge of foreign places gained from living abroad and travelling extensively. She currently lives on the Kent coast.

You can connect with me on:

🌐 https://janetpywellauthor.wordpress.com

🐦 https://twitter.com/JanPywellAuthor

📘 https://www.facebook.com/JanetPywell7227

🔗 https://www.subscribepage.com/someone-elses-dream

🔗 https://www.instagram.com/janetpywellauthor

Subscribe to my newsletter:

✉ https://www.subscribepage.com/janetpywell

Printed in Great Britain
by Amazon

71104584R00190